the not to do list

Wentworth Ravens Hockey

viera hope

a note from the author

Welcome to the world of the Wentworth Ravens! A fictional team, set in a fictional town in Colorado, at a fictional college. While I am a fan of hockey, and I did research on the game to stay authentic to it, I may take some liberties occasionally. I apologize and in no way mean to offend. The found family and the friendships are authentic as they get, and the romance is sweet. Which is ultimately what we're here for, so happy reading!

one

. . .

KENNA

I've been staring at my phone for a full minute, reading over the email as if I might be hallucinating. There's a slight breeze today, sending some of my hair into my face, but I can't even be bothered to push it away. It's happening, it's actually happening. My plan is coming to fruition.

"Kenna! I have the greatest news!" My best friend and roommate rushes up to me, and I finally tear my gaze away from the phone as I look at her, my face breaking into a grin.

"I have the greatest news too!"

"You go first!"

"No, you go first!"

We stop talking over each other and burst out laughing. A few people glance our way, and I take her by the wrist and pull her to the side, away from the front door of the café.

"Should we rock, paper, scissors for it?" I ask.

"No, please go."

I smile and then take a deep breath.

"I got it, Evie. I got the job!" I grab her arms, bouncing on the balls of my feet, regardless of the stares. She squeals, pulling me into a quick spin, and I throw my head back and laugh.

When I applied for the barista position at the campus café I had very little hope I would get the job. Not that I don't believe in my awesome abilities when it comes to making coffee—I'm a professional coffee connoisseur—and my work ethic is off the charts. These are direct quotes from previous employers, not me just tooting my own horn.

But getting a job on campus is like entering the Hunger Games. A little dramatic of a description, but very legit. The competition is incredibly fierce and it's basically a free of all. I don't know how many times I've heard of people trying to bribe the administration for favors.

Everyone wants to work on campus. Not only do you receive a—admittedly small—paycheck, campus staff get their room and board half off, and I could really use the extra money.

I shouldn't complain, but my father can barely take care of his own finances, let alone mine. It took a lot of long barista shifts in high school to get here on top of helping with his bills. Wentworth University might not be as pricey as some of the bigger colleges in other states, but my savings are dwindling, and I need a job.

Starting my sophomore year by checking one of the top three items on my to-do list is exactly the positive vibes I'd like to take with me into the rest of the year.

"No way! I mean, I knew it, but, ahhh!" Evie jumps up again, completely disregarding the stares from passersby. We probably shouldn't be doing this on the sidewalk on a weekend, but Evie's excitement cannot be contained. I think when you're five foot eight, as a girl, you get used to the staring anyway. I'm only five foot six and it seems like a stark difference between us. People definitely notice Evie.

I may be biased, but I find my best friend gorgeous. Short blonde hair—at the moment, she changes her hair style a lot —green eyes, curvy, with a confidence that shines through everything she does. She's also the only one in her core science classes that dresses in colors. The rest of the soon-to-be veterinarians take the white lab coat very seriously. So does she, but she makes sure there are patterns and color underneath it. She's one of my favorite subjects to photograph, and we do random photoshoots all the time.

I, on the other hand, am more muted in my wardrobe choices. My brown hair is long and messy, my outfits more business casual than anything else. I find that it's easier for me to blend into the background, especially since I want to be a professional photographer. It's not really about me; it's about my subjects. But somehow Evie and I still fit together like we were always meant to be friends.

We met our junior year of high school when we both went to an assembly regarding college admissions and chose Wentworth University as our goal. We've been inseparable ever since. Well, besides the very long freshman year when we didn't end up in the same room. Or even in the same dorm. But Evie worked her magic this year, and we're back to being joined at the hip.

"Okay, we're getting cake. No arguments," she hurries on to add when I open my mouth. I've been trying to cut down on my spending while I've been looking for a job. "We're celebrating. Just wait till I tell you my news."

It's Sunday, so as usual, we're off campus at one of our favorite cafés, before we head outside for our weekend walk through town. Living in Knightley, Colorado, for school has its perks, particularly the weather and all the parks within walking distance in every direction. The city and school's on-the-nose name is not lost on me, but I feel like it adds character. There are quite a few areas that pay tribute to famous Austen couples and that always makes for a fun outing when I want to explore and take pictures.

We head inside the small café, and I'm already reaching for my phone to take a few pictures. Here, the design heavily features floral elements, with pink, white, and red flowers adorning the corners and some of the ceiling. I think they took their inspiration from English tea houses, although they only serve matcha lattes and Earl Grey here. They change up the flower arrangements and colors every few months or so and this is the first time I'm seeing all the pink.

Once we've grabbed our lattes, as well as a caramel cheesecake for me and a very delicious looking donut for Evie, we find a seat near one of the front windows.

"Okay, I can see you're bursting at the seams," I say as soon as we sit down. Evie is grinning like she's won the lottery, a conspiring twinkle in her eye. "Spill."

"Oh, Kenna, darling, what is the one thing that would bring you utmost happiness in this moment?" she asks, drumming her fingers against her chin dramatically.

I narrow my eyes, having absolutely no idea where this is going. I already told her about the job, and it can't have anything to do with my photography, because I haven't been able to apply for any contests or scholarships yet. So it's not as if she saw a posting for me winning first place somewhere.

"I have no idea. I'm already thrilled."

"But Kenna, how about the downfall of your arch nemesis?" she mock whispers, leaning forward. My heart thumps in my chest, making sure I'm paying attention, because there's only one person she could be talking about.

"Are you really bringing him into this very joyous moment?" I ask, taking a bite of my cheesecake. It's delicious, but I can't even savor it properly because now my mind is on him.

Reese Dawson. Captain of the Wentworth Ravens—our school's hockey team—and everything I dislike in a guy.

"Yes, I am bringing him into this moment, because WentworthWhispers posted an update an hour ago that you have to see!"

"Evie, you are much too obsessed with our school's gossip Instagram account," I chuckle, trying to distract her, but I should know better. There's no way it'll work.

"I'm not ashamed of it," she announces, then thrusts the phone right into my face. "Look!"

I pull back a little to get a better look, and I'm greeted by a blurry picture of two guys fighting. The big letters across the bottom of the picture announce "the new school year starting off with a bang as the campus's star player gets into a brawl".

Even though the picture is blurry, I recognize one guy immediately. Reese is hard to miss, even with this picture quality. Sometimes I wonder if I should volunteer for WentworthWhispers just so I can teach them to take better pictures, but that's neither here nor there. I avert my gaze, trying to push down all the emotions seeing him bring up.

"You cannot tell me that seeing Mr. Ice Man in hot water isn't the greatest. We hate him, remember?" Evie raises her eyebrows.

"Ugh, I thought you forgot, since you brought him up and we agreed he's not allowed to be the topic of our conversations."

"Look, baby girl, I am always on your side in this. I know he messed up badly. He basically told you that you were his perfect girl and then when it was time to actually meet, he stood you up. Add insult to injury, I'm never forgiving him for announcing to the world that you're not his type—"

"Evelyn, please get to the point." I'm not exactly excited to be reminded that I thought I had finally connected with someone on a deeper level, only to have that blow up in my face. My experience with a previous relationship ended with my self-confidence completely shot and my ex made sure that I associate athletes with the horrible way he treaded me. Add in my issues with my family, and I'm callous when it comes to love. And when I had a glimmer of hope snuffed out very painfully in my face, it's really no wonder I carry so many unresolved emotions for this guy.

"Okay, McKenna," she replies, huffing at my use of her full name whenever I'm annoyed. "But all of that just makes this fact so much sweeter; the golden boy fought someone. Even on the ice he's a perfect picture of calm, cool, and collected. But now the world sees he's just human. Something serious must have set him off."

"I'm sure it was something serious, like someone not getting his cheeseburger order correct."

By the looks of that picture, it appears they're in a food establishment. Which is honestly one of only three places I've seen hockey players hang out.

"There's no leeway with you," Evie says, placing her phone on the table and picking up her donut, saluting me with it. "I love that about you. But be honest, you're happy, aren't you?"

I shake my head, but I can't help the smile that blossoms on my face. It's very petty of me but seeing Reese fall from his pedestal brings me a sense of vindication. I lean forward, dropping my voice.

"It does make me happy. He's not so perfect after all." Evie grins, satisfied, and I dig into my sweet treat.

Pushing all thoughts of the hockey player out of my mind, I focus on the facts. This is going to be an exceptional year, I can feel it. I have a few more photography classes this semester, which is a pleasant change from all the required classes I had to take our freshman year. And now, I have a job.

All in all, there are three things on my to-do list for the beginning of the school year:

One: get the job at the campus café

Two: grow my photography account, and

Three: stay away from hockey players—specifically Reese Dawson. The guy who stood me up and since then forgotten I exist. I think I'm off to a fantastic start.

two

. . .

REESE

"What do you mean they're pulling my sponsorship?" I sit up in my chair, nearly toppling it over. My coach shoots me a sympathetic look as the representative from the sport goods store keeps his expression stoic.

Early this morning, I got called into the coach's office only to be met by the most unsmiling man I have ever seen. Now, by his lack of empathy I wonder if he's even human or GoGo Sports sent a robot.

"Unfortunately," the man says, his voice monotone, "the CEO has a very strict policy for individuals he works with and after your recent bout with the law, he believes it would be best if we part ways."

It wasn't even a "bout with the law". Some of my teammates and I were out at Raisin' Canes for dinner when one of the guys from a nearby school came over and started causing problems. He was a big dude, but still not anything to fear by the three of us. But then he dumped a cup of coke on Austin before taking a swing at him, and I had to step in. I took the original hit and then pushed him back. I called Coach afterward, letting him know what happened. But then WentworthWhispers thought it would be fun to broadcast it on their page. However, our school's gossip Instagram account only caught that second part, and now I'm in the hot seat.

"Sir, we understand your concern," Coach Warren speaks up, "But Reese is an exceptional individual, and the picture doesn't show what actually happened."

"I understand," the representative—Mr. Willis—says, "but unfortunately, a picture speaks a thousand words."

This dude really likes the word unfortunately and every time he uses it, my worry rises. I've done my best to keep myself in check my whole life. My mom has always been big about appearances, because her job requires her to be, and she appreciates me keeping my nose clean. Which I have done from an early age. I've barely ever fought on the ice, which is very surprising for most people. But it takes a lot to rile me up. I don't remember the last time I got angry enough to lose control. But I will never stand by and watch if one of my teammates is being harassed for no reason. Those are my brothers, and I will protect them.

Apparently, to my own detriment.

"Will they give me another chance? I promise my image is good. I'm solid," I say, keeping my tone leveled, but I can feel the desperation creeping in. I've worked so hard to come this far. Years of training, of keeping myself in check. This is important to me. It's my first ever sponsorship, and it's one of the biggest sporting goods stores in the state. GoGo Sports are recognized for being directly involved in the community and they hold a huge pull on a national level. This gives me a significant advantage when scouts come as well. Everything about me is an image—it's why NIL is so important. Name, image, and likeness is what I base all my decisions on. I need this.

The coach is saying something, and I turn just in time for the representative to face me once more, his eyes hard.

"You make a valid point," he says, addressing Coach. "I can speak to the CEO, but in the meantime, you need to fix this."

With that, Mr. Willis stands, giving Coach Warren a firm nod and then sees himself out.

"I'm sorry, Coach," I say as soon as the door shuts. "I didn't think of the aftermath."

"I don't think that would've changed anything. You watch out for your team, you always have."

The Wentworth Ravens have a reputation for playing clean, on and off the ice. Coach Warren has always been very outspoken about his stance on how a man should live his life, and it always comes down to someone with good thinking, good habits, and an open heart. Since I've been taught by my uncle for most my life that emotional romantic attachments lead to distraction, and hockey is to always be my "one-true-love" because "hockey never fails you". Basically, I'm not into romantic relationships. The rest, I stand by.

"We'll figure this out, Reese. Not all is lost. I'll make a few calls and see where we stand."

I nod, but my mind is already trying to come up with a way I can fix it. It's what I do after all. Ever since I was young, the first time my uncle made a scene, I tried to be the good kid that fixes things instead of breaks them. There have been plenty of arguments with me in the middle. I've been the go-between with my family, and I've become that to my teammates as well. But when I'm in trouble, everything takes a much darker outlook. My phone vibrates, pulling my attention, and I take it out to glance at the reminder.

"I'm due at work, Coach. I'll see you at practice."

I leave the office behind and head toward my job. This year is a big one for me because a lot can be decided by the end of it. Even though I have another semester to go, I'm still in that stage of my life where everything is either falling apart or coming together. The scouts came to a few games last year, and I have preliminary offers on the table. But with some rumors and issues circling around the league, and with the state of the world, things are moving much slower. While I would love to play hockey professionally, I also understand not everyone gets that chance, which is why I'm getting my physical therapy degree. Honestly, I'd be happy just to have hockey be part of my life, but my uncle doesn't see it that way. He's putting a lot on me to get into the big leagues, even though it's not exactly my ultimate goal. I've always thought that I owed Uncle Dan a little, for taking me in while my parents weren't around. He's given up enough that I want to give back a little. Right now, I won't just sit around and not give it my all when it comes to the game. Which means I have to make this season count. I have to keep my nose clean, and I have to find a way to get back on the good side of GoGo Sports.

"You're here!" Alan greets me as I step inside the café. He's one of the few people who works at the café who isn't a student. He's in his late twenties and graduated a few years ago, but hasn't really found his passion yet. Or he decided that bare minimum at Coffee & Books is his passion. I honestly can't tell. Mrs. Lowery hired him in his junior year, and he just stuck around. I like the guy fine, but sometimes he can be slightly condescending and flaky.

"I'm here," I reply, smiling at a few people waiting in line as I walk around the counter and head to the back room. It looks like he's alone right now. I thought they hired someone else to help during the midmorning rush, but maybe they're still looking.

I drop off my bag and shed my hoodie before I step back out to the main room. Coffee & Books is a campus staple. Large open floor area, floor-to-ceiling windows around three-fourths of the room, with the counter in the middle, and a more closed off seating area at the back. The decorations are mostly books and plants, but it doesn't seem overwhelming. It's pleasant and comforting here, and it feels like a bit of a sanctuary for me.

My favorite place is being on the ice. It has been since I was four years old. But there's something nice about being able to work with my hands, especially in a familiar place such as this. After a year behind the counter, there's a sense of comfort to my movements. I know what is expected of me and I know how to deliver on those expectations. Even when it gets busy, I still feel like I have everything under control.

"Finally," Alan says, and I glance at the clock hanging over his head behind him. I'm twenty minutes early.

"If you missed me so much, just say so," I say, making the girls ordering giggle. I flash one of my signature smiles and glance at the orders pinned to the machine. Without a second thought, I wash my hands and start preparing them, while Alan finishes up with the current customer.

"The new girl is supposed to start today, but I can't exactly have her doing anything without training. And Seth didn't show up. Again."

Oh, well, I guess Seth is going to be losing his working privileges. Not that I'm all that surprised. The guy barely shows up to work anymore. I think he was here as a punishment, and now he's worked off his sentence. I have no idea if that's true, it just seems like it because that was his whole attitude.

"No worries, I'm here. You can train."

"Actually, since Mrs. Lowery promoted you to manager, it's your responsibility to train her."

That makes me pause. "You're the senior manager."

"And I have an appointment in thirty minutes, so this one is on you."

"Wait, you're leaving me here with the newbie during rush hour?" I place the finished coffee at the pickup area and call out a name, before turning to make the next one. I don't even know why I'm surprised. This is so Alan.

"The rush has almost finished. Classes are starting up, so it'll be quieter for a few hours."

He's not wrong, but it still seems like I'm getting dumped with his responsibility. I finish preparing another order before I turn to him.

"When is she getting here?"

"Oh she's been here for almost an hour now. She's at the back tables."

Alan walks around me as I work on the next order. I swear this guy is allergic to making coffee. He will do literally anything else.

"Have a good one," I say to the couple as I hand them their coffee, just as Alan comes back.

"Kenna, meet your trainer. This is Reese, he'll show you the ropes."

I turn around, my smile in place, and then I freeze. The most gorgeous girl I have ever seen is standing in front of me. Dark brown hair, slightly wavy in some parts, slightly curly in others. Brown eyes so dark, they look almost black, framed by long lashes. She can't be more than five-six, coming up to right under my chin, and curvy in all the right places. When my small perusal makes it back to her face, I find surprise and something akin to dislike there. I blink, momentarily stunned, before I grin.

"Nice to meet you," I say, watching as her beautiful eyes narrow. The hostile expression on her face is really sending me spinning. This is not the typical response I get, especially not from girls. I know I look good, and girls don't shy away from telling me, either. But Kenna looks like she'd like to dump a scorching cup of coffee on my head before she pushes me off the nearest cliff.

"Well, I'll leave you to it," Alan says, completely oblivious to everything that's happening in front of him. Kenna watches him leave, before she turns her attention back to me.

"Don't worry, I'll take good care of you," I try again, and she huffs—actually huffs—as she shakes her head.

"Don't make any promises you can't keep," she mumbles, her voice a little low and raspy, shooting straight through me. I'm almost sure she didn't want me to hear that. She appears to dislike me and while I have no idea why, I'm suddenly more interested in keeping her attention on me. Her voice is scratching an itch in my brain—like a memory trying to come to the surface—and I'd like her to simply keep talking. Even if it's just to figure it out. Which makes this a very interesting development.

And an unexpected one.

three

. . .

*R*eese. Freaking. Dawson.

Everything about this is terrible, horrible, unbelievable… where's an English major when you need one? I need more descriptive words for him.

How did I not know he worked here? I basically live in this café. Okay, that's a slight exaggeration, but I tend to spend a few of my evenings during the week here, tucked into one of the corners as I edit pictures. I've never once seen him. I would've noticed, if only by the flock of adoring fans that seem to follow him everywhere. He is a walking dream, with his six-foot-one frame, dark blue eyes, and wavy dark hair that seems to somehow look styled and messy simultaneously. I have eyes, I'm not oblivious. In my case, it's more of a nightmare, but I can understand it…objectively. Even now, as he prepares one of the orders, I can pinpoint five different people staring at him as if he hung the moon.

Of course, I know who he is. Hockey might not be a

favorite sport of mine, but I'm not oblivious to the ways Wentworth University operates. And one of its pride and joys are the Wentworth Ravens. I actually wanted to give them a chance, but then all of that crashed and burned my first semester here when Reese stomped on my very fragile self-esteem and then forgot about me.

Clearly. Even looking at me now, he has no idea who I am.

It's better this way, anyway. I can get through the training period and then hopefully never have to work with him again.

"The midmorning rush is basically over now," Reese says, turning back to me. It's very annoying that such a horrible guy has such a soothing voice. Focus, Kenna. "I can show you how to make this order, and then we'll go over everything. I'm assuming Alan showed you nothing?"

Well, at least he's aware. I arrived on time, and Alan put me in a corner for an hour. Not exactly the best way to start my day.

"I know the basics of the machine," I say, nodding toward the coffeemaker. "I worked with one like this at a café back home. But some of these" —I point to a list of coffees offered— "I've never even heard of, except on this menu."

"If you have the foundation, you'll have no problem picking the rest up," Reese replies, that easy grin back on his lips. I can see he's trying to win me over, but I'm unaffected. I'm a stone wall; nothing is getting through. He narrows his eyes for a second, and I think he's about to ask me something, but then decides against it at the last moment.

"You'll also get to know the regulars, and those are the easiest coffees to make. We do serve some baked goods, which are delivered fresh each morning. For the afternoon crowd, we serve hot sandwiches, but a different crew typically handles that. You'll only need to worry about the coffee if you work in the mornings. Hi there, what can I get you?"

He doesn't even run out of breath delivering all that information before he turns to take the next order. There is no hesitation in the way he speaks, pushing the buttons on the register before scooting over to make the coffee, not missing a stride. He also seems very unbothered by the fact that Alan basically dumped me on him.

I know his nickname is Ice Man—in that he's always the most levelheaded in the rink. I suppose you have to be if you're going to be the captain. Although I have read plenty of gossip on WentworthWhispers that covered other captains not being so... stoic with their emotions. There were a couple of games last season that were very memorable to the fans. Mostly because the fighting got out of hand. Evie quickly pointed out that college hockey leagues prohibit fighting and penalize it very strictly. But apparently, it did not matter to these teams. Not to the Ravens, but to two other schools. I know enough about hockey to know gloves come off often enough, at least on a professional level. But somehow Reese keeps his team playing the game without shedding unnecessary blood and keeping to the rules.

My mind goes back to what Evie showed me on WentworthWhispers and how it must've been bad to get to him. I wonder what would set him off. He seems almost unshakable in his ways. At least from a distance.

"Are you listening?" he asks. I blink a few times and realize that I've been listening to him in the background while he was explaining the white mocha latte.

"Of course. Make it foamy, but not too much. Sprinkle chocolate powder on top."

He looks mildly impressed, and I almost high-five myself for my multitasking listening skills. It comes in handy when you shoot big weddings and you have to filter out unimportant information like the second uncle thrice removed shouting out horrendous ideas for poses, while keeping the rest of the guests smiling nicely.

"This one is a big hit on campus, so you'll be making it a lot."

"It's delicious."

"Oh, is this your preference for coffee?" he asks as he makes another cup, and I make sure I'm actually watching what he's doing as I answer.

"Mornings, yes. In the afternoon, I go for a more standard oat latte."

"Ah, of course. Can't overdo it on caffeine and sugar. Not when you're plenty sweet already."

He flashes me a grin, and I bite my lip to keep my snarky response in place. I'm sure there are plenty of people who would fall at his feet for such a cheesy line, but it definitely won't be me. I need this job, and I doubt I can get away with dry sarcasm when I'm supposed to be nice.

He finishes serving the group and then turns to me. For someone so big, he sure moves with an annoying amount of grace. I'm only noticing from an outsider's perspective. Know your enemy and all that.

"When you think about it, there's probably more caffeine in the oat latte, since it comes standard with two espresso shots versus one, so your logic is flawed," I can't help but point out.

"That can't be. My logic is never flawed." He flashes me an a pleasant grin that ruffles all my feathers. If he truly believes that, it means that when he chose to stand me up, it was a calculated move. It would be great if I could tell that self-deprecating voice inside my head to shut up, especially at a time like this. But Reese's amiable smiles and cocky state-ments are making my tongue loose before I can stop it.

"Maybe you think that, but I think it just makes hockey players less logical than I thought," I reply, turning away to study the machine in front of me. The range of emotions running through me right now is very confusing. I thought I'd dealt with all of my anger already. Okay, fine. Anger and disappointment. In my mind, it was just a little simmer, an unpleasant memory, nothing more. But apparently not, because I'm getting all kinds of riled up and cannot stop myself from speaking out.

What is this behavior, Kenna? You're an adult. Put your hurt aside and act professional.

"So you've thought of me?" He grins, raising an eyebrow at me. "Are you a big hockey fan?" Reese moves closer, sliding across the counter so he can peer down at me. It's actually quite maddening that I have to look up at him any time I speak.

"Not even a little bit. I tried watching it once and found it boring."

"Ouch," he places a hand over his chest, stumbling back against the counter. "Straight to the heart."

"If you had a heart, you'd know it's on the other side of your chest," I say, raising an eyebrow. Thankfully, my tone is coming out a lot more teasing than mean, or I'd be in hot water.

He surprises me by laughing. My whole body jerks at the sound, as if it affected me physically. The sound is rich and carefree, and it gets right under my skin in the most frus-trating way possible—sending goose bumps down my spine.

Don't get distracted, I repeat firmly to myself three times. His laugh is partially why I was interested in him in the first place, and look how that ended up. I'm not getting sucked in again.

I roll my eyes at him, leveling him with my deadliest glare. He watches me narrow my eyes, and the spark in his eyes turns into something else I can't quite name. But I ignore it all the same, because it doesn't matter what he's thinking or doing. I just need to get through this training with him.

"You know how to wound a guy," he finally says, and I shrug.

"I thought hockey players had thicker skin than that."

"Maybe I'm a softy on the inside." He leans down as he says that, eating up some of the space between us, and I do everything in my power to stand my ground.

Lifting my chin, I raise an eyebrow. "I'm sure your organs are just as mushy as everyone else's, but that's where it stops."

Goodness, Kenna. Hold your tongue. You're going to get fired before you even get started.

There's that chuckle again, and he leans even closer, with only a handful of inches separating our faces now. I think he expects me to move, but I don't. The flash in his eyes is unmistakable, and I tell my traitorous body not to react to it. I'm not going to lie, it's very annoying that my chemical reaction is overriding my common sense, if only for a moment.

"I gather you don't like me very much."

"Oh, there is a brain in there after all. I guess those helmets are good for something." My eyes flash and I don't mean to, but I end up a bit closer as I square my shoulders. His proximity makes me lose all my self-preservation instincts, and if he fires me right now, I wouldn't be shocked. But then he surprises me again.

"Didn't anyone ever teach you to be nice to your supervisors?" he says sternly, but there's amusement in his tone, and

I try to match it. If I can make him think I'm teasing, maybe I can get by until I can get a grip on myself.

"This is me being nice to a supervisor. You don't want to know how I'd treat you like if we met on the street. That's when you truly need to watch out." I give him the tiniest of smiles, hoping to lessen the blow of my words.

He blinks at my words, momentarily stunned, and I use that pause to take a step back and inhale fully. Then, before he can recover, I step around him and toward the register, a smile plastered to my face as I face the next customer.

"Hi, ready to order?"

four

· · ·

REESE

"**A**re you with us, Captain?"

I shake my head, bringing myself out of my thoughts and to the present. Leo is our goalie and the only guy I have ever met who is so attuned to others. It's almost downright creepy at times. He's looking at me with slight concern in his eyes, and I immediately sit up straighter.

"What was that?"

"I asked if you wanted me to spot you," Leo says, his eyes narrowing a little as he studies me. Whether he ends up playing hockey professionally or simply becomes a psychologist, he still doesn't know. But we all know he'd be great at both.

We're in the weight room this morning, as we are most mornings during the week, and my mind has clearly been wandering. The season doesn't start for another month or so, but the guys have been working hard. This year we're having open tryouts for the first time, as most of the team is in the last two years of their college career, and our coach wants to try something different. Everyone is a little all over the place regarding the upcoming months, and I definitely don't need to be distracted.

But I am. Boy, am I distracted.

There's the whole sponsorship dilemma, of course. But what's more surprising is that I cannot get Kenna out of my mind, even if I tried. Which I have, albeit not that hard.

In the last two days, we've spent two four-hour shifts together training, and she's been quick to pick up the way the café operates. Honestly, she's supposed to train for a week at least, but I don't think she'll need to. Which is making me feel a bit bummed, uncharacteristically so.

In the last three years of college, I have concentrated on two things: hockey and my studies. Sure, I've been on a few dates, but nothing serious. I've definitely never got hung up on anyone after the first meeting.

Well, there was that blind date last year that Leo dragged us to, but that's different and not something I'd like to think about. The girl and I connected—or so I thought—and I never even saw her face. I still think about the feeling I got when I talked to her through the dark screen that separated us. Well, I try not to, but it happens.

"Yeah, thanks, man," I nod at Leo and move toward the bench press. We both get into position after rearranging the weights, and I make myself focus on what I'm doing. I welcome the burn in my muscles and try to concentrate on my body's reactions instead of what's going on in my head.

"Do you want to talk about it?" Leo asks after a few reps.

"Not particularly."

"Is this about the mystery girl?"

This time I do grunt out loud, and Leo chuckles. He's the only one I've told about the whole experience because I needed someone to talk to. The other knuckleheads would've had a field day with it. Well, maybe not Don, our center, who has a younger sister, so he's almost pre-programmed to be a bit more understanding. But telling Leo was enough. However, now I think maybe I should've just kept it to myself and said the experiment failed.

"No, it's not."

Which is true. This is about Kenna. And the fact that I dreamed about her last night. The details of this dream are going to stay behind lock and key in my head forever. It was the strangest dream I have ever had: a house full of kids with her and me at the center.

I don't think I've ever thought of having a family. Which is weird, because my parents are happily married. Not that I've spent much time around them growing up. It's only in my adult years that I got to know them. I think they love each other deeply, but I wouldn't really know from personal experience. What I know is that it *seems* like everyone around me is *not*" so in love". It has also always felt like lightning doesn't strike twice, so while my parents got their happily ever after, I should focus on my career instead, because there's not a chance it'll happen to me.

This may be slightly influenced by my uncle, his horrible marriage, and his very vocal ravings about love since the moment I can remember him speaking. He was also my hockey coach growing up, so I was around this mindset a lot. Make that constantly and without reprieve. Which started as annoying and then became rules I lived by.

My first memory of Uncle Dan and Aunt Mary was them snuggling under a blanket in the backyard, looking at the stars. I remember them tugging me to them, holding me close, then sneaking a kiss when they thought I wasn't looking.

Then, Aunt Mary abandoned Uncle Dan—the word he has used to describe it—and he became the coldest, toughest man I'd ever met. As a coach, he ran my practices like a drill sergeant, and as an uncle he would rant about unfaithful women and love being a joke that is sold to us as kids. If I grew up knowing it was all a scam, then I couldn't fall into the trap. Such ravings stick with a child, especially when they see people's marriages break apart around them constantly. One of my friends from back home just had a falling out with his girlfriend of five years. I thought they'd get married. So did he.

When you're constantly told something as the truth, you start to believe that it is. I think that's why I've never actively sought to create any lasting romantic relationships. Keeping to casual dating is safer.

But now, suddenly, my brain has other ideas.

Leo, thankfully, doesn't press the subject, and we finish up our sets in silence. However, when I stand to wipe the equipment, he doesn't move away. Resigned, I glance up, meeting his gaze.

"I'm here if you want to get something off your chest," he says after a long pause, then walks off. I glance around and realize we are the last two in here. I arrived a little later than usual, after meeting with Coach this morning, and the guys have all scrambled off already.

I head to the showers, hoping the water helps me clear my mind.

"Are we grabbing a bite tonight?" Micah asks, intercepting me as I walk into the locker room. Him and Austin are heading out, but both stop to wait for my answer. Micah, the right defenseman, is easygoing to the point of annoying at times, and Austin, the left defenseman, is basically his opposite. Where Micah is loud, Austin is quiet. They're both about six feet, with dark brown hair and light amber eyes, and if I didn't know any better, I'd think they were brothers. But they met at tryouts the first night of our freshman year and have been close ever since. They're also notorious for going out to eat while the rest of us are trying to save money.

"Not tonight. I have a late shift at the café."

The guys nod and after a few goodbyes, they head out as I walk to the showers. I was hoping the workout would help, but apparently not. I rarely work night shifts, but tonight the café is hosting one of their special events, and since I'm officially one of the managers, I'm scheduled to work. Alan will be there, but as always, he'll be mostly useless.

Since the café hosts events throughout the year—it's something Mrs. Lowery thought would be good for campus life—we're often roped into working different hours. Once hockey season starts, I won't be able to take part as much, so I feel obligated to do as much as I can before then.

I wonder what event it is tonight. It's honestly up in the air, because this campus seems to thrive on the unexpected. Last year, we hosted a themed bachelor party for a seventy-year-old groom and his buddies. It was fun, and I learned that I'm fantastic at rummy.

I'm not all that excited to work tonight, but on the plus side, I get to see Kenna and try to figure out once again why she seems to have such a dislike for me. And why she seems oddly familiar. I glimpsed her smiling at the customers once or twice yesterday. Maybe if I convince her I'm not so bad, I'll find out what it feels like to have that smile aimed at me.

five

. . .

KENNA

"I'm sorry, I'm confused. What are we doing?" I stare at Alan as if he's been speaking an unfamiliar language. Either that or I need more sleep, because there's no way the words that came out of his mouth are what he meant.

"We're hosting a magician's dream." He says it like I'm supposed to know what it means, or why there are a bunch of kids currently running around the café after hours.

"Alan, you're going to have to explain what you mean, instead of just assuming people speak your language."

The deep voice sounds from behind me, just as a kid rushes by, and I stumble back. Strong hands catch me at the elbows, and I look up over my shoulder to find Reese's amused eyes staring down at me.

"Falling for me already? That took less time than I thought."

"In your dreams," I snap, extracting myself and taking a step away. Something passes over his face, but I'm already turning away. I need to start acting more poised, or I'm going to lose this job before I even get started.

"Alan, please can you explain to me what I need to do?" I ask, using my best customer service voice.

The senior manager sighs, acting as if I'm asking him for something unmanageable, like fetching the stars from the sky, before he ignores my question and looks at Reese.

"It's a party of thirty-five, and the magician is arriving in ten. Watch over Emma. I'll be in the back." He turns away and weaves through the crowd of kids like his tail in fire.

"It's Kenna," I say to his retreating back, but he doesn't even pause his escape. I glare at him before I roll my eyes. How he even has a job here, let alone as a supervisor, is beyond me.

"Oh good. I'm not the only one on the receiving end of those glares."

It's hard to ignore the hockey player next to me, but I'm still determined to try. Except that I'm an adult with an adult job and I need him to explain what in the world is going on. So I take a deep breath and turn to face him.

How someone can wear a simple hoodie and jeans and yet look so put together is beyond my comprehension. His slightly wavy hair is disheveled by the wind, and he's wearing one of those cocky grins these guys seem to be born with. But his eyes are tired… or maybe troubled? I'm not sure. But he looks like he would welcome a hug. I flex my fingers to snap myself out of such foolish thoughts. He is obviously never getting one from me.

"Don't worry. You're still special. I've reserved my most lethal ones for you," I say, keeping my tone as light as I can manage.

"Weird way to propose, Eeyore, but yes?"

I glance up, my eyes locking with his. I seriously cannot get a read on him. Is this his idea of flirting?

"Did you just call me a donkey?"

"If the pessimistic shoe fits——,"

First, I need to point out that Eeyore wasn't pessimistic; he was depressed. Second, I'm not depressed. Just… tired." And very overstimulated by Reese's proximity. Not that I would admit that out loud. I wasn't expecting to see him, not when he told me yesterday that he rarely works nights, which answered my question on why I never saw him in the café. As a customer, that's when I'm usually here.

"Maybe also a bit grumpy?" he asks, cocking his head to the side, and I press my lips together. He's clearly teasing, but I'm simply annoyed.

"Do you tall people just get away with everything because you tower over most humans?" I sigh, and Reese grins.

"Is that the best comeback you've got, Shortstack?"

"I knew hockey players weren't that smart. I'm five-six, genius. That's above average."

"The perfect height."

He bends at the waist as he says it, bringing us eye to eye, and I immediately lean back, my eyes narrowing.

"Personal space isn't a suggestion, it's an established boundary."

"Aren't boundaries meant to be pushed?" he asks.

"Only if you want to lose something important to you," I reply, giving his face a quick once over. How would he fair playing hockey with one eye?.

I wish it wasn't frowned upon to hit people, because I'm feeling violent. It might have something to do with the fact that I barely slept last night. I'm extra snarky when I'm exhausted.

The school year has barely begun, and I'm already feeling the pressure. Wentworth University's Bachelor of Arts is an excellent program, so it feels like a battle against my peers at every turn. Our portfolios need to be impressive, and that requires a lot more than only taking photographs.

For example, last night, my mind was in overdrive trying to come up with ways to build my Instagram following. Technically, I know it's not a requirement, just a very firm suggestion from our teachers. But I also understand the way the world works, and having a social media following will land me much better opportunities.

Reese surprises me when he leans back, taking a step away, hands raised in surrender. His eyes flash with something akin to respect, but that doesn't let him off the hook.

"I'm sorry if I made you uncomfortable. It wasn't my intention." He's sincere, I can tell. The apologetic look on his face might be enough to melt a less stubborn heart, but I'm not giving in.

"Not uncomfortable. Just annoyed."

"That does seem to be your factory setting," he says.

"Don't you forget it," I reply and receive one of those goose-bump-inducing Reese chuckles.

"I'll just have to keep on my toes around you, Grumpy."

"How about you please stop with the nicknames and focus on whatever is going on here." I turn my attention to the quickly rising chaos of children around us.

"Nope, I'm determined to find the right one for you."

I don't dignify that with an answer as I watch three kids run circles around a table before one of the parents grabs them and pulls them to the side.

"Could you explain to me why we're in the middle of a children's birthday party. Please?" I add the last part like a good little employee, and I can almost feel Reese's grin. But thankfully, he gets down to business.

"Mrs. Lowery, the owner, has a dream of making Coffee & Books a community space. Since it sits on the outskirts of the campus and people from the community, use it as their local coffee spot, she's opened up the space for events, birthday parties included." Reese's voice takes on a bit of a serious note, which I appreciate. Staying on the business side of things might help me keep my cool better.

"We don't host many parties, since most employees are students. But now and then, we get hit by one of these."

"So what do we do?"

"Mostly just supervise." I glance over at Reese as he folds his arms across his chest and takes on a bodyguard pose. Immediately my brain registers how nice the lighting is in here at the moment, and how he's outlined by the twinkly lights and the setting sun at my back, peeking through the window. He'll probably find me strange if I simply pulled out my camera and took a picture. Not that I would. I don't need him clogging up my limited storage space. But it's a reflex I've developed after years of training my eye, and I can't even lie to myself that he doesn't look good.

He sends me a wink as if he can read what I'm thinking, and I shake my head before turning back to the crowd. The kids seem to have settled down around the tables, devouring the cupcakes placed in front of them by the parents. Oh good, more sugar. The noise levels inside the café are already making my head hurt.

I really do need to get some sleep. I typically enjoy kids, even though I'm not the greatest with them. I shouldn't be so… grumpy.

"We'll make coffee and tea for the parents, but the kids are taken care of by whoever hosts the actual party. We're in charge of the cleanup at the end," Reese continues, just as the door opens and a man dressed in a lime green velvet suit steps inside. I blink a few times, blinded by the atrocity. The kids squeal in delight as the man whips out a bouquet of fake flowers out of his jacket, raising it high in the air.

"Greetings, little humans! Let the fun begin!"

six

. . .

I'm honestly not sure how I found myself in this situation. It's been about forty-five minutes since the magician—and I use the title generously—showed up. The kids are having a blast, and Kenna and I have somehow been roped into helping with the big act after making coffee and tea for the parents.

Kenna is looking around like she is ready to bolt at any moment, and I honestly don't blame her. Alan is ridiculous for making her work one of these crazy events on her third day. Speaking of which, he has completely disappeared. I'm pretty sure he snuck out the back door while no one was looking. Which is so like him, leaving the new hire to deal with the chaos. I wouldn't be surprised if she quits after this. It's happened before. They hired someone last year who lasted three days. I'm almost positive Alan now throws newbies into the deep end just to test them.

But I will say that Kenna doesn't seem to be a quitter. I've only known her for a few days, but she seems like the type of person who takes things head-on and doesn't back down from challenges. She hasn't backed away from me once, and I usually intimidate people. Maybe that's why I'm finding her such a breath of fresh air. Which is a ridiculous thought. I cannot let any of the guys hear me speak like this. I'd never live it down.

This party is definitely not what I expected. Case in point, the magician is now making us stand in front of the crowd, facing each other.

"Let's give our friends a big round of applause," the guy says—I've honestly forgotten his name already—and the kids clap with enthusiasm.

"It's time for one of my favorites. Are you ready?"

"Yeah!" The chorus of kids' voices is so loud I can't help but grin. My eyes transfer to Kenna, and I find her smiling as well. Her gaze meets mine and I'm stunned into a stupor. She's always gorgeous, but with that smile? Holy crap I think my heart just skipped a beat. It's possible that all those cliché books and movies my uncle always ranted about being a bunch of crap were actually correct. I'm not sure what to do with that information, but now I want to see her smile all the time.

She's clearly forgotten her dislike of me for a moment, but then seems to realize what she's doing, schooling her features back into indifference. I kind of like how she does that. I'm sure she wouldn't appreciate me pointing it out though.

"Now, my little assistants." I grunt at his use of the word little when he's shorter than Kenna, and he rephrases, "Little big assistants, join hands."

"What?" Kenna's question comes out an octave higher than her typical voice, and I suppress a smile.

"Hands. Join them. Come on, don't be shy." The magician

pushes me toward her, and I stop about three feet away, offering my hands palms up.

"I don't bite," I say, nodding at my hands.

"I don't believe you," she replies but then places her hands over mine. This time, my heart definitely skips a few beats, making me lightheaded. Her hands are smaller than mine, soft, and a little cold at the fingertips. Automatically, I slide my thumbs over her fingers, tugging her closer. She stumbles a little, and then there's only about two feet separating us.

She's watching me warily, as if she also can't quite get a read on me. She's braided her hair, but some of it has escaped in the day's madness, and now I fight the urge to reach over and push the rogue locks behind her ear.

It's such a new-for-me experience, I've never been so fascinated by someone before. Well, maybe once, but even though that whole experience still haunts me, I can't really count it. We never even met face-to-face. Water under the bridge, as they say. I'm more interested in the girl in front of me right now.

What I wouldn't give to know what's going through her mind. She's watching me watch her, and for the first time there's a bit less hostility and more curiosity in her gaze. It disarms me, just like everything else about her.

"Voilà!"

I jerk at the magician's proclamation just as I glance down at a set of handcuffs now linking mine and Kenna's wrists.

"Umm, what did you just do?" Kenna asks, pulling her hand out of mine only for me to be jerked toward her. Our bodies clash, and she stumbles back. Automatically, my arm wraps around her, catching her around the waist. Except that my hand is attached to her hand, so now we're flush against each other, with her arm behind her back and me holding her in place, while I try to catch my breath.

We stand frozen for a long tense minute, before she jerks, grabbing my hand from her waist and moving it back around us, as she takes a step back. A tiny one, but still.

"Watch carefully, or you'll miss it. The magic, magic, magic, coming to free you!" The magician makes a big show of waving his wand in the air, before he twirls in place. Somehow the kids are eating it up.

"I thought his spells were supposed to rhyme," Kenna mumbles, and I chuckle.

The magician makes a bunch more sweeping motions with his hands, sending some confetti into the air—that we will have to clean up—before he skips around Kenna and me in a circle.

"What is happening?" Kenna asks.

"No idea."

The magician returns, taking our bound hands and raising them up in the air, so everyone can see the handcuffs. "Do you see it? No escape!" The kids shout yes again and for some reason, I'm feeling a little concerned.

"Can we free them with our words?"

"How about we use a key?" Kenna comments, and the magician laughs.

"There is no key!"

"What?" Kenna and I exclaim at the same time.

The magician just laughs again, then points to the birthday boy. "Come, come. Use your magic to set them free!"

The little boy, who's just turned six, runs up to us with the most adorable eager expression on his face, and the magician brings our hands in front of him.

"Concentrate really hard and when you're ready, blow, blow, blow."

I'm starting to think this guy has never performed an act in his life because what is this? Kenna glances at me, and I shrug, because at this point it's all I can do.

The little boy closes his eyes, concentrating before he blows on our hands. The magician grabs the chain, yanking it up and then bringing it down. Our hands follow, because of course nothing has happened and we're still attached to each other.

"One more time!" the magician says, and if I'm not mistaken, the dude's voice sounds a little shaky.

The little boy does it again and once again the magician raises his hand, bringing it down on the chain and yanking it up, making our hands go up as well.

"It's not working?" the little boy asks, concern on his face, and when I glance at the magician, my concern also rises.

"It seems these two are powerful magicians and have a bond of their own. But, oh what's that now? Your magic has created a new thing!" The magician reaches behind the little boy and produces a large candy bar. The boy's face lights up with glee and he grabs it, rushing back to his seat.

The magician steps around us, blocking our hands from the view, and throws more confetti into the air. I have no idea where he keeps pulling that out from, but I bet it's just like glitter, something we'll be finding in cracks for years to come.

"That's it, folks! Now watch me disappear!" he yells, then throws a little smoke flare to the floor. He grabs me by my free wrist, and I instinctually take Kenna's hand and pull her behind me as we rush around the bar to the back area.

"Hello, what was that?" Kenna asks as soon as we're out

of the room. She drops my hand, but can't go far, considering we're still handcuffed together.

The guy in front of us looks a bit nervous.

"Dude, where's the key to these?" I ask, and he takes a step away, before he replies.

"There isn't a key. They're supposed to come apart with a hard yank upward." I take a step toward him and he backs up again. "Sorry, sorry. It's never happened before. Maybe try yanking it a few times?"

"What do you mean just try yanking it?" Kenna asks, her voice low but outraged. "Help us get out of this!"

"You might need a set of pliers, but—" His phone dings and he pulls it out, gasping at whatever he sees there. And then he starts backing up. "I'm sure it'll be no trouble taking it apart though. But I gotta go. I have to return this outfit. Sorry!"

He doesn't even wait for us to say anything before he runs out toward the back door, leaving Kenna and I staring after him.

seven

. . .

*T*his isn't happening. Maybe I did actually fall asleep last night, and this is just a nightmare. Yes, definitely. My subconscious is simply working out some issues.

By handcuffing me. To the guy I can't stand.

"Don't panic. It's fine."

"I'm not panicking," I say, peering over at Reese. "But you're looking a little green around the edges."

He's not. I'm trying to make myself feel better. He looks very calm—ice man on and off the ice, clearly. But I might be a little green around the edges because how in the world are we supposed to get out of this without a key.

"These look legit," Reese says, shaking his hand a little, making mine shake as well.

"Can you not? It's digging into my skin."

The genius magician, Greg—I'm going to remember his name forever—put mine on too tight and then kept pulling it up and down. Reese picks up my hand and places it carefully in his for a better look. He's so gentle it throws me for a loop. His hands are so large compared to mine, yet he's taking the utmost care as he looks over my skin.

"We should—" Before Reese can say whatever he's going to say, one of the parents sticks her head into the room.

"Could we get those trays out now?" she asks. I almost forgot we still have a job to do.

"Of course. This way."

Reese turns toward the tables in the back room, and in the same moment slides his palm over mine, entwining our fingers together. I jerk at the contact, this being much more intimate than when we held hands moments ago. I try to pull back, but he pulls me back to his side.

"You'll hurt yourself. Just stay close while we finish up, then we'll get these off."

He keeps his voice low, and somehow, that soft whisper goes directly through me and zeros in on the anxiety I'm feeling. I'm frustrated by the whole situation, but I can't argue with him. My wrist is already hurting from the metal.

When I catch you, Greg we'll see how magical it'll be when I make you disappear…

Reese leads the parent and me toward the tables at the back, where trays with cupcakes await. Not that these kids need any more sugar. The volume has gone up tremendously since this party began, and it just continues to climb. I do not know where Alan has gone, but it would've been way more helpful if he were here to help with this.

The woman picks up one of the trays, not even giving Reese's and mine entwined hands a look. But I'm concerned for a plethora of reasons, the most current one is how we're going to carry the trays. We each need to carry one. I suppose it'll be too much to ask one of the other parents to come and grab them. Maybe they don't realize there's a problem, and it'll create more chaos if we go out there and the kids see us like this.

I unlock my fingers from around Reese's slowly, making sure not to yank at the metal bracelet again. It can rotate around my wrist but won't move up or down.

"We'll go slowly," Reese says, bringing my attention to him. "Side by side."

Seeing no other option, I nod before I reach over to grab the tray. Reese moves quickly, making sure he's right beside me and not pulling on my arm. The small ways he considers me are not going unnoticed, but I can't concentrate on that right now. Truth be told, he's a walking contradiction. Which is messing with my mind in ways I am not prepared for. Better just shut all those thoughts away and keep my distance. At least mentally, while I'm handcuffed to him. We'll work on the actual distance later.

We pick up the trays and head out into the main area. We have to shuffle to the side, keeping each other at our shoulders and somehow, miraculously, we make it to the table and set the trays down with no accidents.

The kids are up and grabbing the cupcakes before we can move. Suddenly, Reese's hand is once again intertwined with mine, but this time, he swings it over my shoulder, stepping right behind me. His other hand lands on my hip and he moves us backward as one unit, dodging the tiny children.

My entire body warms at his closeness—the sensation of his arm around my shoulder, his other hand around my waist, holding me close. I can't even remember the last time I held hands with a guy. Reese's words come back to me earlier —perfect height—and I have to agree. Somehow, I fit against him as if I'm supposed to be here. Which is an incredibly wild thought to have about my arch nemesis. Maybe I need to see a doctor.

What is wrong with you, Kenna? Shut it down.

I glance up to find him already looking down at me, and something passes between us. There isn't a word for it, at least not one I can find at the moment. But it's like the surrounding air is so heavy, someone can slice it with a knife. I don't think I've ever been this on fire before in my life. Suddenly, every molecule is combusting.

There's a moment of stillness around us, and then I remember where we are and who this is. But before I can move, a small body slams into me, and I glance down to find one of the girls has run into me. She stares at her hand and then at my jeans, and I sigh. I am now wearing the cupcake.

"I'm sorry," the little girl says, and I smile at her as I try to lean down. It's a little difficult since Reese's hand is still around me, so I use my free elbow to nudge him in the stomach. He unhooks his arm from around my shoulders, dropping it between us, but he doesn't let go of my hand.

"It's okay, sweetie. Go grab another cupcake. I'm keeping this one."

The little girl smiles at me and takes off immediately. I stand back up, just as Reese hands me some napkins. I take them with a nod and then proceed to clean up the mess.

My hand is sticky and so are my jeans. I just want this day to be over already.

But even as the party winds down, I realize it's far from over because I'm still attached to Reese and we have this whole mess to clean up.

eight

. . .

REESE

don't think Kenna will appreciate me saying this but I kind of want to high five the magician for this mishap. There's no way she would've spent this much time in my presence otherwise, so I'm calling this a win. A part of me doesn't want this party to end, even as the kids and the parents are getting ready to leave.

"Are you sure you're going to be alright?" one mother stops to ask, glancing down at our entwined hands. Kenna has stopped fighting me on this, mostly because her wrist is really suffering any time she moves. Actually, I take back my earlier desire to high-five the magician; I need to hunt him down and handcuff him to something, painfully.

"We'll be just fine. Don't worry about it, but thank you," Kenna replies, her customer service smile in place. She's being a real hero about this; I haven't heard her complain once.

"Please call me if you need anything. Thank you!" The

mother reaches for her son and then they're off, leaving Kenna and I alone. The moment the door closes, I lean forward to lock it with one hand, as Kenna tugs on my other hand.

"I need this off immediately," she announces, raising our clasped hands between us. Once more, I get distracted by how well her hand fits into mine. It's been a very long time since I've held hands with a girl and this feels like… well, like we've been doing it for ages and not just the last hour.

"Would you stop pulling on it?" I ask, my anger at the magician rising with every second at seeing Kenna's very red wrist.

"I don't see how you're so calm about it. What are we going to do?"

"Not panic?" I shrug.

She gives me her best death stare, before she straightens.

"Wait, can you pick the lock with a bobby pin or something?" She asks. I press my lips together, before glancing up at her hair and the way it's escaping her braid.

"I'm all out of bobby pins," I say.

"Oh, what about dislocating your thumb? Or can you rip them apart?" I'm probably not supposed to be finding this as funny as I am, but I can almost see her mind working out different scenarios.

"I'm very pleased to hear that you think I'm that strong, but unfortunately, Oscar the Grouch, my strength lies somewhere below Hulk," I reply, and this time I nearly cough to cover up the smile that's trying to fight it's way out,

"This is serious," she says.

"I'm not arguing," I reply.

"You're also not being useful. Oh, I've seen this in a movie once, you know," she continues, as if she didn't hear me.

"How would you fair without a hand? Can you play with one?"

"Umm, no. I need both of my hands to stay attached to my body. Exactly what kind of movies are you watching?" I ask, watching her very serious face examining our hands.

"The educational ones, of course," she replies.

"So, horror then?"

She finally looks up at me, and I can't even pretend to keep the amusement off my face. Every single side of her I meet, I want to know more about.

"Ha, you do find this amusing. But you should know I *do* know how to dispose of someone. I have a friend in the medical field. The authorities would never find you." She lowers her voice, leaning closer while not breaking eye contact. I know she's trying to be intimidating, but that's not the effect she's having on me. When I don't comment, she straightens, rolling her eyes.

"Seriously, this needs to come off. Now!" she says.

"Just trust me."

"Never."

I don't think laughing will help my case, so I fight the urge. Instead, I flex my fingers around hers, rearranging our palms into a more comfortable position. I really shouldn't like this whole situation as much as I do. I'll have to think on this later.

"Well, while you were concocting a plan on how to best get rid of my body, I texted a friend," I say, tugging her behind me as I head for the counter.

"Wait, what?"

About twenty minutes ago, while Kenna was busy talking to one of the mothers about kindergarten pictures, I texted Leo. It might've been faster to text the group chat, but I don't need to give the guys any more fuel to hassle me. At least I know Leo will keep my secret.

"One of my teammates will be here soon. Do you want to wait or clean?"

I'm leaving the decision up to her, since my wrist isn't irritated like hers. She looks around at the mess, then at the large clock hanging on the wall, before she sighs.

"Let's stack the dishes at least," she says, and we get to work.

Somehow in the last hour, our movements have become synced. It's almost like we've begun to anticipate each other. We stack the dishes on the tray in silence, shifting around each other like it's a dance and we know all the steps.

I've always thought of hockey in this way, a coordinated dance. It's a flow of movement, taking me from one side of the rink to the other. With Kenna, it seems as if I'm dancing a different genre, but it's just as fluid of a motion. It's soothing in a way I would never expect.

My phone vibrates in my pocket, and I tug Kenna to a stop as I pull it out. She watches me check the screen, and I try to keep the disappointment in check. It's selfish of me to feel any sense of it.

LEO:

back door

"My teammate is here," I say, sending a quick reply. "Come on."

I step around the tables, heading for the back door. When I unlock it, I find Leo's face on the other side of it, looking slightly apologetic.

"What—" I begin, but don't get to finish as Micah pops his head around the corner. So much for keeping this out of the group chat.

"Our very own damsel in distress. Let me get a look at you!" Micah says by way of greeting.

"Keep it up and you're doing an extra bag skate or ten," I reply, but he's not even listening to me anymore as his eyes zero in on Kenna. She's standing slightly behind me, her hand still in mine. I tug her closer, because I don't like the gleam in Micah's eyes.

"And here is the hero of the moment. We've all been wondering who was finally able to lock Reese up. The guys will not be disappointed." Micah grins, and I have a sudden urge to push him backward and slam the door on his face. "Hi, I'm Micah. You might know me as the best right defensemen on the Ravens. Can I apply to be your new favorite player?"

"Hockey isn't her thing," I say, keeping my tone neutral, but I don't miss the way Leo is studying me. I simply ignore him.

"I'm Kenna," she replies, taking a tiny step forward and lowering her voice. "Application accepted."

I gape at her as Micah bursts out laughing. Even Leo can't help but smile. I stare at the girl beside me, and she transfers her gaze to me with a proud lift to her eyebrows.

"What? Are you going to make me bag skate too?" she asks.

"You don't even know what that means," I reply.

"That's okay. Micah will teach me," she says with a slight curve up to her lips.

"I absolutely will," Micah announces, but then takes a tiny step back when I turn my attention on him. Most of the time it takes a lot to get me riled up, but if Micah doesn't knock it off, I'll have to knock him out.

"Leo, why is he here?" I turn to my goalie and find him still watching me with an intense look in his eyes. I always forget just how well he can read me, so I narrow my eyes in warning. He suppresses a smile but ignores my question.

"Hello, Kenna. I'm Leo. I'm sorry it took longer than I thought to get here. Is your wrist okay?" Leo asks.

She raises her handcuffed hand, which I'm still holding, and shakes her head.

"No, it's currently trapped. Help me get it out?" She asks.

"I'll help you." Micah steps forward and I block his path once more, staring him down.

"Maybe don't attack your right defenseman before he can help you?" Leo comments.

"Yeah, Cap, I'm just making friendly with your lady friend —" his words are cut off when Leo pulls him slightly back from my death stare.

"Micah, I suggest you tone it down," Leo say and then looks at me. "Reese, let him help. He can pick the lock."

"What?" That's definitely not what I expected Leo to say.

"Oh my gosh, really?" Kenna exclaims, taking a step round me toward Micah. "Finally, someone with some actual useful skills."

"Hey, I texted Leo." I feel inclined to point out.

"Mhhm, sure." Kenna waves me off with her free hand. "Can we get this off now?"

Leo motions for us to take a seat at the table, and Kenna and I sit down side by side, while Leo and Micah sit opposite of us.

"Hands, please," Micah says, and I place our entwined hands on the table. Kenna's wrist has become much redder in the last thirty minutes, and I'm angry all over again.

"You'll need to let go," Micah says. Kenna and I glance at each other before I straighten my fingers. We separate just enough, placing our hands palms up on the table. Micah takes out a paper clip and starts bending it.

"Where did you learn how to do this?" Kenna asks, watching him closely.

"Back in high school. There was a girl I wanted to impress," Micah replies, glancing up and wiggling his eyebrows at Kenna. I nearly growl at him, but when he meets my eye, his grow round and then he gets down to business without meeting my eyes. I guess my death stare finally got to him. What is actually going on with me? Maybe be also need to follow Leo's advice and tone it down, because this is very unlike me.

"How exactly did you end up like this?" Leo asks, as Micah starts wiggling the paperclip inside the keyhole. I try not to focus on how he's cradling Kenna's hand for easier access. I'm just hoping he can actually get them off.

"Greg said these were trick handcuffs. They were supposed to open with an upward yank," Kenna replies.

"Oh, good. You remember his name. It'll be easier to abracadabra him for some good old fashioned retribution," I mumble, and Leo presses his lips together to keep from smiling.

"These are definitely real handcuffs," Micah announces. "But thankfully, they're not double locked because I'm done!"

The lock clicks, and the cuff around Kenna's wrist is pried open. She pulls her hand toward her immediately, cradling it to her chest.

"My hero!" she exclaims, leaning forward and sending a big smile Micah's way. "I owe you."

None of those words sit right with me, but I suppress the urge to say anything as Micah grins back at Kenna.

"You should probably hurry and take care of that one," Leo comments. Micah moves immediately, reaching for my wrist. It seems to take him less time before the metal bracelet falls away from my skin.

"Did I earn myself favor in your eyes too?" Micah asks, but it's Kenna who answers.

"You did. He won't make you do that bag skating thing. Right?" She turns to me with the question, her eyes big as she waits for an answer. I think this is the first time she's given me this much undivided attention and I can't lie; I don't hate it. But I suddenly can't make my mouth form any words, so I simply nod.

"See," Kenna says, turning to Micah. "Thank you for your service. I now need to clean up about one billion confetti bits. I'll see you later."

She waves at the guys, then stands, heading for the front of the café. I watch her go until she disappears around the counter before I turn to my teammates. Both of them are watching me with an amused look on their faces. There's no way this isn't getting broadcast in the group chat. I'm screwed.

nine

. . .

KENNA

It took us about an hour to clean everything up. Mostly because Micah and Leo stayed to help. Which I appreciated, because after being that close to Reese, I needed a buffer. My brain was having a very hard time reconciling the guy I knew from before with the one that was in front of me. And my sleep-deprived brain was definitely not helping.

Not that this morning is any better. I woke up late, and I have work before class.

"Wow, you sure know how to make headlines," Evie yells from her bedroom.

I hurry around the living room, trying to figure out what I did with my notebook when Evie steps out of her room.

"What do you mean? I have a shift at the café, and I have to finish this essay. Have you seen—" I spot the notebook underneath the cushion and pull it out triumphantly. "Never mind. Now I just need my pencil case."

"I have no idea how you can think of anything else right now." I can't quite place the tone of her voice, but I'm only half focusing.

"Evie, I'm tired. What is it?" Evie rushes up to me, halting my search, her phone in her hand. The look on her face is complete shock, and I narrow my eyes in confusion.

"What it is, is you," she starts, her voice rising higher with every word. "All over WentworthWhispers, holding hands and looking all snuggly with Reese Dawson!"

I stare at her as if I've never heard words spoken before and transfer my gaze to the phone she's thrusting into my face. It takes me a moment to come to terms with what I'm looking at.

It's a very blurry, slightly obscured photo of Reese and I holding hands, while I look down at a child and Reese is looking at me. Evie reaches over the top of the phone and swipes to the next picture which is of us, holding hands and looking at each other.

There's no way this is real. I must still be sleeping. I take the phone out of Evie's hands and zoom in on the picture, but the handcuffs are nowhere in sight. We look like we're holding hands because we want to be holding hands. With the party decor and the low light, everything looks very... misleading.

"Kenna, why are you and Reese holding hands and gazing lovingly at each other?" Evie's head peaks over the top of the phone and I nearly drop it at her words.

"We're not gazing. We're looking..."

"You might not be gazing, but he definitely is." I glance at the picture—and image now embedded in my brain forever—and then thrust the phone back into Evie's hands.

"Please stop hallucinating, I need to go to work," I say.

"Kenna, how can you care about work? You're the hot

topic of conversation. Did you see these comments? Why do I have to find out my best friend is dating the hottest hockey player on campus from a gossip account? A hockey player? And Reese of all people? I mean, what is even—"

"Evie, breathe. In, hold, out." I grab her by the shoulders, looking her in the eye. Her voice has risen to record high octave, and I'm truly concerned she's going to make herself pass out. We take a breath together, hold it, and let it out. "Better?"

"Not better!"

I roll my eyes and let go. She's better. I spot my pencil case, grab it, and stuff it in my bag while she continues to stare at her phone.

"Kenna—"

"We're not dating," I say. "We worked a birthday party at the café and got handcuffed together."

"No way." I watch her zoom in on the picture, narrowing her eyes in concentration. "I don't see handcuffs."

"Which is why people are making stuff up online," I sigh. This is already giving me a headache. I glance at my watch and realize I need to hustle if I don't want to be late.

"I'm coming with you," Evie announces, rushing after me as I turn toward the door. "I think you might need a bodyguard."

"I think you're exaggerating," I say, but she simply waves me off and dashes into her room to grab her bag. I could protest some more, but it would be pointless.

Turns out, she was not exaggerating. The moment we step out of the door, I am assaulted by whispers on every side. If there is one thing WentworthWhispers excels at, it's unverified information and grainy pictures they can spin to fit their own narrative, and now I'm smack dab in the middle of it.

"I told you," Evie whispers, linking her arm through mine

as we head out the front of the building. It's late enough in the morning that even people who don't have classes early are out and about. Which means more stares that I care to be noticing.

"Don't people have anything better to do?" I grumble.

"Not when it comes to Reese. Come on, Kenna. You know he's like campus royalty. He hasn't dated at all since freshman year, and now he's publicly holding hands? It's newsworthy information."

"It's gossip, is what it is." I send a glare at a couple walking in our direction, who don't even hide the fact they're looking at the phone and then at me. Because of course WentworthWhispers made sure to tag me in the photo, for maximum identity verification.

"Gossip or not, it's hot. Now tell me how this happened."

Which I do as we head toward the café. From where our dorm is, it's about a fifteen-minute walk, since we're pretty close to the outskirts of the campus. By the time I'm finished with the story, Evie's eyes have grown three sizes. It seems like a scientific miracle, but the way she's looking at me isn't helping the situation. People can clearly see I'm giving her some juicy information, even if they can't hear it.

"Evie, please control your face or people are going to be asking for a wedding registry next," I say, trying to keep my own face void of emotion. I don't need people speculating even more.

"Sorry, I'm just… how does that even happen? And to you, of all people. Reese is not exactly your favorite person." She whispers that last part.

"The universe has a sense of humor, apparently." I sigh, shaking my head as I look up at the sky for a moment.

I don't even know how to feel about the whole thing, because last night felt like a strange out-of-body experience, and now I'm dealing with the aftershocks of it in the most bizarre way possible. I don't think there's a user manual on this.

"Are you okay?" There's genuine concern in her voice because she knows my history with gossip and people assuming things when it concerns me and athletes. My ex made sure I was nice and traumatized when he publicly dumped me. I can't lie, this is stirring up all kinds of memories that I am not equipped to deal with at the moment. I just need to push it all away and compartmentalize. I've gotten good at it; I can do it again.

"I'm fine," I say, but I can tell Evie doesn't believe me. But she doesn't press. For now.

"So what are you going to do?" Evie asks when we reach the café. From what I can see, there's no sign of Reese inside. He's not supposed to be working this morning, but a part of me thought he'd be here.

"I'm going to go inside and work my shift," I say, turning to face my friend. "I have a class at noon, but I'll meet you after?"

She nods, more worry lines appearing between her eyebrows.

"You sure you'll be okay?" she asks, and I shrug.

"I can handle a few gossiping busybodies. It's not the first time." She nods, the concern not leaving her face, because she was there back in high school when all those rumors about my break up were going around. I've lived through being the center of conversation once, I can do it again. If I repeat this enough times, I'm bound to believe it.

Now I'm just curious what Reese is thinking. I'm sure he's not too happy to be associated with me. After all, he said it himself that day, I'm not his type.

ten

. . .

"If you don't shut your mouth right this second, I'll make you scrub the showers for a month," I say, keeping my voice low and steady, even as my heart is trying to jump out of its chest.

We had practice this morning, and although I was exhausted, I pushed myself enough that I'm ready to collapse. My plan was to take a nice shower and a nap, but then Austin and Micah burst into the locker room, phones pulled out and laughing their heads off.

"I'm sorry, Captain. But only you can send Wentworth-Whispers into chaos twice within that many weeks," Austin replies, his face bent over his phone. "You have to admit, this is… pure talent."

In reality, it's actually my very new and not yet fully recognized desire splashed all over the school's gossip Insta-gram account. I haven't even had a chance to win her over yet, and I'm already getting sabotaged. I wanted to get to know her slowly and figure out why I've started to experience these unfamiliar feelings—which are still so very confusing to me. I kind of always thought that relationships have been conditioned out of me in light of career and hockey, but apparently not? But now, I don't even get a chance to explore that before everyone on campus is in my… our business.

"Did you see the comments on this?" Micah asks. "Apparently the way to Reese's heart is a whole bunch of cupcakes." Wait, I like this one. 'But Reese was supposed to marry me!' Did you see that, Captain? Your future wife is lamenting her loss publicly."

I grab the phone from Micah's hands and scroll through the comments. Half of them are various comments of surprise and shock, while the other half is speculating about Kenna.

"Does anyone even know this girl?" is a common theme, followed by comments on her hair, clothes, everything about her, and it makes me want to throw the phone across the room. I'm used to this kind of scrutiny, but I doubt she is.

"Is there a way to take this down?" I look up, focusing on Donovan, our center. Out of everyone, Don knows the most about social spaces, since he's studying public relations.

"You could put in a request with the account, but you know how these things go. I'm sure plenty of people have saved that post already," he replies, a serious look in his eyes. His presence on social platforms, personally and regarding his major, makes him extra sensitive to the way things are perceived. He doesn't know Kenna, but I'm sure he doesn't like this.

"They'll never take it down," Tyler, our right wing, says, pulling a hoodie over his head. He's been gone a few days taking care of some family stuff, but he's usually pretty level-headed when it comes to conflict, so I'm happy he's back to offer his opinion. "They didn't take down the picture of you pushing that kid, and *Coach* made that request. Pretty sure they'll care less about you making it."

He's right, of course. Getting this off the internet is out of question. I need to find a way to fix this. My first instinct upon seeing it was to rush over to Kenna and make sure she's okay. But one, I think that would just make things worse of her, and two, I need to bring her a solution before I see her.

"She seems like a capable person," Leo says, breaking through my thoughts. "I'm sure she can handle herself."

"Doesn't mean she should have to," I mumble, running a hand over my hair.

"This really sucks," Austin says. "And it sucks because we can't even make fun of you for the handcuffs thing now."

I reward him with one of my best glares, and he raises his hands up in surrender immediately. Before I can say anything else, Coach appears at the doorway.

"Reese, can I see you?"

I nod and stand immediately, handing Micah his phone back. I can't really blame the guys for finding this amusing. I probably would too if I wasn't in the middle of it. Well, if Kenna wasn't in the middle of it. We haven't known each other all that long, but I already feel very protective of her.

"Close the door." I do as Coach says, then turn to face him.

"I know what you're going to say, but it's not what it looks like," I feel the need to say, and Coach smiles.

"Take a seat, Reese." There's something in the way he says it that sends some of my warning bells ringing. "I just got off the phone with Mr. Wills." I immediately sit up straighter. "He saw the post and thinks this is a positive step in cleaning up your image."

Out of all the things I thought Coach would say, this was not one of them.

"What does that mean?" I ask carefully.

"It appears that the CEO is very old school and a big fan of romance. He believes, according to Mr. Wills, that a man in a relationship is a far more reliable man. It seems he likes the idea of you being in a relationship. They'd be willing to give you another shot, but they want to see how you handle this gossip first."

My mind is spinning. This is definitely not what I expected. But I have to be honest with Coach Warren.

"It's not what it seems. Kenna and I aren't in a relationship. We just work together and had an incident last night."

"I understand, but you can see how people are getting the wrong idea. Even with the picture zoomed in and sort of grainy, you don't just look like coworkers." It appears I'm not hiding my intentions toward this girl very well, but hopefully, no one but my teammates and coach can see right through me. That part doesn't matter right now, though, because I need to fix this.

"So what am I supposed to do?"

"I can't tell you that. But maybe you can talk to her, see if she'll be willing to come to a game or two. Maybe take some pictures with you to post online. I don't know what you kids do these days. But her presence is currently giving you a boost in your standing with GoGo Sports. Maybe this girl can help you out?"

I nod, just as Coach's phone rings. He picks it up, motioning me to the door, and I stand and walk out. Once the door is closed, I pull out my phone and open Instagram. It doesn't take long to find Kenna's account since the picture has her tagged.

I expect to find pictures of herself or her friends, but

instead, I'm met with a very cohesive grid of various shots that look much too good to be on a simple account. She clearly loves photography, and she's good at it. Even to an untrained eye like mine, I can see it. When I glance at her bio, it makes sense. She's a photography major. I refresh the page once and watch as her following jumps by a hundred people. An idea pops into my head. I might have completely lost my mind, but it could work. Maybe it could even work for the both of us.

First, I'll need to talk to Leo, and then I need to find Kenna. Maybe this isn't as much of a disaster as I think it is.

eleven

. . .

Today's shift is only three hours, and it's been the longest three hours of my life. I've had about thirteen different people come up to ask me if Reese is the best kisser ever, eleven people ask if I blackmailed him into a relationship, four straight up would not stop glaring at me and just held up the line without ordering. My favorite was definitely the one who told me I was a home-wrecker because she was supposed to marry Reese. This is not the response I could've ever imagined from normal people, but apparently, this is the life of the famous. I'm ready to start snapping at people. When you're sleep-deprived and stressed about classes, your emotional state is shaky at best.

None of those people really bothered me though, because right now all my emotions are zeroed in on one person: Alan. Who, after seeing the state of the questions I was getting, lectured me on workplace relationships and then disappeared, leaving me to handle the midmorning shift alone. I really can't stand that guy. He never even apologized for ditching us at the birthday party.

When Mr. Popularity shows up at the end of my shift, I'm not really surprised. Reese seems like someone who wouldn't run away from conflict, but I'm still annoyed to see him. Thankfully, Seth arrives on time to take over for me, and I can escape. I didn't even know he worked here until this morning, but apparently, he's known to be a bit flaky.

"Can I get a latte?" Reese asks, coming up to the counter.

I motion to Seth.

"He'll check you out. I'm off."

I don't wait for a response as I pivot and step out from behind the counter, heading to the back. Not that I think I've actually escaped. I can feel Reese moving behind me, and I can see people staring. Thankfully, there are only a few students present at this time, or I would be dodging more cameras. I truly never imagined just how obsessed people are with Reese's life. I step into the small office at the back and head for my locker. I just need to grab my stuff, and I'll be out of here.

"I have a proposition for you," Reese comments from behind me.

"I don't make deals with the devil," I reply, not turning around. Instead, I unbraid my hair and run my hand through it, before I brush through it with my trusty brush. It's taken me a long time to get my hair to this length, and I take excellent care of it. And right now I'm using it to stall for time, so I don't have to face Reese just yet.

"You've got me confused with the college up north. I'm a Raven," Reese says. He sounds so proud of that fact I can almost picture him slapping his chest a few times with the announcement.

"You're annoying."

"That too."

I turn around at that and find Reese leaning against the wall by the door. I make sure he sees me roll my eyes at him before I turn back around, swipe some tinted ChapStick on my lips, and finally pull my bag out and shut the locker. He doesn't look like he'll leave me alone until he gets to his point.

I sigh once.

"Please say what you need to say. I have class in an hour."

Reese grins, pushing away from the wall and taking a step toward me. For a second, he looks unsure of himself, which is so uncharacteristic of him. I almost forget myself and ask him what's wrong. But I control myself at the last moment and instead wait him out.

"We should date," he says, his voice catching on that last word slightly. He places his hands in his pockets, his eyes on me.

My whole body freezes at his words, an array of emotions rushing over me like a tidal wave. Confusion followed by disbelief and back to confusion. I blink a few times, trying to figure out how to respond, when he takes a step forward again and hurries on.

"Just hear me out, it could work for both of us. I need to clean up my image and apparently, being in a relationship makes me seem more stable."

"You, stable?" I manage, but he's unrelenting.

"And I heard through the grapevine you're into photography and need to build a bigger audience. There's some contest you can be eligible for, or something of the sort? What's bigger than the audience of a hockey star?" He takes the hands out of his pockets, spreading them out in front of him as if he's presenting himself to me. I shake my head.

"Do you hear yourself when you speak?'

"Come on, think about it, Kenna. This could work. We just need to go with what everyone is already thinking. Let's do a little more hand-holding and we both benefit from it. It doesn't have to be for long, just long enough to be worth it."

Ah, of course. He's not actually asking me to date him. This would be just pretend. I can't tell if I'm bothered by that or not—no, actually, I am bothered by that. Maybe it's the use of my name instead of his many nicknames for me that gets to me. Or maybe it's the fact that he thinks I need him in order to grow my account. As if I need a pity fake date to get noticed.

"You're implying that I can't get myself a hockey player boyfriend on my own?" I ask, raising my chin, and Reese immediately straightens. Oh good, I'm getting to him. This will help me get back to solid ground.

"I—"

"Hmm, Micah seemed like he would be willing to go on a date or two, no? I wonder how many followers he has." I tap my chin as if in thought, trying not to smile at the way Reese's eyes narrow at my words and the puppy-dog expression is replaced by something a little more serious. I drop my hand, as he takes a step toward me, eating up the small amount of space between us and suddenly, it feels like all the oxygen has left the room.

"If you want to date a hockey player, I am your *only* option."

The statement is delivered with no argument, sending goosebumps down my spine. My body really is out to get me, isn't it? I stare at Reese, trying to figure out what he means by that exactly. It's frustrating because I can't quite read him, but it's not like I want to date Micah anyway. The thought does seem to rile up Reese enough, which is an added bonus. But

I'm running out of time, and he doesn't seem like he'll be dropping this anytime soon. I need to try something else.

"You're not my type," I say, but Reese is already shaking his head.

"What? I'm everybody's type."

I roll my eyes. "In your dreams, maybe."

He grins back at me.

"Hey, what happens in my dreams is not up for discussion in public." He leans his face closer, mischief shining in his eyes, and all I can do is stand frozen at his proximity. And argue. I can continue to argue until he gets it through his thick skull.

"Fine, I'm not your type. No one will ever believe it."

He doesn't say anything immediately, just leans back to give me a quick once-over before meeting my gaze again. I raise my chin a little, daring him to admit it, but he shrugs instead.

"They already believe it. Haven't you seen the comments?" he asks.

"No, I try not to stay away from gossip." I also didn't need to see the comments, considering they walked themselves into the coffee shop all morning. But I don't think it'll help my case if I share that.

"Kenna."

The way he says my name stops me, and I meet his eye before I can talk myself out of it.

His full attention is on me, eyes earnest.

"This is beneficial for both of us. You help me clean up my image, and you get a real shot at building a following for your portfolio," Reese says, not breaking eye contact.

He's more serious than I've ever seen him, not that I've looked *that* often.

"What grapevine shared that information?"

He shrugs. "I know a few guys in your program."

Of course he does. It's annoying because he is correct. Having over ten thousand followers would qualify me for some pretty good contests and competitions. I could use new equipment, I could—no, I'm not giving into this.

"This feels like it will be more beneficial for you. While I simply suffer," I say, crossing my arms in front of me.

"Suffer is a little dramatic don't you think?"

"Not dramatic enough."

I would like to say that I'm very set on this, but he's giving me his best pleading puppy dog eyes again and it's truly messing with my resolve. Not that anyone could blame me, I'm not a robot. I'm a pretty sensitive soul, if I allow myself to be, which is why all of this is just a bad idea and nothing more. I turn to the side, placing my bag on the table as I rummage through it to find my phone.

"Fine, let's look at the numbers," Reese says, pulling out his phone. "You have three thousand followers—"

"No," I nearly laugh out loud, "I have four hundred and fifty-seven. I don't know whose page you're on."

"You have three thousand and two." He steps up behind me, holding his phone in front of me, and it feels like I'm hallucinating. Again. I think I've fallen into a pattern of hallucination when it comes to Reese.

There's my page, my small little bio, one hundred and seventeen posts and… three thousand and two followers.

I grab the phone, including Reese's hand, and pull it toward me. I stare at the numbers, convinced they can't be right. Maybe it's another account, maybe—

"What do you say?"

The question comes from my right, and I glance up to find myself pressed against Reese's chest with my shoulder. He's so big and sturdy and—

I jerk away from him, but he follows, nearly stumbling into me before I realize I'm holding his hand and pulling him with it as I go. I let go immediately, straightening. He's smiling at me, not one of his cocky grins I expect, but something softer. Which is probably why I say what I say next.

"You really think this will help me?"

"I do. There are over ten thousand students on our campus alone. Times that the schools we visit for games, plus the endorsements and fans across the league and outside of it… you've seen my page, right?"

Of course I have. Over one hundred thousand followers, the punk. He knows it too, because his smile becomes more self-satisfied, as if he can see me caving.

"We'll go to a few parties, you'll come to a few games, we'll take a selfie together. People are curious creatures; they'll seek your information. And when they do, you can wow them with your skills. I mean, your pictures are good, really good. All you need is the right exposure. I'm not saying you won't have people dropping off after we break up, but not all of them will. This will give you a good boost, so why not take advantage of it?"

My brain is still stuck halfway back to when he said my pictures were good. Somehow, he's moved closer again, as he was delivering his speech. I can't even fault his logic. If I can get to ten thousand followers, I'm eligible to enter a few contests I've been eyeing. This could be the break I've been looking for. I'm just not sure how we're supposed to sell this to the public.

"You sure you're not going into politics? You're very persuasive," I say, grateful my voice comes out normal.

"Wait, does that mean I've persuaded you?" He moves up and down, off the balls of his feet, in an excited little jump.

He genuinely looks so hopeful and excited I almost forget myself and smile.

But this is not a place for that because this is a business deal and nothing more.

"Not yet," I say, holding up a hand. "I want a written set of rules and a deadline. And a way out. If it gets too much for me, I want to be able to pull out."

"Okay, like what?" He asks and I pause.

"Like…one outing a week?" I ask, trying to think of what else I can put on the list. "In a public place."

"You come to my hockey games," Reese counters and I nod.

"No gift exchanges," I say and he opens his mouth immediately.

"But—"

"No buts," I say, pointing a finger at him. "I don't have time or money to go shopping. And no public confessions."

Reese shakes his head at me.

"Why are you taking all the fun out of this?" He asks.

"This is not supposed to be fun. This is a business deal," I reply and he shakes his head.

"Fine, then I have a rule," he says. I motion for him to go ahead. He takes a step forward, his eyes suddenly serious.

"My rule is that you…can't fall in love with me," he says and I raise my hand in front of his face, fighting the urge to push him back.

"You're a walking cliché, you know that right?" I ask and he shrugs.

"But what a package, am I right?" He asks, pointing to himself. Before he turns to the right and then to the left, showing off. I make sure to keep my eyes on his face and not get distracted in any way.

"Are you sure you need me?" I ask. "It seems that you and your ego are in a very committed relationship."

He sobers up immediately.

"Yes, I absolutely need you."

The way he says that, his voice low, but sure, runs over my skin, sending a bunch of goosebumps to follow. I clear my throat, pushing those unwanted body responses away and focusing on the facts. He's right, I can make this work in my favor.

"I still want a written contract," I say.

Reese gives one fist pump into the air before he bends at the waist, bringing our faces on the same level. Our eyes are in line and the intensity in his nearly makes me move forward.

"It's a deal," Reese says, and for some reason, my heart leaps in my chest. What have I done?

twelve

. . .

The gossip mill seems to be extra active, because I'm halfway through my patient management class when my phone tries to vibrate itself off the table.

DON:

miracles do happen, or is it the end of the world?

TYLER:

come on, man. Don't rain on his parade. The boy's got himself a girlfriend.

REESE:

what are you two hens clucking about?

DON:

the one and only captain of the Wentworth Ravens, off the market. Never thought I'd see the day.

REESE:

where are you even getting your wild information?

MICAH:

according to Suzy, her roommate's friend saw you and Ms. We-got-handcuffed-together coming out of the back room in the café, looking mighty cuddly this morning

I swear no one has anything else to do on this whole campus but gossip about other people.

REESE:

we weren't even touching

TYLER:

but you were together!

REESE:

what are you, in kindergarten? Does walking together count as third base now?

MICAH:

no actually third base is when

LEO:

don't worry, I have confiscated Micah's phone

TYLER:

we actually overheard coach saying you should date the girl and then you talked to Leo and then you rushed off, so we just assumed

REESE:

stop assuming

DON:

come on dude just spill. Are you bringing her to Clay's party?

I nearly forget I'm in class and groan out loud. That's right, that's happening. It completely slipped my mind. The party is tomorrow night and since I don't have to work, I'm required to make an appearance. Which isn't the worst thing. We can get this fake dating off the ground immediately. There should be a way I can talk her into taking a quick selfie with me. If I post it on my account, that'll look nice and respectable to the CEO who apparently is a big fan of online stalking.

REESE:

I'll ask her.

AUSTIN:

I knew it! Tyler, you owe me 50 bucks.

DON:

wait, why wasn't I in on this action?

REESE:

I'm muting you now

AUSTIN:

aw Cap don't be like that, we're just happy
for you.

REESE:

go be happy in class, I gotta focus

They're definitely not going to stop hassling me about this one, but even I have to admit, it's a worthy bit of news. I'm known for not dating. Apart from my uncle's voice constantly berating relationships in my head, I simply never met anyone for whom I wanted to break my own rules for. This could possibly be good for me too. I don't even know if I'm boyfriend material.

If I were to sit down and reexamine my stance on the whole romance thing, I'd say I'm not cut out for it. My whole life, I've had a very standoffish view toward relationships and have no actual experience in them. I never thought I'd want to. Yet, suddenly, after meeting Kenna, all I want to do is learn how to be what she needs. Is that crazy after knowing someone for a week? Maybe. But does it really take that long to realize someone seems to fit in the spaces that have been empty? After this week, I say it doesn't. It was like something clicked and now I just want to know her. I have no idea where that'll take us, but it would be foolish of me to take myself out of it just because Uncle Dan's voice is unrelenting at the back of my mind, screaming that she's going to ruin me.

I don't have such a narrow-minded view of people. I believe we're all different and people can surprise you in various ways. After all, I've met plenty of pretty girls before, but no one has intrigued me the way Kenna has, and that has to count for something. It's a very big bonus that I get to do this fake dating thing with her, because I actually want to be in her presence. Which means I am determined to stick to our agreement and be the best boyfriend Kenna has ever fake dated.

I should probably tell the guys it's all for show, but I'm not sure they're good enough actors to pull it off. Leo is the only one I trust with this information for now. He tried talking me out of it but then couldn't fight against my logic. Especially when I showed him Kenna's page.

If I can make this work for both of us, then it's worth it. I can't lose out on the GoGo Sports sponsorship, not when I need the national recognition it brings. I had a few official visits and offers come through my junior year, but since I'm determined to finish my college career with a diploma, it's the rest of this school year that truly matters. This is the season that makes it or breaks it for me in the big leagues, and I can't disappoint my parents or my uncle by not giving it my all.

Regardless of whether I play minor or major league. They've supported me this far; I want to be able to give back when the time comes.

Most importantly, I can't disappoint myself. I've worked hard and made enough sacrifices to bring myself this far. I owe it to myself to do my best. This whole situation has taught me that I have to be even more careful about the decisions that I make. But even as I try to find reasoning for why the deal with Kenna is wrong, I can't. It feels exactly like what we both need. I'm not going to cloud that fact with my own regrets or second-guessing. I'll treat her right, and then I'll win over GoGo Sports and get the offer I want. These are facts I'm determined to live by.

thirteen

· · ·

KENNA

"You're not serious."

"I'm one hundred percent serious."

Evie and I are on the couch in our living room, takeout tacos on the table, and the TV on in the background. Evie is currently holding a taco halfway to her mouth, her eyes wide as she gapes at me.

"Kenna, but you hate him."

"Yes, this is a valid point. Which means it's perfect, because then I won't be catching any unnecessary feelings."

She stares at me like I've lost my mind. Maybe I have. But the more I think about it, the more I believe I've made the right choice. In a way, he owes me, and this is a way for me to get my payback.

Evie, on the other hand, is very protective of me and might lock me in my room for the duration of the semester. I sigh. I had to tell her. There's no way I could keep this from her. Especially since she's been fighting off questions about me all day. If Reese and I are going to make this work, she has to be on my side.

"Are you sure you can deal with this? I know you have a good reason for disliking him. And it... this might not be the wisest decision."

I do. Sometimes Evie blames herself. After all, I didn't want to go to the mixer. Evie dragged me to it. Third week of freshman year, I wanted nothing more than to figure out my classes, get comfortable on campus, and start setting up some photoshoots to beef up my portfolio.

But according to Evie, the psychology majors enjoyed putting together different experimental events, and she couldn't miss out. She begged me for days until I finally caved.

What I didn't realize at the time was that the particular event was an extreme case of blind dating. They set up small boxes, like confessionals, with a number system for the rooms and the people taking part. A wall obscuring their vision separated the two parties, which required them to get to know each other blindly. We filled out small cards with our preferences upon entering, and then we were led to one side of the room, into a corridor. So we never saw our partners.

The gist of it was testing how quickly someone could connect with another human being. Once we were inside the small booth, we had five minutes to make a decision. We could stay in the room for up to twenty minutes if there was genuine interest, or we parted ways after the timer ran out. The hypothesis dealt around the phenomenon of love at first sight and if sight was actually needed (for those who typically relied on it). I have to admit, it was an interesting hypothesis and it didn't hurt to see how it played out.

When Reese walked into the other side of the box room, I had no idea that's who was there. I knew of him—anyone who's been on campus for longer than five minutes would know who the Wentworth Ravens were. But inside the box, we weren't supposed to exchange names or any identifiers that might clue us in on the other person's identity. We only exchanged our assigned numbers. We started talking about our favorite childhood movies and trips on our bucket list, and twenty minutes passed before we knew it.

He was so easy to talk to. I've been on dates before, but have never clicked with anyone the way we seemed to click. Not even the one boyfriend I had in high school. Not that it's surprising. My ex was a jerk. But I truly felt a connection with my number partner. When our time was up, he left first just like was supposed to.

But I cheated.

I didn't go the way I was supposed to, and I ended up catching a glimpse of him when I rounded the box room. I can't even lie to myself that I wasn't pleased with who he was. He was exactly my dream type in that way that I wouldn't even allow myself to dream about, lest I'd be disappointed.

The next part of the experiment was setting up a date. We were supposed to turn in our cards with our votes and information. I made my way to the front table when I saw him with some other guys standing on the other side of the room. Even before I got too close, I could hear one guy talking about the experience.

I should've left. I should've kept going and never paused, but I couldn't help myself. Not when one of the guys directed his question at Reese.

"So, did you find your special girl?"

"I'm not sharing."

I don't know why, but his answer made me blush.

"Let me guess, she sounded tall and blonde?"

"Obviously, and don't forget athletic," Reese replied, and the guy slapped him on the back.

"I knew it, you're very particular. I can't even imagine you with anyone but…" The guy laughed, and Reese nodded.

"Well, you know, that's my type," Reese laughed, and I felt my heart sinking. I dodged around them and kept going, my mind racing. I was nothing like his perfect type, but that shouldn't matter, right? My old insecurities based on my ex began to rise, but I pushed them all away. Reese and I clicked in a way that was beyond all that, didn't we?

I turned in my card and was told they'll be in touch. Not even an hour later, I received a text with information regarding a date. I was surprised, but also incredibly hopeful. I stared at that message for hours, trying to remind myself that not everyone was like my ex, that Reese wouldn't just disregard me because I didn't live up to his expectations visually.

Two days later, I had my favorite green dress on and had even curled my hair. I waited at a café off campus for our coffee date. I was excited, and I tried to tell myself that it would be fine. Sure, his statement about his type didn't sit all that well with me, but that was my own doubts and experiences that tried to creep in. I wanted to give him the benefit of the doubt. If nothing else, he'd come, and we'd see if our connection was anything beyond a twenty-minute conversation. Then I could decide where we stood.

But he never came.

I sat in that café for two hours like an idiot, checking my phone. By eight o'clock, I knew he wasn't coming.

I made my way back to campus and just when I was walking past Coffee & Books, he walked out with a girl. Tall, blonde, and much fitter than I could ever be.

Reese looked up and I swore our eyes met, and then it

was like I didn't even exist. They kept going. And I stood there, trying to rationalize what happened. The scenarios my mind came up with were not pretty. But the one that stuck? It was that Reese came to the café, took one look at me, and left.

When I got home, Evie had a lot of questions, but I couldn't deal with any of it. So, I simply told her it didn't work out. It was only a month later, when she wanted to go to a hockey game, that I admitted it was Reese who stood me up.

Now, thinking about that whole experience, I realize it's not his fault that I'm not his type. It's a matter of preference. I can't even hold him accountable for my worst-case scenario because I made that up in my head. I don't think I'm ready to forgive him yet, but time has definitely made me more level headed about the whole thing.

The one thing I can't get over is that I could never respect someone who doesn't communicate and would simply stand a person up. It reminds me too much of my mother and the way she treated people around her. Of the way she disregarded my dad when the time suited her best. And then, of course, there was my ex, who used me up and then threw me away like garbage when it suited him.

It's not fair to put all that on Reese. Maybe that's the real reason I agreed to this little deal of ours. To give myself a chance to be open to possibilities past my own prejudice. My chance to be a Lizzie at the end of the book, instead of the beginning.

"I'll be okay," I turn to Evie now, determined to stay true to an open mind. "It's not like there are actual feelings involved, so I'll be fine. I just need to make sure I use this to my advantage while I have the chance."

"If you're sure." Evie doesn't sound convinced, but she

knows better than to try and talk me out of it. I can be pretty stubborn.

"I—" my phone vibrates with a notification, interrupting me. I've muted most of my notifications for the day, just because I've been getting a pretty steady flow of followers and comments. Granted, those comments had to do with Reese, mostly. But there were a few who liked my photos and commented on them. Since it seemed to die down a little, I turned the notifications on again. Mostly out of curiosity. I pick up my phone now and see a message notification. I click on the DMs and my requests folder when I see Reese's name.

Of course he wouldn't have some obscure username. He uses his own name. He's a walking brand, after all.

> ReeseDawson_13: I don't have your phone number. Here's mine. Can we talk?

I stare at the set of numbers and his demanding tone for a moment before accepting the request. I grunt out loud and Evie shoots me a questioning look. I turn the phone toward her briefly, and she scoots closer.

> picsbykenna: most people start with a hello

His response is almost instantaneous.

> ReeseDawson_13: Hello, Moody Judy. How was your day? Can you please text me so we don't have to resort to the public platform?

"Moody Judy?" Evie asks, leaning over on the couch to look at my phone.

"He has stupid nicknames for me. I don't even know how many he's used already."

"Mm-hmm."

"What is that supposed to mean?" I look at my friend and she only shrugs, moving back to her side of the couch.

"I said nothing."

"Your face said plenty," I comment, then get another notification.

> ReeseDawson_13: having each other's phone number is part of dating

> picsbykenna: we're not dating

> ReeseDawson_13: Moody Judy! What if your FBI agent is checking on you this very moment?

> picsbykenna: he'll be proud of me for making good choices

"Just text the poor man already," Evie comments, and I look up to find her eyes on the TV. She's unpaused our show, and I didn't even notice. "He's going to bug you until you do."

She's not wrong. I glance down just as another message pops up.

> ReeseDawson_13: I apologize for my lack of tact, now please? Pretty please? with all the cherries on the top? Or if you're allergic to cherries, insert your favorite berry here...

I can almost see him making begging eyes at me. He's fantastic at that expression, I'm not going to lie. I shake my head a little, but then copy the phone number into my phone and send him a text.

KENNA:

what is it?

REESE:

ah! The begging worked. Good to know for
the future! But what is your favorite berry?

I roll my eyes, but I also almost smile. He's confusing me,
and that's making me more annoyed.

KENNA:

speak or forever hold your peace.

REESE:

Fine, Grumpy Gus. I know you're not
working tomorrow night, but do you have
any other plans for your Friday?

KENNA:

how do you know I'm not working?

REESE:

I have my sources.

By which he clearly means Alan, that traitor. He can't be
bothered to help with work but gives out information no
problem, apparently.

KENNA:

before I tell you, why are you asking?

This time, he doesn't reply right away. Almost like he's
thinking over his words first.

REESE:

> I was thinking we can kick off our
> partnership right. There's a party tomorrow
> at the soccer team's house off campus.
> Clay's. I have to make an appearance, so I'm
> thinking we should go together. Solidify our
> public image. Maybe even take a selfie.

"Why is your face doing that thing?" Evie asks, and I shift my attention to her.

"Reese wants to go to a party tomorrow. To solidify our public image." I show her the message.

"A man of action. You like that." I glare at her, and she chuckles. "Sorry, slipped out. But if he's down, I can come with. In case you need backup."

"You just want to see Clay," I smile. There are a few athletes on campus Evie has mentioned by name, and Clay is one of them. She does like soccer more than hockey, or so she's said in the past. Evie shrugs, completely unfazed. But I can also tell she's worried about me, since I don't do so well at parties.

"A girl knows what she likes," she says.

Evie turns back to the TV, and I look down at my phone. It needs to be done. Better now than later.

KENNA:

> I'll go, but I have some stipulations.

fourteen

. . .

REESE

Fridays are always really long days for me. Between practice, three classes, and a shift at Coffee & Books, I'm ready to collapse by five p.m. I've never been that big on the party scene, but I do know I'm required to keep up with the appearances, so I promised Clay I'd be there. I'd be regretting it if it didn't mean I get to see Kenna.

She's been invading my thoughts a lot more than I'd like to admit. There's something familiar about her—no, maybe not familiar. Comforting? Even when she's teasing me, I'm intrigued. The glimpses of her I've seen, when she's not taking shots at me, leave me curious. I want to get to know her and now I have a chance. It feels like she wouldn't give me one if we didn't need each other.

The party isn't until eight, but Kenna asked to meet earlier to go over a few things. Even though I would've loved a nap before I had to socialize, I'm sitting in an café off campus, waiting for her now. We could've met at Coffee & Books after I finished work, but she insisted we needed to go off campus. Preferably somewhere less popular with the students. So, I drove thirty minutes into town and found a place where I didn't recognize a single person, and no one paid me any mind. Which is a bit rare in this town, and I'm kind of enjoying it. Kenna texted and said she'll be here in twenty minutes. Maybe I should've taken a nap in the car.

I'm contemplating if I have time to squeeze in a small one when the door opens and Kenna steps inside. It's windy outside, and her hair lifts around her like a halo as a gust follows her inside. She's wearing an oversized sweater that's somewhere between light pink and maroon, and a short gray skirt, plus combat boots with long socks peeking out of the top. It's the first time I've seen her in anything other than business casual, and the sight throws me off-kilter. When her eyes find mine, I see that she's added some sparkle to her eyelids, and her lashes are longer and darker than usual. I don't even realize she's moved toward me until she's standing right by the table.

"Hi," she says, and I shake my head to restart my brain and motion to the chair opposite me.

"Did you find it okay?" I ask as she rearranges her hair around her head, my eyes following the movement. I have the sudden urge to reach over and do the job myself, so I link my hands together on top of the table and force myself to focus on her answer.

"You really found a good one. I don't think people from campus would stumble in here."

"You told me it needed to be discreet."

"And you listened. I'm very proud." She flashes me a tiny smile before she reaches into her bag, pulling out a folder. Just then my name is called, and I stand to grab our drinks. I ordered them when I came in, but I asked them to wait about fifteen minutes before making them.

"You got me a coffee?" Kenna asks as I place a cup in front of her.

"Thankfully, they had oat lattes here. Since it's after five and all," I reply and take a sip of my own. She's staring at me like she can't believe the words that are coming out of my mouth. "What?"

"You… nothing." She shakes her head once and then takes a deep breath. "Thank you."

"You're welcome."

I'm not sure why this seems like such a big deal to her, but she's back to staring at the cup as if it's full of treasure. I decide not to push; I don't think she'll tell me anyway if I ask. Instead, I motion to the folder.

"What's this?"

"Oh, our contract."

I nearly choke on the sip I've just taken, swallowing quickly. I glance between the folder and Kenna, thinking I haven't heard her correctly.

"A what?"

"Our contract. You didn't think I was kidding, did you?"

I absolutely thought she was kidding. But I don't think I'll earn any points with her if I admit that now.

"You're just very prepared, is all."

"Well, you're the one taking me to a party before we even set ground rules. I had to be proactive." She opens up the folder and produces two pieces of paper, stapled together. "We can go over it now, make any amendments needed, and sign. Here."

She hands over the papers, and I start reading.

This is a relationship contract agreement which has been formed between Party A, Kenna St. James and Party B, Reese Dawson for the purpose of fake dating in order to grow Party A's Instagram account and give her portfolio more exposure, and to clean up Party B's image, to restore his good name and help him with his sponsorship.

This partnership is entered on this date and will end within no more than three months of signing this contract. If it needs to be terminated early, both parties will have a discussion prior.

Party A and Party B are formalizing the rules of this partnership, and they are as listed below:

- there will be no unnecessary physical contact.

- there will be one public outing a week.

- Party A will attend Party B's hockey games

- there will be no discussion of the relationship outside of pre-approved people.

- there will be no unplanned events and outings, unless both parties agree otherwise.

- there will be no disruption of their personal lives.

- there will be no commitment made, and both parties are allowed to explore their own feelings if they meet someone they are interested in.

"Absolutely not," I stop reading and look up only to be met with Kenna's confused expression.

"What's wrong? This is a standard contract."

"No, this is a 'not-to-do list' and for us to be believable, we need to do some of this."

"Okay." She pulls out a pen and reaches for the contract, but I snatch the pen out of her hands and begin crossing out some lines. Starting with the last one.

"Hey!"

"This one is an immediate no," I say, not even looking up. "Fake or not, you are my only girlfriend. I will not be exploring anything with anyone else."

I keep my voice level, but I can feel myself getting upset. It doesn't sit well with me at all. It also seems that my nickname needs to be updated because when I'm around Kenna, I'm anything but an ice man.

"Okay, but what if you meet someone? I don't want you to feel obligated to me—"

"I'm not obligated. I'm your boyfriend, you are my only girlfriend. That's how this works," I say, looking her straight in the eye. She looks shocked, and I have the sudden urge to kiss that slightly open mouth and show her just how committed I am to this. Obviously, I won't, but the fact that she wants to keep her options open is making me feel some kind of a way.

"Okay, but what's wrong with the first one?" Kenna asks.

"Physical contact is necessary if we're to present a united front in front of everyone."

"Fine, but we have to discuss it first."

"Fine," I mimic before adding to the bullet point. No physical contact unless previously agreed upon. "How's that?"

She reads over the document, her brow furrowed in concentration, and I think I'm actually holding my breath. There's a possibility that she'll back out now. We haven't signed anything. But then she says:

"Agreeable."

And I can breathe again.

I reach for the paper and sign it at the bottom, ready to have this locked down. I hand the pen over and she, thankfully, doesn't hesitate as she signs.

fifteen

. . .

KENNA

"Come on, I'll drive us."

Reese stands up as I hurry to put the contract away, then holds the door open for me as we step outside together. There's a very big possibility that this will blow up in our faces, but right now, I just keep thinking about those five thousand followers on my account and the few people that have already commented that they'd love to do a photoshoot with me. This is good. I can handle a hockey player for a few months if it means I'm closer to reaching my goals. It's not any harder than handling a big family reunion photoshoot.

"Have you ever been to any of Clay's parties?" Reese asks as he leads me toward his car. I didn't even know he had one. Most people on campus don't. But I suppose since he lives off campus, albeit not that far, he needs transportation. According to Evie, a lot of athletes live off campus in nearby neighborhoods. Just one of the perks, I suppose.

"No. Is there anything I should know?" My question comes out casual, but my anxiety is already rising. The last time I was at a party was when my ex publicly humiliated me, so needless to say, I have not attended one since.

We reach the parking lot, and Reese walks over to the passenger side of a dark green SUV. He opens the door and motions me inside. I stare at him dumbfounded before I hurry over and get in. He shuts the door and then walks around the hood of the car to the driver's side, while I try to force my heart to stop trying to jump out of my chest. I mean, he just opened a door for me. He didn't lasso the moon.

Granted, no one has ever opened a car door for me and shut it after, like one of those gentlemen in old movies. It's one of those gestures I've always found incredibly sweet. I just didn't expect it from Reese.

But then again, he's different from the version of him I have in my head.

"The party can get pretty wild," Reese says, answering my earlier question. "Just stick with me and you'll be fine."

"My friend is also coming," I remind him, and he nods as he puts the car in reverse.

"Don't worry. The guys will be there. We'll look out for her too."

I can't admit it out loud, but that's also sweet. He says it so nonchalantly, as if it's the most natural thing. After my mother left and my dad became mostly focused on work and nothing else, I forgot what it means to have people around you that care about you. I did all the caring. I took care of my dad. I took care of the house. I worked to save up for college, and I forfeited a lot of friendships. It became easier to keep people at a distance because I simply didn't have time for anything or anyone. Which is why when one of the guys in class asked me out, I thought that someone had seen past all my defenses and wanted to get to know the real me. But he ended up being a shallow excuse of a human who took what little I had left of my self-confidence and poured gasoline all over it before setting it on fire.

I met Evie right before the crash and burn, and she has been the only constant presence in my life. She looks out for me the way I look out for her. Having someone else step into that role, even if it's just for a party, even if it's fake, feels… nice.

"What got you into photography?"

At first, his question doesn't register fully, then I turn to glance at him in surprise. But of course, he needs this information. He's not asking because he wants to know.

"I'm asking because I'm really curious," he continues, shattering my predisposed idea, and I press my lips together for a moment.

"Am I that easy to read?" I ask and am rewarded by one of Reese's soft chuckles.

"Not at all. Which is quite frustrating at times. But just now, yeah, I figured you out just fine."

I cock my head to the side as I lean a little against the passenger door so I can see him better.

"That's a whole lot of honesty in an answer," I say.

"I don't see any reason why I wouldn't be honest. You seem like someone who's upfront about her thoughts, so why wouldn't I be upfront about mine?"

I open and close my mouth, completely disarmed. Most people don't appreciate me being so blunt, and I constantly have to make sure I'm filtering my responses instead of going into protection mode. But I suppose when I look back at our interactions, I've been more blunt with him than I usually allow myself to be. He doesn't seem intimidated, which is rare.

"I don't really just walk around being mean to people," I decide to keep the honest streak going. "But—"

"You don't like me. Or you don't like hockey players. I get it, being in the presence of someone so amazing can bring out the worst in people."

The laugh escapes me before I can police it, and Reese whips his head in my direction right as we come to a stop at a red light. I slap my hand over my mouth, surprised at myself, but he looks like he's won the lottery.

"I knew I'd get to you eventually," he announces, and I roll my eyes immediately.

"Your ego truly has no bounds. I'm surprised you can walk around, carrying so much of it around."

"I work out." He shrugs, and my eyes shift to his chest, almost on their own. He clearly does. His shoulders are broad and sturdy looking, the arm that's resting on the steering wheel is well-defined. I'm a big fan of forearms, and he's got very nice ones. The shadows of the passing streetlights dance over his skin, and once again, I want to take a picture. I clear my throat and avert my eyes, hoping he didn't notice.

"When I was ten, my dad got me my first camera." I decide that I don't mind offering up this bit of information. "It was one of those point and shoot ones, but no digital screen. Just a viewfinder. I thought it was cool seeing the world through this tiny square. It sort of took care of all the noise, giving me a chance to focus on what's in front of me, of what was important in that moment. I started taking it with me everywhere. Learning about composition and light by practice, before I got older and started to look into the technical side of the art."

I pause, surprised at myself for giving away so much. But when I steal a glance at Reese, he seems genuinely interested, even while keeping his attention on the road.

"What's your favorite subject to take pictures of?" he asks.

"It changes depending on my mood," I reply automatically. "I went through phases when it was only still life or only nature, but then I started doing themed photoshoots and weddings. Each time I pick up my camera, it brings me a sense of peace and a chance at adventure. It's hard to explain, I suppose."

I stop, a little embarrassed by my outburst, but can't help it. Photography has always been my escape, especially when things became difficult at home. It's been my creative outlet, my friend, the only time I felt like myself, but I can't exactly tell Reese all of that. I would probably sound like a lunatic.

"I get it," he says, and I shift my eyes to him. A small smile is tugging at the side of his lips, and it's almost like he's looking at something I can't see. "It's how I feel about hockey. When I'm on that ice, there's nothing but me, my teammates, and the game. The noise of life kind of disappears, and I can focus on this one thing that brings me happiness."

His words pierce through me, the sheer honesty taking my breath away. I've never understood hockey, but hearing him talk about it makes me want to. This is the exact reason why I felt such a strong connection to him when we were in that booth last year. He has a way about him that's dangerously magnetic, and I have no idea how I'm supposed to fight against that pull. Maybe Evie was right, maybe this wasn't a good idea.

"We're here."

Once again, he pulls me out of my thoughts, and I realize we've parked. We're off campus, in a subdivision near the east side of the school. I haven't been here before because I've never had the need to, but I do know from Evie that this is one of the subdivisions that houses athletes from the school.

"Is this the neighborhood you live in as well?" I ask,

peeking through the front window. There are cars parked up and down the street, and I can see people walking into a house about four houses in front of us.

"Actually, the guys and I are in the neighborhood on the other side of campus. As you know, freshmen and sophomores cannot live off campus, but the team grants some soccer players leniency because they are with the team. So, this neighborhood houses almost the entire team."

"Ah, I see."

Now that we're here, I don't want to get out of the car. I don't think my brain realized how many people come to these things. Maybe Reese and I should just stick to hanging out on campus in a café or library to fuel the rumors. I think that's much more manageable. I think—

"You're freaking out."

I turn to find Reese leaning on the armrest between us, studying me.

"Stop reading my thoughts!" I reply, glancing away before I decide to give him one of my deadly stares instead.

"Can't help it. It's cute. The way you press your lips together and your brow furrows right here when you're concentrating so hard." His finger pokes me ever so gently between my eyebrows, and I freeze.

"That was unauthorized touching. You're breaking the rules already," I say, my voice breathless—the traitor. Reese leans farther in, his face only inches from mine now, but I don't move. I can't tell if it's because I'm determined to hold my ground or if my body has stopped responding to my commands.

"I think we need to amend the rule while we're at the party," he says, keeping his voice low and sending another plethora of goose bumps up my arms. "You can't tense up every time I touch you."

"Are you planning on touching me a lot?"

"Yes."

"Oh."

I need my brain to come up with something more, to bring up some kind of argument, but when he's looking at me like this, I find that I can't think at all. In the low light, his eyes look almost black, framed by long eyelashes, and there's so much intensity it takes my breath away.

"What… what's the plan?" I manage when Reese doesn't move. He just continues to study me. I need to get us back to our corners, and maybe a little breakdown of what to do and not to do will be good for us. His lips curl up slightly at my words.

"I'll need to stay by your side, so we'll need to hold hands," he says.

This is expected, I'm just not sure why it's making me breathless all of a sudden. I clear my throat softly.

"Just palms pressed together," I say.

"Or an arm swung over your shoulder."

"For how long?"

I'm not exactly sure when it happened, but we've moved even closer to each other. Our faces are inches apart, the noise outside the car completely forgotten, as we whisper the rules to each other.

"Five to ten minutes at a time," Reese replies, his voice just as quiet as mine.

"Two to three minutes, in short bursts."

"You drive a hard bargain, St. James." Reese grins, and my lips curl on their own.

"Gotta keep you on your toes, Dawson."

He's watching me in that intense way of his, and I have no idea what would've happened if my phone hadn't vibrated, breaking the moment. I fall back into my seat, my face on fire, and I duck my head as I open the message.

"Evie is here," I say, making sure my hair stays covering my face. I have no idea what that was, but it was unacceptable behavior on my part. It's like playing with fire, and I am sure to be burned, so I need to douse myself in some cold water and remember this for what it is: a mutually beneficial agreement.

"Then let's go wow the masses," Reese says before he opens his door, but then pauses. "Wait, one more important question."

I freeze, my hand on the handle as he leans back closer to me.

"What's your favorite berry?" He whispers and I nearly snort as the chuckle tries to burst out. He raises his eyebrows at the noise, and I shake my head once, while he nods in encouragement.

"Strawberries," I reply, and he grins, blinding me.

"Now we're ready to wow the masses," he says and gets out. I give myself one solid, deep breath and let it out. Professional and unattached. I can handle it.

sixteen

. . .

REESE

$\mathcal{I}$t has taken every ounce of my self-control to not simply close the remaining distance between us and kiss her right then and there. I'm not sure why, but my brain is now wondering if she'd taste like strawberries too. Which is so irrational I'm not sure how this train of thought is even possible.

A part of me wishes we could've just kept driving around, so I can ask all the questions piling up inside my brain. There's something incredibly attractive in seeing her in the passenger seat of my car. And when she started talking about photography, her passion for the art was clear on her face, making her shine in the dim light of the streetlights.

I want to know more. I want to know everything.

Which is not something I thought would ever be an issue for me. But it's almost like Kenna breaks down all the doubts so deeply instilled in me by my uncle and shows me a different way of looking at things. She's making me reeval-

uate my stance on a belief I've held onto my whole life. I am so curious about her; it's driving me crazy.

Even now, I want to know what she's thinking. She's walking quietly beside me, her eyes trained on Clay's house as if it'll disappear if she looks away. Even though she's only a foot away, she seems too far and I can't resist the urge anymore, I reach for her hand. The next time our arms swing, I simply wrap my fingers around hers, pulling her right into me.

"What are you doing?"

"Practicing," I reply without missing a step. "So you don't look so spooked in front of our peers."

She glances up at me, and I almost turn us around and walk us back to the car. She looks so beautiful, I don't want to share her with anyone else.

Maybe I should go get my head checked. I haven't taken any hits lately, but I feel as though someone has slammed me against the glass a time or two.

We step onto the driveway and my eyes zero in on my teammates. Micah sees me first, pushing away from the wall and taking a step toward me.

"There you are! You..." Micah freezes as he gets a look at the girl beside me, and then at our clasped hands, and meets my eye long enough to give me a sly grin before he transfers his attention. "Kenna! It's so lovely to see you. Is Reese holding you hostage? Blink twice if you need help."

"I suggest you tone it down before Reese breaks his rule about physical violence against teammates," Tyler says, coming up beside Micah and wrapping his arm around his neck to pull him back. "I'm Tyler."

"Kenna." She gives him a small smile before glancing over at the other two guys with him. "Hi, Micah. Hi, Leo."

The goalie gives her a nod in greeting before looking at

me. I can see the concern in his gaze, but he doesn't voice it. Thankfully. He's the only one I told my idea to, and while he didn't physically restrain me, he's not supporting this madness. He said it was dangerous, but I disagreed. But now that I've spent just a few hours with her alone, I don't disagree anymore. But I'm not about to admit that out loud.

"So what's the deal here?" Micah glances between the two of us.

"What does it look like?" I ask, and Micah shakes his head dramatically.

"It looks like I missed my chance and will forever carry a wound in my heart," he replies, earning a small chuckle from Kenna. I glance down at her, and she meets my eyes, hers full of amusement.

"It looks like the dramatics run among the teammates. Is that a prerequisite to being a hockey player, or did you train them yourself?" she asks, but there's nothing but teasing in those eyes, and I want to break all the rules, right here and right now.

"I don't know what you're talking about. I have never been dramatic a day in my life," I reply, leaning down just a bit so I can inhale more of her sweet scent. It's familiar, I noticed that before, but I can't place it. She smells like a fresh bouquet of wildflowers, and I hope she was in my car long enough to leave some of that behind. The idea makes me smile.

"Anyway," Kenna says, turning back to the boys. "Have you seen a tall blonde with short hair and a dazzling yellow dress come through here?"

"No," Leo replies, and then pauses. "Maybe?" He's looking over my shoulder, and I turn to watch a girl coming up the driveway. She's exactly how Kenna described her. Her eyes zero in on Kenna, and then they're reaching for each other. Kenna clearly forgot we're still holding hands because she pulls me right along, then stops and stares up at me in shock.

"What are you doing?"

"Following you."

"Well, can I have a moment with my friend before we go in?"

"Sure. But then you'd have to let go of my hand."

She glances down and drops my hand like it's on fire. She takes a step away, looping her hand through her friend's and then leads her back down the driveway. The friend, Evie, meets my eye, a very amused expression on her face, before she focuses on whatever Kenna is whispering to her.

"So what's the deal, Reese?" Tyler asks, coming up beside me. I glance at him and find him watching the girls. Refusing to acknowledge just how much I don't like the fact that I had to let go of Kenna's hand, I turn to my teammates instead. The three of them are watching me, waiting for me to reply.

"The deal is that Kenna and I are dating. Which you already know because you've hassled me enough by text." But I like how that sounds and suddenly I want to tell everyone. Micah hollers and whoops and Tyler claps, as if I've received an award.

"I had to hear it out loud," Micah says.

"It was bound to happen, eventually. The Ice Man's heart is melting," Tyler says, and I level him with a look.

"You're not funny."

"And you're not as slick as you think you are. You're smitten. It's all over your face." Tyler turns to Micah. "Let's go find the others and tell them. They've got to see this."

Tyler and Micah start toward the house, leaving me alone with Leo. A few people move past us toward the entrance, but we're far enough to the side of the driveway that we're not in the way. And not within anyone's earshot, either.

"Are you sure about this?" Leo asks as soon as the guys are gone.

"Yes."

No, I can't back out now though. This is important for her, and I'm determined for it to work. Leo can clearly see through my words, but thankfully, he doesn't call me out on it. For now.

"Just be careful," he finally says, and I nod.

"I always am."

Which is true. My parents expect me to be a good representative of our family. For my mother's business, image is paramount, and I have consistently made decisions that match what's expected of me. My uncle expects me to excel in hockey in the way he never got to after his injury. Coach requires me to be a leader, on and off the ice. My teammates look to me to make decisions. In every aspect, I've been careful. But now, after meeting Kenna, I suddenly don't want to be careful. I want to see what happens when I let myself go against everything I've ever been taught and take a risk. She seems like she's worth the risk. I suppose spending more time with her tonight will show me if I'm right or not.

Now I just need her to come back because my hand is feeling kind of empty without holding hers.

seventeen

· · ·

KENNA

"I can't lie to you, he looks so yummy up close," Evie whispers, and I shush her as I glance behind us. No one seems in earshot. There are a few people walking up to the house from the other side. I can see Reese through the bushes talking to Leo.

"The guy he's talking to is also yummy." Evie leans her head against mine for a better look.

"Evie, focus."

"I am focusing."

"Evelyn."

"McKenna."

I grunt at her grinning face, and she finally sobers up.

"What is it? You look a little freaked out, if I'm to be honest," she says, peering down into my face.

"It's because I am freaked out. I didn't realize how many people were going to be at this party. And Reese made this rule about holding hands, and I have to go in there with him, and—"

"Okay, breathe." Evie turns me toward her and places both hands on my shoulders. I inhale and exhale twice before my heart rate seems to even itself out. "Now, talk me through it."

Of course, she sees the core of the problem. But I'm not sure I'm ready to put into words the wild rage of confusing emotions coursing through me after spending just a few hours with Reese. I can't keep putting him into the same box I've always had him in, and I don't know how to deal with that. But then, the memory of the last time I was at a party creeps in, and I can't forget just how much that event in my life shaped a lot of my responses. When Rob, my ex, broke up with me, he did so publicly and loudly, and he wasn't nice about it. He made sure everyone at the party heard him. The house, the music coming from inside, it's all bringing back those memories.

I'm so terrified I'm just going to be crushed again, my stomach is hurting. And my face is hot. I'm having an actual physical reaction to the situation. Which is beyond wild, since Reese and I aren't even actually dating. But it seems my brain cannot separate the two.

"He's the center of attention, everyone is going to be looking at him. And in turn, at me. What if..." I don't know how to voice my fears, but I try. "You've read the comments. Not all of them are kind."

Evie studies me for a long moment, understanding shining in her eyes. She knows my struggles, knows how hard I work to quiet the voices in my head of people in my past who have told me I'm not enough. Every time I think I've won the battle, I face it again.

"What is it you always tell me? Basically, since the

moment we've met," Evie asks. I'm not sure where this is going before it clicks.

"That you are an incredibly capable person and you have talents you're not even aware of yet?" I say, and she nods.

"When we first became friends, I was floundering. You were so sure about your career path, so capable of taking care of anything that came your way. I thought I was the only junior who still felt lost," she reminds me.

I remember some of our earlier conversations, back when we first connected. Especially when everything happened with Rob, I had to put on the bravest face.

"But I was lying to you. I didn't feel capable of anything."

"You didn't *feel* capable, but you were. You taught me that our brains lie to us all the time. You pushed me to sit down and figure out what I wanted to do with my life, what dreams I was allowed to have for myself. Now, it's my turn to return the favor."

"I don't think this is the same," I say, and Evie shrugs.

"It's all part of life, so it counts," she says and then squeezes my shoulders once, as if to make sure I'm paying attention. "Tell your brain to shut up and remind it that you are capable and amazing and you're doing this because it brings you closer to your dreams."

Evie hasn't been the greatest supporter of this fake relationship, but it's because she's worried about me. I'm not making it any easier on her by having a tiny panic attack in the bushes. But I was the one to tell her that I needed this, maybe even more than Reese does. So I was going to be selfish about it. Now she's repeating all of this back to me.

"Does that help?" she asks.

"Yes. I think the freak-out is over."

"Okay good, because I'm pretty sure if I don't return you to Reese soon, he'll be coming to collect you."

I shake my head and take a few deep, calming breaths.

"Evie, what are you even talking about?" I ask as we turn back to the house. When we step back onto the driveway, Reese's gaze locks on me, and he immediately moves toward us.

"That. I'm talking about *that*," she says, just as Reese reaches us.

"Everything okay?" he asks, his eyes on me.

"Yes," I reply, offering him a tiny smile that I hope doesn't look as crazy as I feel. "This is Evie. I don't think you've met."

"No, we haven't. Nice to meet you," Reese says, briefly glancing at my friend before transferring his gaze to me. I have no idea what he sees, but after a moment, he seems to come to a decision. Or something.

"We're in this together, right? I got your back," he says. In one fluid motion, he moves beside me, tucking my hand back into his and turns us to the house. The gesture is so natural, it takes me by surprise. I'm still trying to process his words when I feel myself wrapping my hand more tightly around his. Reese is watching closely, which means I need to put my game face on.

"Shall we?" he asks, and I nod.

"We shall."

eighteen

. . .

REESE

She's definitely nervous about something, and I'm annoyed with myself for promising to come to this party because we could be somewhere else right now. Where fifty pairs of eyes are not on us the moment we step inside the house. Although I doubt Kenna would agree to hang out with me on her own merit, so maybe I should be thankful for this opportunity.

"Want something to drink?" I lean down to ask, and she looks up at me, her eyes big. They dart around us and then back to me, and I give her hand a little squeeze. If I were a betting man, I'd bet good money that she'd bolt the moment I let go of her hand. Which is all the more reason for me to keep it firmly in mine. Just in case.

"Soda, if they have it," she says, and I turn us toward the kitchen immediately.

"Hey, the girls from the lab are here. Is it okay if I go say hi?" Evie says, pointing to a couch. Kenna nods immediately.

Evie seems very protective of Kenna, which means I'll have to work at winning her over, just like I'm trying with Kenna. But I'm also glad Kenna has someone like that on her side. I know how reliant I am on my guys and I think everyone should have a good friend in their life. But I'm also noticing some undercurrent of history as the girls look at each other, and that makes me even more curious to find out all I can about Kenna.

"Do you want a drink?" I ask, and Evie shakes her head.

"Are we good here? Don't leave her side," Evie says to me and I don't miss the serious tone.

"I wouldn't dream of it," I say and there must be something in my eyes that convinces her, because she gives me a solid nod and then looks at Kenna. Whatever they're communicating silently, Evie seems satisfied and moves away. I feel a sense of pride in the moment, as if Evie has deemed me safe enough to leave her friend with.

I'm stopped and greeted by a bunch of people, and I don't miss the curious looks sent Kenna's way. She doesn't cower, keeping her head high, but I can feel the tension vibrating off her. I realize that since I don't know much about her, there might be an issue here I'm not aware of. She could have social anxiety, and I didn't even think to check.

I don't pause on our way to the kitchen and once there, I tuck Kenna in the corner against the counter before I fetch us drinks.

"Don't move," I say. She nods, and I feel her eyes on me as I grab two sodas from the fridge. When I return, she hasn't moved. People are going in and out of the kitchen, but it's the quietest place in the house. I open the can and hand it to Kenna, and she takes a few sips instantly.

"What's wrong?" I lean down to speak directly into her ear, and because we're so close, I can feel her tense. Pulling back a little, I stare into her eyes, realizing I constantly forget to keep my distance. Even now, I've caged her in with my body against the corner of the counter, but unless she tells me to move, I don't want to. Instead, I wait for her to speak up.

"Just a little overstimulated," Kenna finally speaks up.

"Do you want to leave?" Because I will. I'm ready to lead her out here this moment if she says it.

"No. It's just, it's been a while since I've been to a party. I wasn't… prepared."

There's definitely more to what she's saying. I want to push, but I don't think now is the time. What I want more than answers is for her to feel safe enough to confide in me. But I don't think we can accomplish that in the short time we've known each other. I'll just need to make sure to become that safe space for her, so she will feel comfortable enough to share.

"If you're sure?"

"I'm sure. We came here with a purpose."

She gives me a tiny smile, and it squeezes at my heart. Before I can stop myself, I reach up, but stop at the last moment. I don't want to make her uncomfortable. She watches me and then leans just a bit closer, almost like she's giving me permission. I push some of the hair off her forehead, letting my fingers linger down the strand, and over her shoulder. She grips the soda can slightly tighter, but that's the only indication she gives that she's affected in any way. I've noticed this when she's serving customers or talking to Alan, she thrives on staying in control. Sometimes I think she lets herself lose some of that when she's with me and I want to keep that up.

"Shall we make our rounds then?" I ask, and she gives me a firm nod. I chug my drink quickly, probably too quickly for a carbonated drink, and then reach for Kenna's hand again.

She meets me halfway, as if she's anticipating me, and then I lead her out of the room.

When we enter the main living room, my teammates are in the corner talking to Evie. I lead us over there, just as Micah offers Evie his hand.

"Oh hey, Cap. We're going dancing. Are you joining us?" Micah asks, and I glance at Kenna.

"Maybe later?" she says to me, and I nod.

"Maybe later," I repeat to Micah. He simply shakes his head as he and Evie head to the dance floor.

"Where are Don and Austin?" I ask Leo, and he motions to the opposite side of the room. My two other roommates stand with Clay, Don waving his hands in the air as he talks about something I can't hear.

"How did Austin get roped into that?" I ask.

Leo shrugs.

"Don bet him twenty bucks that he wouldn't last an hour."

"Don should know better." I say and can't help but chuckle. Austin can last longer than that on just pride, but if there's money involved, he's all in.

"Do you—" I turn to Kenna, just when my eyes land on a familiar head of blonde hair. "Okay, don't freak out, but we're about to be ambushed."

Kenna's eyes snap to mine immediately and I motion toward the door slightly with my head. She looks around my shoulder, her eyes narrowing as she's trying to pinpoint what I'm talking about.

"See the tall blonde?" I ask, keeping my voice low. "She… has a tendency to get handsy."

Alicia is studying to be in marketing, and last season, she worked as our PR person as part of her internship. I like her fine, but she is one of those girls who dates for status and status only. She also has no concept of personal space whatso-ever. She's been after me for a while now, and I've been doing my best to dodge her.

"The one with the red top?" Kenna asks, cocking her head to the side. I turn just slightly to glance and nod.

"How handsy are we talking?" Kenna continues her gaze still on Alicia.

"I don't know, she—what are you doing?" I ask when her Kenna steps right into my personal space.

"Making a statement?" She glances up at me with a smile. "If it's okay with you, we're about to have some extended touching."

"Umm, yes, it's okay with me." I somehow manage to get the words to sound normal just as Kenna snakes her arm around my waist, pulling herself right into my side. I don't have a moment to process because Alicia is suddenly right in front of us.

"Reese, it's been a hot minute. How have you been?" Alicia asks, her lips curled up in a smile, her signature red lipstick in place.

"Alicia. How's senior year going?" I ask, my entire body hyper focused on Kenna's frame pressed against mine.

"Oh you know, it could be better." She takes another step toward me, nearly brushing against my arm. Kenna shifts her body, as my arm comes around her shoulders, pulling her to the front of my body. Alicia's eyes drop down, as if she's just noticing her.

"I thought I knew all of your friends already," Kenna says, smiling up at me softly.

"This is Alicia. She worked as PR for the team last season," I say, my attention entirely too focused on how perfectly Kenna fits against me. It's like this space between my arm and my chest has been Kenna-shaped this whole time. She's looking up at me, a mischievous gleam in her eye, and I wonder how she'd react if I simply lean down and kiss that scheming mouth of hers. I clear my throat and try to push away the assault of images that thought enticed. It's a good thing no one can read my mind.

"It's nice to meet you," Kenna says, completely oblivious of me losing all brain function, as she gives Alicia a bright smile. "I'm sorry to cut this short, but the light near the fire outside is perfect right now. Reese and I have a prior engagement."

I look outside and then down at Kenna, and I'm probably grinning like an idiot when I turn back to Alicia.

"Sorry, my girl is a photographer, and I promised her a picture by the fireplace."

"Hmm your girl?" Alicia repeats. "I didn't think WentworthWhispers ever got anything right."

"Well, we wanted to keep things on the DL for now, but we got caught," I say, shrugging a little. "Now, if you excuse us."

I turn myself and Kenna away from Alicia and start moving toward the back door. My eyes meet Leo's briefly, and he gives me a slight nod but doesn't comment. Not that I could focus on anything but Kenna's body pressed against my side. Even the way we move together seems practiced, comfortable, as if we've been doing this for a while, like two people in a relationship would.

We step outside and toward the fire, but when we reach it, I'm not sure what to do.

"Take out your phone," Kenna says and then steps away just long enough to tug me behind her. She picks a spot and takes a seat, taking me with her. I follow suit without a word, pulling out my phone.

"Here," she motions to my left, "hold it out just a little

more to the left and slightly down. There you go. See, perfect lighting."

I stare at us on the screen, just as Kenna snuggles closer, placing a hand on my knee as she leans a little forward toward the camera. Her touch is barely there, but I feel as if I've been branded. I smile and tap the button a few times, hoping to prolong this moment.

"Let me see."

I hand over the phone and watch as she scrolls through the pictures, her face bent in concentration over the screen. Her hair falls into her face, and I don't even hesitate to reach over and tuck it behind her ear. She glances up at me, freezing as she realized how close our faces are to each other. I don't dare breathe as her eyes round bigger and hold my gaze. Everything around us seems to disappear, and for this one, long moment, it's just Kenna and I in the whole universe, and it feels right somehow.

She seems to snap out of it first, pulling back just enough and rolling her shoulders back as she straightens. Then she rotates my phone so I can see the picture she picked.

"Look at that, not half bad," she says.

She gives me a wide grin, and I lose all sense of coherent thought. We signed a contract. We agreed to this fake relationship, and I haven't even made it a full day before realizing that I might be far more gone than I thought.

nineteen

. . .

KENNA

*M*aybe I need to rethink my resistance to Reese's charms, because he's kind of winning me over. And I'm not even directly involved. He's just being nice and considerate to everyone around him. It's clear his teammates respect him, but so do others in the room. Except for that blonde girl, who looked like she was ready to climb him like a tree. There was a moment when a million doubts crept into my head. She looks like his type. But then, I couldn't resist pulling him away from her. The way Reese responded, immediately turning his attention to me, gave me the confidence to act. I've found solid satisfaction in watching her watch us.

We've migrated to the couch, where Clay is rehashing some game from the last season with a lot of exaggerated flair. He's very animated, and probably, a good storyteller, but I can't focus on anything but Reese's body pressed up against mine. I'm in the corner, with Reese's arm stretched out on the back of the couch. If I breathe too deeply, in case my elbow will brush against his chest.

"Exactly how long are you going to stay in that position?" Reese's breath ruffles my hair as he leans closer to whisper directly in my ear. I'm thankful for the low lighting in here because I'm sure my face is turning red. I turn my head to look at him over my shoulder and find him much closer than I expected. I press my lips together and raise my eyebrow.

"I'm comfortable." Even though I'm not, I have to stand my ground. He keeps winning, even though he probably doesn't know we're competing. I desperately need us to get back to our corners. But then he smiles that annoyingly cocky smile at me.

"I don't believe you."

Thankfully, I'm saved from replying when Evie comes back. She's been checking on me continuously, but I keep sending her out to have fun. Even though she'd stay by my side if I asked her, I don't see any reason for her to do so. I've calmed down enough that I seem to be able to handle the noise and the stares.

"Want to sit?" Tyler addresses Evie. He's on the other side of Reese, and there isn't really any room left on the couch.

"I'm good," Evie replies, moving to stand beside me. Reese leans a tiny bit closer, his full focus on me once again.

"Are you sure you're comfortable?" He asks.

"Don't I look comfortable?" I whisper back.

"You look tense," he says and I turn my head just a little bringing us face to face and much closer.

"Pay attention to your friends," I say, keeping my voice low.

"I rather make sure that you're relaxed and enjoying yourself."

I nearly gasp at his words, because once again, he delivers

the statement with no lightness, as if he wants to make sure I know he's not joking. I can't stop staring at him, at the way he constantly seems to consider me and my feelings. I'm so not used to that.

Reese's lips are at my ear again, sending goosebumps down my skin.

"Do you trust me?" He asks.

"Yes, but what are—"

"Good, because I'm about to break a rule."

He doesn't give me time to respond further as his arm lands around my waist, and he lifts me with him as he stands. We don't go far, because in the next moment he's sitting again, right along with me. Except I'm on his lap.

"We made room," Reese says, motioning to the spot between him and Tyler. I'm too stunned to speak, and I keep my gaze on Reese, hoping the rest of the room doesn't notice my shock. Evie takes a seat, and I can see her shoulders shaking slightly from my peripheral vision.

"What are you doing?" I hiss when Reese's arm wraps even more tightly around my waist, pulling me more comfortably across his lap.

"Being considerate to your friend."

"And breaking rules."

Our faces are barely inches apart, our voices low, and I'm sure to an outside observer we look very cozy. But inside, I'm freaking out. His hand is firmly around my waist, his palm splayed out on my hip. I'm fully on his lap, my feet barely touching the floor. It takes all my self-control not to bolt. I know I'm heavy, I've been told I'm heavy. Repeatedly. This is just one of the many insecurities my ex exploited. But if I run now, I'll make a scene, and I—

"Kenna, are you uncomfortable?"

Reese's whisper in my ear breaks through my anxiety. I

turn my head just slightly so I can look at him. His eyes are full of concern, almost as if he could feel my freak-out. His eyes soften even more, and I feel his arm flex.

"I didn't ask, and if you're uncomfortable, tell me, please. I didn't mean to—"

"No." The word is out of my mouth before I can process it. His eyes round for a moment, as if I surprised him as well. The state of my being has nothing to do with him. It's on me. But what I'm finding is comfort in the circle of his arms. It feels as if he can protect me from anything. I'm not ready to admit this, but I like the way he took charge. I haven't been around anyone so assertive with his actions before. Maybe that's why I add, "I'm not uncomfortable. But..."

He gives my hip a tiny squeeze, as if encouraging me to go out. I can't believe that I'm about to admit this, but there's something about Reese that tells me he'll understand. Or maybe simply listen without judgement. Just the fact that this thought comes into my mind is crazy. This is only a mutually beneficial partnership, not an actual relationship. But with the way Reese is looking at me, I want to confide in him. The rest of the party has all but disappeared in my mind, and I'm completely locked in on the here and now.

"I'm okay, but if I'm too... heavy... just let me know. It might be uncomfortable for *you*. I don't mind standing, or I can perch on the end, I just..."

I trail off, unsure how to finish my admission. I'm not looking at him as I say it, staring at the wall behind him instead, but I feel his body grow tense with each word. I'm not sure if there's a way to take the words back now. I have no idea what he's thinking, but maybe I shouldn't have told him. Why did I tell him?

A loud shout comes from the other side of the room, and I turn my head to watch a bunch of guys jumping and hollering. During the time Reese and I were talking, some people sitting with us had moved on, and it's mostly just his teammates and Evie in our little circle. My friend meets my eye right before her mouth falls open. In the same moment, Reese's arm comes below my knees, and I'm lifted straight up in the air as he stands. My hands wind around his neck automatically as I gasp, and he hoists me up a little so we're nose to nose.

"Excuse us for a moment," he says loudly, but his gaze is still on me. "Kenna and I need some fresh air."

"Put me down." I gasp, wrapping my arms tighter around his neck.

"No," he chuckles and I can't even blame him because I'm sending mixed signals. But I can't help it, he's enticing a lot of confusion from me. I keep expecting him to ask something of me, just like everyone else before him, but he continues to surprise me.

He moves forward and I catch a glimpse of the guys, broad grins on their faces, before Reese maneuvers us around the bodies. My eyes are focused on his neck, and I know my face is on fire, because there's no way people aren't staring. Even as I try not to freak out, I can't help but appreciate the way his arms feel strong and sure around me. Even though he towers over me, I oftentimes forget that he's strong. He doesn't seem to care at all. He calls out a greeting to someone, and then we're out the front door and down the driveway.

"Put me down," I repeat. Now that we're out of the house and earshot of people, my firmness is returning and so is my panic. I need to breathe through it and not just lose it, but I'm struggling to stay calm.

"I don't think so. If I put you down right now, you might run." He spares me a glance and continues down the road, heading toward his car.

"I'm not going to run," I say, even though I'm kind of thinking about it. Maybe I can transfer schools, that sounds like a fun activity mid-semester.

"You are. It's written all over your face, and before you do any kind of escaping, we need to talk."

"We couldn't have just done that inside?"

"Nope, this was the only way." There's so much determination in his words, I suddenly have no fight left in me. A tear slips through and I don't have a hand to wipe it away because I'm still clinging to Reese.

He reaches over and catches the stray tear, holding me up with just one arm and the damp opens.

"Well what would you like to talk about? How terrified I am of parties? Or how I'm a complete mess the moment someone is nice to me? I keep waiting for the other shoe to drop or whatever that expression is. And I do actually want to run away. I've never been a runner, but with everyone staring, and all the memories, I just can't—couldn't—"

I pause because I've run out of breath, wanting to hide so badly. I turn my head into Reese's shoulder, silently hoping Greg the Horrible Magician shows up and makes me disappear.

Reese's arms flex around me, somehow pulling me even tighter against him and my frantic heartbeat calms a fraction. I feel Reese's cheek press briefly against the top of my crown and I lift my gaze enough to find him watching me. The care in his gaze feels heated somehow and I want to cry all over again.

"Reese, what are you trying to prove?" I ask, my voice small, even to my own ears.

He pauses, meeting my gaze and holding it. There's that concern again, mixed with a bit of anger, and another emotion I can't place. A big part of me wants to look away or hide. This is too real for our fake agreement. But I can't. When Reese answers, there's not an ounce of teasing in his tone.

"What I'm trying to prove is that whoever told you whatever lie that makes you feel small or invalidated is a complete weasel who was insecure about himself and took it out on you."

His words punch right down to the core of the problem, and I'm apparently a crybaby around Reese because I'm struggling to keep myself together. I've carried these scars of insecurity and self-doubt for years now, and just when I think I've got a grip and they're finally healing over, it takes one party and a bad memory to set me off again. But somehow, it doesn't feel as bad or scary as before. Not when Reese is here, holding me as if I weigh absolutely nothing.

"Aren't you getting tired of carrying me around?" I ask, my voice wavering slightly as I try to keep myself from crying. He's given me an enormous gift, and he doesn't even know it.

"Just say the word, and I'll carry you anywhere."

twenty

. . .

REESE

t this point, I'm basically confessing my feelings out loud. This is the exact thing Leo warned me about. It hasn't been fake for me since the moment I turned around and saw her frowning at me. But clearly, someone has wronged her, and I would like to personally meet that someone and then repeatedly punch him in the face. No Mr. Ice Man about this. I want to crush whoever put this look on her face.

We're reached my car and even though I want to keep holding her like this, I know it'll be best for me to set her down. I stop near the passenger door and gently place her feet on the ground first, before I unwind my arm from around her shoulders. She's gazing up at me with the most open expression, and if she asked me to jump on top of this car right this minute and start singing some obscure love song, I'd do it without a second thought.

Control yourself, man. You'll scare her away.

"Thank you," Kenna says, her voice soft and a tiny smile on her lips. My self-restraint is really something, because all I want to do is lean down and kiss her like she's meant to be kissed. I suspect no one has ever truly adored her, and this makes me extremely angry. She needs someone who will, although I don't like imagining anyone in that role.

"Who knew you can be a good friend?" She continues and it's a good thing I have restraint because kissing her would be awkward after that.

"You're welcome," I say instead of giving into my impulses and reach for my keys. "Would you like to go back to the party or—?" I don't know how to finish that sentence, because I would like an option that doesn't end the night just yet.

"Do you *need* to go back to the party?" she asks.

"No, I made my appearance, we're good to go."

Anywhere you want, I'll drive us.

I don't add that last part out loud.

Way to go, Reese. You get a medal.

I really need to get a grip before I make a fool out of myself. But honestly, I have no idea how I thought I could pretend this is fake when I've been smitten from the beginning. This one is on me.

"I'd definitely rather not go back in there. Let me text Evie."

I nod and she takes out her phone. Now that I'm thinking about it, I'm pretty sure I scored some major points with Evie if the impressed look she gave me when I carried Kenna out of the room is any indication.

"Evie says she wants to stay awhile. She's catching up with her science buddies. The guys offered to take her home."

Just then, my phone vibrates in my pocket, and I pull it out to see one message come in after another.

MICAH:

that was the most beautiful display of chivalry I have ever seen. I'm crying.

TYLER:

seriously the way he just carried her out of there... all the girls were jealous

DON:

to be carried by Reese, a truly once-in-a-lifetime experience.

MICAH:

did you carry her straight to the chapel to make an honest woman out of her?

REESE:

idiots, I'm still outside. Do I need to come back in there and rearrange some faces?

AUSTIN:

Micah wouldn't survive without his pretty face

LEO:

just go, I'll take care of these knuckleheads.

TYLER:

and we'll take Evie home

REESE:

thanks guys

I get another text, but I don't even look at it. Instead, I turn to Kenna, who's watching me.

"Tyler said the same, they'll take Evie home. So, shall we?"

She nods and I open the door, waiting until she's inside before I shut it. I take my time walking around the hood, trying to figure out a reason for prolonging the night. There's still so much I don't know about this girl, and with my schedule getting crazier by the day, I don't know when I'll be able to spend time with her like this again. Or if she'll even allow it.

"I was thinking," I begin, starting the car. "We had coffee, but we didn't have dessert."

"What?"

"Dessert. What's your favorite one?" I ask, pulling out into the road.

"Ice cream." There's no hesitation in her response, and I take that as a good sign.

"Prefect, there's a place down the street from here that's got a late-night drive-through. Would you like to go? My treat for you saving me from unwanted advances." My voice is nonchalant, but I'm pretty sure my heart just jumped into my throat in anticipation. I glance over at Kenna, and she gives me a big smile.

"Absolutely yes."

Wow. Her smiles are lethal.

"See, I'm not just a good friend, I'm an amazing friend," I say, trying to convince both of us.

I tear my gaze away and focus on the road, gripping the steering hard enough to make my knuckles white. I'm a complete mess. I'm so far gone I don't think I'm ever coming back. That terrifies me more than a six-foot-five defender coming at me during the NCAA's Division Championship. Somehow, I need to get back on solid ground, or I'll mess this up before it goes anywhere. I'm still not sure if she actually likes me, but we've begun a tentative friendship at least, and I can build on that.

"You didn't seem all that excited to be at the party?"

Kenna asks while I continue my inner freak-out. There's curiosity in her question that feels like a win.

"I'm not a big party person. I much rather hang out with the guys at home or have a smaller get-together."

"But you go anyway."

"I told Clay I would. I try not to break promises when it's important, and I think keeping appointments is crucial. When Evie and you went to the bathroom, I had a chance to catch up with him."

She doesn't say anything else as I pull into the parking lot of the ice cream shop. What greets me is a sight I don't want to see. They're closed. I pull up to the window and see a sign stating they're remodeling and the late-night drive-through isn't operational.

"Well, that's unexpected. Sorry about that," I say, receiving no response. I glance over at Kenna and find her looking at something beyond the dashboard. But I don't think she's focusing, she seems far away. I take a moment to study her like this, her gaze unfocused, hair falling in waves around her shoulders, and I really hope she'll give me a chance.

"Kenna?" I call out softly, and she jerks, pulling her attention from whatever she was thinking about.

"Sorry, I-I was thinking about something."

"Did you want to head—"

"Actually," Kenna interrupts, "could you drop me off at the dorm, please? I'm feeling very tired all of a sudden."

"Of course," I say, but my heart sinks. I was really hoping for more time with her.

However, I don't hesitate to pull out to the street and drive back to campus. Kenna stays quiet beside me. I'm not sure why, but I feel like something is wrong. I'd like to ask, but she turns her body away from me, as if making sure I won't, so I keep quiet. Maybe tonight was simply too over-whelming for her. I'll have to do better.

When I pull up in front of the dorm, Kenna turns to me.

"Thank you for tonight. I appreciate you putting up with my little freak out."

There's that tight feeling at the center of my chest again and I want to fight anyone who's ever dared to put that look on her face.

"I'm not sure what you mean, there was no putting up with anything. You gave me a chance to be there for you, I should thank you."

She inhales sharply and drops her gaze to her lap as she presses her lips together. I give her a second to collect herself and when she looks up she looks less sad.

"I guess we're pretty good at this partnership, huh?" She says.

"The best," I reply.

twenty-one

· · ·

KENNA

$\mathcal{I}$'ve spent nearly four hours straight going over the portfolio setup. There's a fine line between overdone and just right and I'm teetering on it. My teacher gave us very loose instructions, which is a bit frustrating. I think he was trying to give us creative freedom, but I would like to know what's expected of me. I'm thinking I need to go back and start over when my phone dings with a message.

REESE:

come outside

I stare at the words for a full minute, as if they're going to magically become something else, before I decide to reply.

KENNA:

no

It takes Reese less than five seconds to respond.

REESE:

pretty please? With a cherry on top? And maybe even sprinkles?

KENNA:

is this your idea of begging?

REESE:

idk is it working?

KENNA:

no

REESE:

come on, Grumpy Gus, walk away from your computer for five minutes and live a little

How does he know I'm on my computer? I sit up and look around as if he's going to suddenly appear behind me. But no, just a lucky guess.

KENNA:

I'm actually currently training to become a circus acrobat, so I have no time for whatever it is you're thinking

REESE:

a circus acrobat? This I've got to see. If you won't come down, can I come up?

KENNA:

no

REESE:

you really like that word, don't you?

KENNA:

no

When my cheeks start to feel tense, I realize that I've been smiling at my phone like an idiot. What is happening to me?

This is definitely not the response I should be having to Reese —or anyone for that matter.

REESE:

you wound me. Don't you want to see the fruits of your handiwork?

KENNA:

fruits?

REESE:

you enjoy seeing me in despair, no?

KENNA:

you ARE speaking my language…

REESE:

hurry then, I'm laying on the ground in front of your dorm, tears streaming down my face

KENNA:

if there are no tears, you're in trouble

I don't even realize I gave in until I send the message. Reese's response is instantaneous.

REESE:

victory is mine!!! Hurry, now. I'm wasting away.

I shake my head at the phone, but I do get off the couch. Doing a quick scan of the room, I locate my ID and then head toward the door. At the last minute, I pause, rushing over to the mirror in my room and giving myself a quick once over.

My hair is down and messy because I keep running my hand through it. I'm wearing leggings and an oversized hoodie, and honestly, this is the best it's going to get because I am not dressing up for this guy.

Although we are supposed to be seen together, which

means there's a chance WentworthWhispers will take pictures, so I probably should at least brush my hair. Which I do, very quickly. And then I put on my combat boots and head outside.

When I step out the main door, Reese is waiting. I give him a quick study, annoyed that he looks ten times better in hoodie and jeans than he has any right to, before I meet his eyes and frown.

"I don't see any tears or wounds. I'm going back inside," I announce. I make about a halfway turn before Reese catches my upper arm, stopping the progress.

"All of my bleeding is internal?"

I cock my head to the side and give him my best annoyed look. I'm not prepared when he leans right into my space, his lips at my ear.

"You're supposed to look like we're in love, not like you'd like to murder me." His whisper tickles the sensitive skin at my neck, and I shudder before I can stop myself. He pulls back just slightly, his eyes finding my own, and I can't deny the way he keeps me frozen.

The more time I spend around him, the more confused I become. And I have no idea how to react to that. Instead, I give myself a mental shake and school my features into something more pleasant, because he is right. I do have a role to play.

"Of course, madly in love," I say and his eyes flash, before he finally pulls back. "Now, *darling*, why did you drag me out of my room on this fine evening?" I keep my mouth in a slight smile and Reese blinks at me a few times, as if he doesn't quite know what to do with me.

"Well, I owe you ice cream."

Out of all the things I thought he was going to say…

"Ice cream?"

"Yes, ice cream. Care to join me for a late night, sweet treat?" He grins at me in that Reese way of his and I find that I can't say no. It's getting harder and harder to reconcile myself to the fact that this is the same guy who stood me up. He seems much more somehow. Kinder, sweeter, *likable*. Maybe I'm just a glutton for punishment, but I can't say no. So I give him one solid nod. He smiles like he's won the lottery and then turns to fall into step beside me.

We take two steps when he leans down just a tad and asks,

"May I hold your hand?"

I look up at him sharply and then remind myself that there are people around and anyone could be watching. It would be stupid to refuse, but after the way he cared for me on Friday, I'm not sure physical contact is good for my health.

Which is of course why I say, "Yes."

He watches me for a moment longer, then reaches down and threads his fingers through my own. The gesture is so natural it nearly brings tears to my eyes. My ex never wanted to hold hands in public. I thought he just didn't like PDA. Later I found out he just didn't like me all that much. He just needed me to pass his calculus midterms, so he could stay on the team. I was an easy target, with my own insecurities, and he used that to his advantage.

But Reese seems sure about holding my hand, his fingers strong and gentle while he walks with his head held high beside me. It makes it seem that he's proud of being seen with me, and that ugly voice starts to rise immediately, so I push it down. Reese is such a contrast to Rob that it makes me not know how to act.

When we reach the car, he opens the passenger door and

waits until I'm inside. As he jogs around the car, I give myself a very stern talking to.

McKenna, this isn't real. He's just playing his part. Stop forgetting where you stand with him and get a grip.

Reese opens the door and slides into the driver's seat, throwing a grin my way. I'm reminded of the last time we were in the car and how much it stung to hear him say,

I try not to break promises when it's important.

His admission, maybe it shouldn't have stung as much as it did, but I can't get it out of my mind.

It's hard not to take that personally. Meeting me wasn't important on his list. Technically, I know I can't really make that statement without having all the information in front of me. But my hurt ego is making that conclusion on its own.

It would have been smarter to simply keep my distance and only be around him when we needed to present a united front in front of the school. Yet, I still got into this car willingly, so I have no idea what to make of that. Or of myself. If anyone knew what was going on in my head, they'd run away screaming. Maybe I could use a little screaming of my own.

"All good?" Reese asks, jerking me out of my thoughts.

"Yes, all good," I reply automatically. Because it's a much easier answer than *I think I'm losing my mind.* I just need to remember that we're in this partnership together and this is nothing more than part of the contract. Then, I'll be just fine.

twenty-two

. . .

REESE

She's been quiet since the moment we got into the car and I'm having déjà vu of how Friday night ended. It's been sitting with me the last few days and I can't get over the fact that I'm more than curious about this girl. I'm concerned about her, I want to know what I can do to help, if only she'd talk to me.

Her reactions at the party, the way she's been hiding away since then, tells me that there is some history there that will take time to unpack. I know I'm being impatient but I want to know everything about her immediately.

Which is why, against my better judgement I ended up parked outside of her dorm, staring at the building for about eight minutes before I finally texted her. I was ready with all kinds of excuses to get her to come out, but I didn't end up using any of them. Not after I started talking to her. We don't really have trouble communicating, not when we seem to connect.

Now, I just wish I could figure out what put that thoughtful look in her eyes. If I ask, I think she'll shut down. My best option is to make sure she knows she can be open with me, that I'm a safe space. Even as I think this, I know I'm rushing it. But it seems there's no putting on the brakes in this situation. It's like skating down a slanted ice. You just keep picking up speed.

"How's the follower count?" I ask, thinking this is a safe topic. But maybe not when Kenna makes a little huff sound.

"It's fine. I'm still away from ten thousand though, and there was a contest that just ended that I could've applied for. It's not one of the prestigious ones, just a throwaway, but it would've looked so good on the resume. And they had this —" she stops talking as if realizing she's rambling, and I suppress a smile.

"A throwaway?" I ask, and I can feel her sneaking glances at me.

"Sorry, you don't care about this," she replies, "I was just venting without realizing."

She's apologizing and that just brings up more questions. This is the same tone of voice she used at the party when she told me she's too heavy to sit on my lap. Whoever made her feel that these responses are necessary better never meet me. I'm rethinking my stance on violence.

Right now, however, I need to focus on the girl beside me, not whatever loser in her life made her feel small.

"*I* think this is very pertinent information. What if I'm stopped on my way to class and asked what contests you've been entering? Imagine everyone's shock when I don't know if it's one that looks good on the resume or one that gives you lots of bragging rights with your friends. I mean, people would be appalled!"

There's a moment of silence, and then she laughs, making

a little sound at the back of her throat, which makes her slap her hand over her lips, her eyes big as she looks at me. It won't do me any good to grin like a fool right now, but she's adorable.

"Please ignore that you heard that," she says.

"What? The tiny snorting sound you make when—" her hand slaps across my lips, effectively shutting me up. It's a good thing we've stopped at a red light, or I might've swerved us off the road. I reach up, taking her wrist and slowly pulling it away from my mouth.

"Kenna, it's frowned upon to assault people when they're driving," I say. I have no idea how, but her eyes grow even bigger when she realizes where we are and what she's done. She gasps, tugging on her hand, but instead of letting go, I thread my fingers through hers, effectively trapping it on my thigh.

"This...this is unauthorized touching," she says, and I glance over to find her looking at our clasped hands in concentration.

"You started it, now you have to pay the toll."

Her eyes fly up to mine, just as the car behind us honks, and I grin, as I turn back to the road. I expect her to try to retract her hand again, but she doesn't. But she also doesn't say anything else.

We pull into the parking lot, and I'm happy to see the ice cream shop is operational again. There seem to be a few people inside and even though it'll better suit our partnership to be out in public, I'd like to stay in the car. But I don't get a chance to say anything, as Kenna pulls the door open the moment I park. Having no other choice, I drop her hand and get out of the car. But the moment she's beside me, I reach for her again.

"For the masses," I say and she nods, her entire body

tense. What I wouldn't give to be able to know what's going on in her head for just a second. Since I can't read her mind, I give her a tiny comforting squeeze instead.

I lead her inside, and when we step in front of the counter, I look down to see her watching the people in the shop. There are only five, but tension is radiating off her.

"Ready to order?" I ask, and she jerks, as if she forgot I was there.

"Umm, yes. I'll have—" she studies the menu, trying to find something quickly, and I give her hand another little squeeze.

"How about the strawberry sundae?" I ask. She glances up at me sharply in surprise, and I feel a sense of pride when she nods. I got it right.

I step up and order myself a cookies and cream sundae after ordering Kenna's, and I don't give her a chance to pay, as I hand over my card. She stands beside me, carefully tucked in against my arm, and I wonder for the hundredth time what history she carries inside of herself for these responses. For a girl who radiates confidence, when she's with me, she keeps…hiding, making herself small.

We grab our sundaes and take a seat at one of the far tables. Since this ice cream shop mostly operates as a drive-through, the inside is tiny and not always open to the public.

"Are you going to eat that or just stare at it?" I ask softly when Kenna continues to study her sundae as if she's never seen one before. Without a response, she quickly takes a spoonful that's much too big and I grab her wrist at the last moment, pulling her to a stop.

"What?"

"You'll get a brain freeze. Careful."

She looks at the spoon and then at me, before she takes a

tiny piece of the ice cream. As I watch her, I realize there's no way I'm not asking.

"I'm not trying to pry," I begin, and she transfers her gaze to me. "But do you have some beef with ice cream? Or ice cream shops?"

"I'm not sure what you mean."

"Just that something has you on edge. Is it...me?" I'm afraid the answer *is* me and then I have no idea what I'll do, but she surprises me.

"It has nothing to do with you. It's me."

"How so?"

She sighs and at first I think she won't reply. She takes another bite of her ice cream, before she does.

"My ex...didn't like my love for ice cream. We never had it together."

The anger at this guy is instantaneous. I take a deep breath, trying to keep my voice even.

"He sounds like a loser," I say and Kenna surprises me again by chuckling softly.

"Just from that one statement?"

I nod firmly, leaning closer so I can look her right in the eye.

"That's all the information I need, to be honest. Anyone who doesn't want to have ice cream with his girlfriend is a loser of all losers."

"Hmm," Kenna's eyes seem to have lost that far away look, as she watches me. "Does that mean that you'd buy me ice cream every day if I asked for it?"

"Baby, you don't even need to ask. I'll stock the freezer with all your favorites."

Her sharp intake of breath makes me realize my slip, but I can't even take the nickname back, even though I've never had the urge to call anyone that before.

"Don't make promises you don't intend to keep," she whispers, her eyes on me.

"But what if I intend to keep them?"

This would be a good place to rein it in or put it all on the line, but Kenna laughs, the sound fuller than any of the ones before. She digs into her ice cream more fully and I simply grin. This isn't the time. For now, if I can make her laugh, it's enough.

twenty-three

. . .

KENNA

*I*t's been four days since I've seen Reese and I keep having to remind myself it's for the best.

Our ice cream date has stayed with me this whole time, because once again, Reese is such a conflicting package. What I thought I knew of him versus what I'm finding out is bad enough, but he's also so different from my ex that I'm realizing Rob was never truly a boyfriend. Not if the way Reese is acting is any indication. The way he remembered I like strawberries and ice cream, the way he went out of his way to make me feel good about that fact…I'm not a robot. I can't deny that he's getting to me.

I asked him a bit about hockey, and after we finished our sundaes, he drove me home and walked me to my door. The next day, there was a picture of us on WentworthWhispers, looking cuddly at the ice cream shop. I have no idea how these pictures are getting to them because there were five people there, not counting the workers and I didn't see anyone with their phones out pointing in our direction.

No matter how much I want to control my thoughts, when I look at the pictures, we don't look like enemies anymore. Were we ever? In my mind, we were, but was that just me lying to myself to protect my feelings? I don't know anymore.

The thing is, I can't stop overthinking things. He's getting to me and I don't know how to deal with it. When I agreed to this fake relationship with Reese, I told myself that I could do this without getting emotionally involved. But here I am, emotionally involved.

It's not really *my* fault. He shouldn't be so *likable*. This is on *him*.

I really do need to get a grip on myself. I have plenty to stress about without him constantly disturbing what little sleep I've been getting.

It feels like classes went from zero to a hundred in a matter of days. What started out slow and steady has become fast and furious. Without the cool cars or family dinners.

Today I don't have classes until the afternoon, so I'm hoping some fresh air will help calm me. There's a park within walking distance of the school, but I need to cross one side of the campus to get to it. The air has been cooler these days, and the breeze feels nice on my face when I finally make it out of the dorm.

I only have my crossbody bag and camera with me. If I bring my computer, I know I'll find some café to hunker down in and work on my essay. Never did I think that majoring in photography would require me to write so many papers. Sometimes I don't mind it, like when I have to write a creative reflection to accompany a curated set of images. I kind of like marrying visuals and narratives together. But it's the other type of assignments I'm not so keen on.

In just the last two weeks, the instructor has given us three critical review assignments, and I would prefer we moved on to the hands-on portion of the class. I love studying and analyzing other photographers' styles, especially historically across time, but I would like it so much better if we studied technique, discussed it, and then tried it. I'm a hands-on learner. I'm much better with a camera in my hands than a keyboard.

As I walk across campus, I'm met with a few prolonged looks. In the last few weeks, I have definitely developed a tunnel-visioned focus. If I don't make eye contact with people, they're less likely to approach. And they have plenty to approach me about.

WentworthWhispers doesn't miss a beat. I've become heavily featured on the page, starting with our first public outing. Someone at that party took a picture of Reese carrying me out of the room, and it's going slightly viral. The light was low, and as I thought previously, whoever takes the pictures for the gossip account doesn't really pay attention to composition details. They focus on the subject entirely. My face is shadowed in this case, especially because I'm looking at Reese, who's looking at me. His face in the picture is clear, and more than one comment has mentioned how "smitten" he looks.

I'm not sure what they're talking about, since it's only his profile, but Evie did point out that there might be more to Reese than meets the eye.

Then, of course, there's the ice cream picture. Oh, and one from the cafe, where we're just talking about work. That one, at least, was in the carousel "week of" recap and not the main event.

Evie might be slightly concerned. She told me to be careful. Repeatedly. I don't get her meaning, but it's not like I'm in any real danger. Just a little danger. Where I can't stop thinking about him.

What concerns me more is that he hasn't posted the selfie we took. I thought that would have been splashed all over the internet by now, but there's been nothing. It hasn't affected me, since WentworthWhispers tagged me in their post the steady growth of followers has returned. But since Reese needs this to fix his image, I'm curious. The annoying, self-deprecating voice in my head keeps telling me he just doesn't want me on his feed. But I know that voice is lying because Reese literally carried me out of a room, in full view of everyone, just to prove to me that I wasn't too heavy for him. If he wanted to hide me, he could've made so many other choices. But he didn't.

I would be lying if I said I haven't replayed that moment in my mind a hundred times.

There's no way I could've predicted that behavior, or the way he's constantly considerate of me and my feelings. It's probably why he's the captain of the hockey team. When he leads, people want to follow.

Goodness gracious, I'm exhausting myself with this up-and-down thought process. One moment I'm hurt by him in the past, the next I'm talking myself out of that hurt based on a few kind smiles and a very public display of affection. If anyone could see inside my head, I'd be in real trouble at this point.

My phone rings just as I reach the outskirts of campus, and when I glance at the name, my heart drops a little.

"Hi, Dad," I say after picking up.

"McKenna, how are you?" Just from those four words, he sounds tired. Even though he's in his fifties, he still does manual labor at the warehouse, and it's clear just by looking at him. He looks strong but is constantly worn out.

"I'm good. What about you? How's work?"

It hurts how formal we are, how every time we talk—which is only once a month—we sound like we're reading from a script.

"Work is the same. People always need stuff, you know. I saw your message that you got the job. Congratulations."

I push at the space between my eyebrows, trying to keep the tension at bay. I know where this is going. It's where it always goes.

"Have you received your first paycheck yet?"

Just like clockwork.

"I paid my room and board with this paycheck. I get paid again next week."

"Good, good, that's good."

I close my eyes, moving to the side of the sidewalk so I'm not in the way, waiting him out. He always needs to work himself up for this part. I could make it easier on him, but I won't. Not when I had to use a small chunk of my college savings to pay off his overdue car insurance.

"If you have any cash to spare, I could use some groceries," he finally says.

There it is. I press my lips together, the weight of it all suddenly feeling like too much.

My dad was on his way to becoming an executive director. He had an entire career in front of him, and we were never supposed to be scraping for money. But losing Mom the way we did—by her choice and her choice alone—crushed him in ways I've only begun to understand as an adult. He never recovered from her betrayal and he never sought professional help. He took his trauma and dumped it on me to carry. It was either I step up or we end up losing our house.

It took a lot of therapy for me to not feel like all of this was my fault and something I'm still working through. Mom started to get depressed after she had me, and when I was old enough for kindergarten, she started to seek out other entertainment. It wasn't enough for her to be a mother and a wife. At a very early age, what I learned is that I'm not everyone's cup of tea. She chose herself and other options and left me to pick up the broken pieces left behind. Even as a seven-year-old kid, I remember walking tentatively into my father's room, careful not to spill the oatmeal I made him in the microwave because he hadn't eaten all day. I can still see that dark room and smell the stench of his sadness. That was the year I became hyper-dependent on myself and myself alone. But I think wounds that cut that deep don't really go away. They just scab over and if you're not careful, they'll bleed again. Which is what happened when my ex entered the picture.

No matter how many times I've processed it all, I think that's the reason why what happened with Reese has stayed with me for so long. He touched a spot that was only beginning to heal all over again without realizing it. Even though I wasn't ready to talk to Dad today, maybe it's good he called. Just hearing his voice has reminded me of everything I've learned and how I've pushed past it all.

It's not Reese's fault I'm not his type. It's not his fault we didn't connect. That's just life. My dad has reminded me of that.

"Sure, Dad. I'll send some."

twenty-four

. . .

REESE

The practices have been grueling lately, and weeding out the rookies has taken a lot more time that I would've liked.

"Do you remember us being this fresh coming in?" Tyler asks once the group has skated off the ice, leaving only the starting lineup. The guys and I haven't even had proper ice time since we've been babysitting.

"No, I don't," I reply, meeting Leo's eyes from across the rink. He gives a subtle shake of the head, and immediately I agree—we'll have to cut two of the newbies. Coach has a pretty good record when it comes to recruitment. However, since we are also conducting walk-on tryouts, preseason requires more time to assess these candidates. There were three spots secured for walk-on tryouts, but then two of the recruited guys pulled out. So now we have five spots to fill. It could be worse, but that's a big number all things considered.

Last year, half the team graduated, leaving just the starting lineup in place. It's a tough break and doesn't happen very often, but we're working through it. I never thought I'd be someone who wanted practice to be over, but lately, I'm distracted enough that I do.

It's Kenna's fault. I miss her.

I still have no idea what I said or did when we stopped for ice cream that first time, but I wish she would tell me so I can make sure to never do it again. At least our second attempt at ice cream went better. It would be great if I didn't keep thinking about it like a lovesick puppy, but seeing that sparkle in her eye as she threw her head back and laughed did something to me. Maybe I've become completely unhinged when it comes to her, but I don't care anymore.

The guys and I do a few drills together before we finally wrap it up for the day. Today is one of our afternoon practices, and after we finish our weight training workout, it's film study time. Since the six of us have been playing together for years, we have plenty of past games to go over. We'll do some with the rest of the team another day, but today it's just the starting lineup. Coach Warren has always been good about nurturing talent, and I've done my best to be a help to him in that aspect.

Outside of my uncle, I've only ever had one other coach. During high school, I played on a varsity team, and that was the one time Uncle Dan couldn't step in for control. I liked my high school coach fine, but he didn't show the same care Coach Warren does. Looking back, I think my high school coach was done with coaching and just didn't care, since he thought none of us would go anywhere beyond recreational hockey. Our school wasn't on the list of schools visited by recruiters from colleges. But in my junior year, we won the championship and suddenly we were on people's radar. It's how I was able to secure a scholarship to Wentworth University.

Playing for the Ravens has been a dream come true. A dream I never truly let myself have when I was younger. Uncle Dan put a lot of pressure on me—he still does. In his mind, I'm his second chance. Lucky for him, my love for hockey outweighs whatever ill feelings I have toward my uncle or I would've quit a long time ago. The tension has always made it difficult. That's how it's always been.

When I first started playing for Coach Warren, I couldn't wrap my mind around the fact that a coach could be a father figure and not just a drill sergeant. He spent time with each of us, going over game tape, doing drills on ice. I have never had to question if he cares for this team, and I do my best to mirror that.

"Who is getting the food?" Tyler asks once we're all in the conference room. I've been so distracted I completely forgot. Glancing at the calendar on my phone, I see that it's Austin and Micah's turn. They're not here yet, which I hope means that they've remembered. I'm actually quite thankful that I don't have to babysit the guys as much as some captains do. I have had plenty of conversations with others to know that I'm lucky and the Ravens are a family. A gift I don't take for granted since my own family isn't really close knit at all.

I shoot a quick text to Austin and get a response immediately.

AUSTIN:

heading back in about 10

"They'll be here soon. Micah and Austen went to grab food."

Tyler nods and then settles back into his chair, pulling out his phone. Leo is still in the shower, and Don is on his phone down the table. I stare at my own phone in my hand, trying to find a reason to text Kenna. There has to be one, right?

Instead, I go into my photos and pull up the pictures we took together. The one she picked is the best one because Kenna is smiling fully. Her smiles are rare, and I've been sitting on this picture with a mix of emotions.

One, I want to show her off to the world. Two, I want to keep her to myself.

This whole part where we're not in an actual relationship is really eating at me. I mean, if I show her off to the world and someone else makes a move, I—

"Are you going to stare at it or post it?" Leo asks, taking a seat beside me. He nods toward my phone, and I honestly don't know how to answer. Leo continues to watch me, waiting for me to decide exactly what I want to tell him.

If only it were that easy, right? But I made things complicated, and now I'm paying the price. I know that's what he'll say.

"If you want to say *I told you so*, go ahead and get it over with," I sigh, dimming my screen and placing the phone face down on the table. Leo doesn't comment for a second, studying me silently.

"Do I look like someone who kicks a guy when he's down?" he finally asks, and I shrug.

"I wouldn't blame you."

"Reese, you're not that hard to read," Leo says, leaning slightly forward so he can lower his voice. "I knew the moment you mentioned her this wasn't going to go your way."

"Why didn't you say anything?"

"I did. You didn't listen."

He's right, of course. I went to him to go over my plan, and he tried talking me out of it. But I had already fully committed, even before I talked to her about it. I couldn't help it.

"Well then, that's that," I say, because I really don't have anything else to add. My mind is still on that night and the look in her eyes after we got to the ice cream shop. What I need to do is stop overthinking things and just talk to her. But I would be lying to myself if I didn't admit that I'm nervous. There's a part of me that thinks she'll just end the whole thing right then and there. My time in therapy has taught me that I tend to go to the worst case scenario when it comes to relationships. Something about a "learned response". So, now I'm trying to remind myself that I can't pretend to know how other people might react, and I need to trust that she would want to talk. However, at the moment, I'm just stuck in the overthinking loop.

"We're here! Did you miss us?" Micah's voice booms around the room, and I jerk my attention back to the present.

"No, but we are starving," Don announces, reaching for the pizza boxes. The guys start arguing about who gets the first slice and the chaos of my teammates calms my nerves a little. I grab my phone and open the messaging app.

REESE:

I'm going with "young, beautiful, and in love" for the caption. Hope that works.

Then I pull up the picture of the two of us, post it, and tag Kenna in it. Even before it's up for a few seconds, there are already likes. Between WentworthWhispers posting a picture of me carrying her out of the party, the ice cream shop, and now this, she should get a great boost in followers. It's the least I can do for her.

I dim the phone and put it away, focusing on the task at hand. With our busy schedule, I just hope I get to see her soon. Her presence tends to quiet the doubts.

twenty-five

. . .

KENNA

I'm so exhausted, it's taken all my will to get out of bed this morning. I managed to drag myself to an early shift at the café and then to class. But now, sitting in history of photography, all I want to be is back in bed. I typically really enjoy this class. We've been going over the theory starting from early photography to more contemporary times, and seeing how it has all progressed is fascinating.

But between classes, work, and trying to research scholarship opportunities, I've left no time for rest. After the conversation I had with my father this week, I don't think I'll be getting rest any time soon. He's gotten back into his horrible habit of takeout food only, which made the bills for this month a bit tighter. He asked for grocery money, but when I checked the finances, I realized he definitely needs more than that. He has a tendency to pretend that he doesn't need me to take care of him, so he asks for bare minimum, phrasing it like it's my duty as his daughter. But then, he knows I will look into things, because it's who I am.

He's never been good with numbers, which is why as soon as I could, I started helping. It's not like he's not capable, he just doesn't seem to care to pay attention. But most of the time, I think that after Mom left, he just stopped trying. He now works at one of the warehouses, loading and unloading freight. It's a long way away from his office career. It also pays way less. I'm going to need to start taking on some photoshoots so I can send money home. I also need a new camera, but I'm trying really hard not to think about that at the moment.

"Hey, Kenna."

I don't even realize class has ended until I hear my name called. I look to find one of my classmates, Will, smiling down at me.

"Hey, what's up?" I say as I start to pack up my things.

"So, are you entering?" Will asks.

"Entering what?"

I stand and we fall into step as we head out of the classroom. Will and I have been in almost all the same classes since the beginning of freshman year. I'm not exactly sure what he's planning on doing with his degree, but so far, we're on the same track. He's one of the few students here that I feel like I'm constantly competing against.

"The contest Mr. June announced." I blink at Will, entirely too confused by what he's trying to say, and he smiles. "You know the annual contest the BA department hosts for the photography students?"

"Yes, but we're not eligible to enter until next year." It's always been only open to juniors and seniors.

"Mr. June said the schools are choosing one sophomore class per college to be eligible, and he put us on the list. The final projects we did last year impressed him enough that he chose our class over his other one. He sent us an email this morning." Will pulls it up on his phone and shows it to me. Now I'm wide awake and focused because this is incredible. The winner receives new camera equipment, and one of their pictures is selected for national recognition in one of their magazine spreads. This is an amazing opportunity to get in front of the right people.

"Wow, I'm certainly caught off guard by this. Are you entering?" I don't even know why I have to ask, because of course he is.

"Yes, I've started brainstorming ideas already," he announces proudly.

We come out at the end of the building and, after a quick goodbye, go our separate ways. Will is a talented photographer. His grasp on composition is impressive, and he consistently finds the most interesting subjects. He often experiments with light, aiming for more artistic looks in his photographs, creating pieces you'd buy specifically to hang as decor. He'll be tough competition, but so will the others.

When my dad and I talked about my career goals, he had very strong feelings regarding the choices I was making. He never thought of photography as a valid career path. It's always been more of a hobby in his mind. But times are changing and more opportunities arise all the time. From art to working with models to advertising, there are just so many options. I don't want his negative voice in my head to keep me from exploring these opportunities, even though the thought of competing against the best and the brightest is making my stomach hurt. I've seen the winning entries; I know what's expected. I need to be able to pull it off, but I'm not sure how.

My phone vibrates, and I take it out to see a message from my roommate.

EVIE:

I have to stay later for lab. Won't make it to lunch. Sorry!

KENNA:

no worries, I'll grab something at the cafeteria. I have research to do.

EVIE:

and a boyfriend to see?

KENNA:

you're so funny.

EVIE:

I know.

Truth be told, Reese and I have made no plans to see each other, not since he randomly showed up on my doorstep. Our schedules haven't lined up at the café, and practice has kept him busy. I only know this because he checks in every day, as if we are actually dating. I can't even bring myself to call him out, because I kind of like getting the messages.

There have been no updates on his sponsorship, but the selfie he posted got me to over nine thousand followers. He wasn't kidding, people are curious creatures. Myself included, because I've been lurking in the comments. Okay, mostly I've been staring at Reese's face and thinking about how comfortable we look with each other. For someone who loves taking pictures, I hardly ever take pictures of myself. Most of the time, especially with my self-esteem issues, I just feel stiff and unnatural. But in the picture with Reese...I look happy and carefree. Not a way I thought I could ever describe myself. Reese also looks like he's won the lottery, so basically, it's a very effective selfie.

I'm so close to ten thousand, I can smell it. I've already looked up a few contests I can enter once I hit the magic number. Right about now, I could use the boost.

I don't even realize I've walked all the way to Coffee & Books until I'm standing in front of the door. I was going to go to the cafeteria and then back to my dorm room, but since I have my laptop, I might as well start researching with a nice cup of coffee.

When I step inside, I automatically scan for Reese and then berate myself for such behavior. What happened to being annoyed at him? I'm really failing on that one lately, and I have no one to blame but myself.

Seth is working the counter, and he hands over my oat latte and a ham and cheese sandwich without two words. I find a seat near the window and pull out my laptop. If I can get some research done on past concepts for the contest, I can have a better idea of where to go with my own. I feel a rush of excitement as I think of the opportunities winning this contest could provide. I have to do my best, no matter what.

twenty-six

. . .

REESE

I wasn't going to go to the Coffee & Books today, but for some reason, I find myself stepping through the front doors after my afternoon class. Immediately, I do a quick study of the room, trying to tell myself I'm not looking for Kenna. But I know I am. It's stupid that I'm still trying to fight against that truth.

Seth is behind the counter, looking bored as usual.

"Hey there," I say, coming up to the register. The guy nods and then stares, waiting for me to order. This is his standard. I'm not sure how he doesn't get a hundred complaints per shift regarding his attitude. But I suppose if the coffee is good, people don't care.

"Could I get an oat latte?" I order, and he rings me up before proceeding to make my drink. I walk over to the side of the counter where I'll collect my drink, trying not to feel so bummed. I was truly hoping to see Kenna. Maybe more than I'd like to admit to myself. She's been invading my dreams and my every waking moment. I'm not sure how I'm getting through classes at this point because I remember nothing from the last week. She seems to have made a permanent residence in my head, and she… she's *here*.

My eyes zero in on the top of her head. She's in the corner of the room, at the last table by the windows. Her laptop is in front of her, as well as a half-eaten sandwich and an empty cup.

"Hey Seth, can you make me another one of those?"

"For free?"

"No." I try not to chuckle at his dry tone. I walk back over and pay, then wait until he's finished both drinks before I take them over to her. She's completely oblivious. Her focus is entirely on whatever is in front of her on the screen. She's doing that cute thing she does with her lips when she's concentrating, pressing them together and apart. I noticed it at the party and then again when we were talking at the ice cream shop. I don't think she realizes she's doing it, but I can't help but stare.

Wow, Reese. Be a bit less of a creep, would you?

I take a deep breath and place a cup on the table, then take a seat. It takes her a moment before she finally raises her gaze to meet mine.

Her eyes grow a little round, and then she pushes at the hair that's fallen in her face, blinking a few times, as if she doesn't believe that I'm here. Her brow furrows, and I can't help but smile.

"Hello, Sunshine, how have you been?"

"What are you doing here?" she replies.

"Building a birdhouse."

"What?" She stares at me as if I've lost my mind, and that's when I notice just how tired she looks. Her face is a bit more drawn in, her eyes are slightly red. Concern overrides my need to tease her.

"I came to get some coffee," I say, before pushing a cup toward her. "And I got you a refill."

"Oh." She stares at the cup as she can't believe it's there, before tentatively reaching for it. "Thank you."

"You're welcome."

She takes a sip, her eyes once again on her computer. She frowns a little at whatever she sees, then looks back at the coffee as if it holds the answers she needs.

"What is it you're looking at so intently?" I ask, taking a swig of my own coffee. She meets my eye once more, and this time I see that she's not just tired, she's troubled. It's like the look I saw in her eyes on Friday night. But maybe a bit more loaded.

A fierce protectiveness rises inside of me, nearly taking all the breath from my lungs. I want to protect this girl from everything. I have never felt this way before. The closest feeling would be me standing up for my teammates. But I also realize this is different. This is a feeling that would make me lose my Mr. Ice Man status in a split second if she so required it of me. Whoever I need to fight, I'm ready.

"A very impressive portfolio," she replies, glancing back down once more.

"Do I get more than vague answers?"

"No," she replies, but there's no bite in her answer. She rubs at one eye, pushing more hair behind her ear, and then sighs a little. My hand curls against my thigh, so I don't reach over and take her hand. I have no idea how she'd respond to physical touch right now, but she looks like she needs a hug.

"Come on, Kenna. Tell me all your secrets," I say, instead of getting up and pulling her into my arms.

She looks up at me then, and something passes in her

gaze. That protective instinct rises again, and this time, I curl my hands around my cup. Our contract states we need to discuss any physical contact beforehand, and I very much wish that wasn't written in ink. Not that it really matters, I would never do anything she doesn't want me to do. I'd need to ask permission, and right now, she has other things on her mind.

"You don't take no for an answer, do you?" she asks, and I shrug.

"Not many people tell me no."

"Maybe they should."

"Nah, why would they when just giving in serves them so much better?" I grin, and she blinks at me a few times. I truly wish I knew what she was thinking because she's basically driving me insane and she seems completely unaffected. I'd like us to be on even ground. I wonder if I can pester her to give in?

No, I don't want to pester. I want her to open up because she *wants* to talk to me. That trust, creating and cultivating it, seems like the most important thing to me now.

"Kenna, I'll listen if you talk," I say.

twenty-seven

. . .

KENNA

He really is unrelenting, which is the energy I need right now. There's a small part of me that wants to give him a chance to fix it for me. No one ever fixes anything for me. I'm the fixer. I take care of myself. Even thinking these thoughts is madness. I really can't give in to these emotions, because they are dangerously close to the ones that will make me dependent on him. Even in the smallest way.

I thought the distance between us this week would make it so I'm more balanced when I saw him again. But the moment he sat down, my emotions went haywire. A defensive approach is my best option right now.

"I don't have time to stroke your fragile ego right now," I say, turning my attention back to the computer.

"It's not so fragile, Fredricksen. Tell me what's wrong." He adds some of that teasing tone back to his voice, but it's a lot gentler. Almost like he can tell I'm on the edge, and he's trying to soothe me.

It takes me a moment, but then the name registers. I meet his gaze and narrow my eyes.

"Fredricksen? Isn't that the old man from *Up*?"

"You get a point. So close to a prize," Reese announces, pointing at my face.

"What's the prize?" I ask.

"I'll tell you later." He winks—actually *winks*—at me. "Now come on, Grumps. Tell me what has you frowning so hard at your computer. You're supposed to be nice to me in public."

"As if I can ever forget with you reminding me every five minutes."

"That's because you forget, but out of the kindness of my heart, I'll keep you honest."

I resist the urge to roll my eyes, because he's right. I *do* forget. We're supposed to be dating, which means I need to make sure I smile at him every once in a while. Just not right now. I'm too riled up by this application.

He continues to watch me like I'm the only person present in the entire room, and I don't think I will ever get used it. His laser focus is something to be admired. He's not going to let this go, and if I'm honest, I don't want him to.

"Fine, because I don't think you'll let me work otherwise," I say, adjusting the computer to the side so I can lean forward.

"That's the spirit," Reese replies, following my direction and leaning forward as well. Which brings us much closer than we need to be, but I don't move away. This is perfect fuel for our little deal.

"Smile at me," I say, and Reese grins immediately.

"I am smiling at you. Maybe you should try it."

Ah, yes, this one is on me. My lips curl up just a tad, and Reese shifts just a fraction closer.

"You look very mischievous and charming when you smile at me like that."

My breath gets stuck in my throat at his simple words, and I force my lungs to operate.

"No one can actually hear you," I manage, keeping my voice low. "You don't have to lay it on so thick." He opens his mouth to say something, but I hurry on. "There's a contest."

I can't believe I'm telling him this. But it seems like he won't leave me alone until I do.

"A contest?"

"A photography contest. It's hosted among the Bachelor of Fine Arts departments across colleges in the state to support the program. There are different categories for photography, video, and imaging departments. Winning one of these would look amazing on a résumé."

"What are the requirements?" He looks so serious when he asks, and I'm helpless to do anything but answer.

"GPA requirements, of course. Also, typically, they're only open to juniors and upward, but this year, they've chosen a few sophomores."

"And you're one of them."

"I am!" I almost forget to keep my voice down. I do a quick survey of the room and lower my voice again. "It's a huge deal just to be eligible. I did a project for my freshman year final and—" I stop myself before I go into too much detail. "Never mind, you don't care about that. But it impressed the right people."

"Kenna—" he watches me steadily, and I narrow my eyes at the use of my name. He shakes his head just a little and I have no idea what he's thinking, but then he says, "Could you stop telling me what I do and don't care about? If it's important to you, I want to hear about it."

His words are gentle, but firm and I fight the sudden urge to cry. So often I've been told to keep my thoughts to myself. My dad is notorious about telling me to leave him alone when it comes to my "silly photography" ideas. But Reese is so different, he genuinely wants to hear me ramble on about these things. When he looks at me like this, I can't pretend that it's fake concern and I don't know what to do about that.

So I simply nod and that seems to satisfy him for the moment.

"When's the deadline?" He asks, as if he didn't just show me an incredible amount of care with his simple request.

"In two weeks." I make my brain focus on the task at hand. "It's actually pretty quick, but it forces the hand in a way. There are five categories, and I have to submit a mini-portfolio for each. "

"Categories?"

"Yes. People, nature, commercial, documentary, and artistic. Each requires a set of five photographs. But they have to be good, Reese. In a way that outshines every other contestant. Which is difficult when the categories are so broad. I mean, do I photograph food or a product or some real estate for commercial? And documentary could literally be anything. And I'll be— Why are you staring at me like that?"

Because he is. He's almost frozen, his eyes on me as if I'm the most fascinating subject.

"I… It's fun seeing you so worked up with excitement. You're nearly bouncing in your seat."

"I am not."

"You are, and it's adorable. Now, how can I help?"

My brain is still hiccuping over him saying I'm adorable, so I don't register his question immediately.

"Help?"

"Absolutely. I *am* the best boyfriend in the world, after all. I need to step up."

"Ah, of course." It shouldn't feel disappointed that he's playing his role well, but for some reason it does. I'm getting distracted. It's his proximity and his eager expression and the fact that I haven't seen him in a week and I wanted to.

Everything is blurry in my head right now, and it's taking all my self-control to stay on task. This seems to be the most loaded conversation of my life and we're talking about a photography contest.

"I'm not sure you can help. I just need to figure something out."

"Have you ever done a photoshoot with hockey players?"

"What?"

"Hockey players," he repeats, his lips curled up once again. "For people. Or even a documentary. I bet you can take some awesome pictures. I've seen some amazing shots before and always wanted to try it out."

"You'd model for me?" I don't think I understand him correctly.

"Sure. I'd get the guys to participate too. You can do whatever you want. We'll be down."

"Just like that?"

"Just like that."

twenty-eight

· · ·

If I knew all it would take to bring that ridiculously bright smile to Kenna's face was my willingness to offer myself as a guinea pig, I would've done it a month ago. She looks absolutely radiant, and I have the sudden urge to be the one taking a picture.

"Are you sure? I know you guys are busy. But if you're sure, then I think this could work. I could absolutely do a photoshoot on the ice. Oh, I can get some nice action shots as well, and then maybe… Sorry, I'm rambling." She gives me that smile again, and I'm pretty sure I'm grinning at her like a fool.

"I'm sure, and the guys will be fine. I'll double-check with Coach, but as long as we're there for practice and do it after, it won't be a problem."

"Oh okay, thank you! This… it really means a lot." Kenna ducks her head, turning back to her computer, almost like she's embarrassed. I can't imagine why. She keeps her eyes trained on the screen, letting her hair fall forward to obscure my view. I'm back to wanting to reach over and push it back from her face so I can see it.

I might be slightly addicted to the very sight of her.

I open my mouth to say something when my phone vibrates. I pull it out and see my adviser's name on the screen.

"I'll be right back," I tell Kenna and stand, heading for the door.

"Hello?" I answer, stepping outside.

"Reese, hello. This is Dr. Stevens."

"Yes, how can I help you, sir?" I've been trying to get a conversation with him since the summer, when I started looking into replacing some of the clinical shadowing that fell through because of scheduling issues. He's a difficult person to meet, because he's overseeing a much larger number of students this year than usual.

"I received your request for clinical shadowing, and I have a spot for you. End of October, you can do up to twenty hours at the Knightly Medical Center. You'll need to contact the physician who is head of their sports medics program. I'll email you the information and you can set up a time that works around your hockey schedule."

It takes me a moment to realize what he's saying. It feels like I've been working toward shadowing at a major hospital since the end of my sophomore year. I can't believe it's happening.

"Thank you, Dr. Stevens," I manage.

"It was your hard work. I'm just delivering the news," he replies, and I can hear the smile in his voice. He's one of the best professors I've had here, and it fills my chest with pride at his compliment. He double-checks my email address, and I thank him again before hanging up.

I stare at the phone for another moment before I make my way back inside. Kenna is right where I left her, now typing on her laptop, but she looks up when I take my seat. She cocks her head to the side for a moment, her eyes flying over every inch of my face.

"What?"

"There's something about you," she says, leaning forward just a tad and narrowing her eyes. "You look very happy."

I almost say something cheesy like *I'm always happy when I'm with you*, but I reel it in at the last moment. It really is insane how I've become the sappiest softy when it comes to her. And I don't even care.

But obviously, now is not the time, so I lean forward, bringing us closer together once again.

"I am very happy. I'm getting an internship at Knightly Medical Center. It's a pretty big deal."

"Oh wow, how did that happen?"

"Well, *I am* a pretty big deal so…"

She rolls her eyes, but I don't miss the way she presses her lips together to keep from smiling. Every time I feel like I've won a prize. I'm getting to her, I'm sure of it.

"This year I'm supposed to be doing clinical shadowing. I need about twenty-seven more hours, since I did a lot of it over the last two summers. But I haven't been able to get in with Knightly Medical Center," I explain, and Kenna stops typing to watch me talk. The power of her undivided attention is doing something to me. I clear my throat and continue.

"Dr. Stevens is the head adviser for physical therapy students, and he managed to secure me a spot. I still have to contact the hospital, but I'm excited. I've shadowed outpatient clinics and nearby high school athletic programs, but an actual hospital was my top choice. I'm a very hands-on learner and I've heard the hospital is great for letting us work, instead of simply observing."

Apparently, it's my turn to ramble. But I can't help it. This was my plan, the one that didn't involve my uncle or my parents. I wanted to graduate with a career outside of hockey, and now I get a chance to do so.

"Is that what you want to do? You don't want to play hockey professionally?" Kenna asks like she actually wants to know, which makes me smile.

"I love hockey." I pause for a moment, because I suddenly don't want to give her my standard answer. I want to tell her the truth. So I do, before I chicken out. "Honestly, I would love to play hockey professionally, but it's not up to me. Growing up, there was a lot of pressure put on me going pro and I don't know, I wanted options. I wanted to choose for myself. When last year ended, I decided that if I don't get drafted this semester, I won't get drafted at all. Technically, I can enter the draft again, but I also need more schooling for my degree, so I would do that next. Basically, I'm ready for anything. I've surprised you." I comment when I notice her staring.

"You did," she replies. "I just assumed all the guys on the team wanted to go pro. You seem to… love the game."

"I do," I reply, because it's true. "But I also know how unpredictable life can be. My uncle…" I pause because I'm not sure how much to share. But she seems genuinely interested, and suddenly, I want to share. This part, only my closest teammates know, because it often feels like a wound I carry. But with the way Kenna is looking at me, I'm ready to tell her all of my secrets.

"My uncle was in the NHL. He played for the Florida Panthers, a few years after they joined the league. He only lasted two years before an injury took him out." It's something he quite often laments about loudly to anyone who will listen. "He didn't have a backup, didn't think he needed one. It ruined his marriage."

I add the last part almost automatically. It's what he's always said, even though it wasn't his injury that did that. It was him. They were college sweethearts, and they fell in love before he was drafted. I don't think my aunt ever really cared about him playing hockey, but I was still young when she left. He always blamed his injury on their problems, but even as I kid, I could tell it's because he wasn't himself anymore.

"He couldn't handle it afterward," I say. "The only thing that brought him joy was training me."

"He was your coach?"

"Since I was about four or five. I lived with him a lot during that time, because my parents were traveling. They both work for the same company. My dad is a business consultant, and my mom was a sales rep. She's the head project manager now."

I always feel weird talking about my parents, because I don't know them all that well. If I'm asked about them, it's almost like I'm talking about acquaintances. A little disconnected.

"So you're getting a degree in physical therapy?"

"Sports physical therapy. If I want to practice, I'll need to apply for a DPT program, so I need to make sure I cover all my bases before then." When Kenna looks at me blankly, I hurry on to add. "Doctor of Physical Therapy. If I don't get drafted this year, it would be wise for me to pursue DPT."

She doesn't say anything for a moment, and I wait. I'm not sure if she wants to ask more questions, but if she does, I'm ready to answer. But she doesn't ask, she just continues to study me with that unreadable look in her eyes.

Our gazes hold for a long moment, and the rest of the

world falls away. There's something potent in this time and space, something that I will hold on to when all's said and done.

Then, Kenna gives me the tiniest of smiles.

"I guess there's more to you than meets the eye."

twenty-nine

. . .

KENNA

*I*f someone told me a month ago that I would be putting together a photoshoot for hockey players, I would've laughed in their faces. But now, this feels like the most natural thing.

Ever since Reese opened up to me in Coffee & Books, I've been actively fighting against my feelings for him. When I listened to him talk about his plans and his family, I realized that he's *nice.* The kind of a nice guy who could be sweet to me just because that's how he is. So basically, I can't allow myself to read too much into anything he says or does. It's simply who he is.

There couldn't be a bigger contrast with how Rob was. It was only after we were no longer together that I realized how much he used me—as his personal servant. I did things for him because I wanted to show I cared, but he never did anything for me. He never remembered my coffee order, or that strawberries were my favorite. He definitely never volunteered to help me with my photography projects. Is it really all that surprising that my emotions are so confused when it comes to Reese? Just the look in his eyes when he volunteered himself and the team for the photoshoot is enough to send my head spinning. I really need to focus on more important things.

Last night, I stayed up late researching what I wanted to do with the boys. With the deadline in a week and their preseason game the week after, we're on a tight schedule. I don't want to take up more of their time than I have to.

"Are you sure you have time to help with this?" I ask Evie. We're in our living room, packing up the last of what I need to bring with me. The contest specifically states that only certain equipment is allowed: a tripod, one extra external light, and two types of lenses, which makes sense. They want to level the playing field, so to speak, and see what we can do with the basics.

It does put a bit of a strain on me, since I've never taken any pictures at the arena before. I didn't even get a chance to do a walkthrough, which is why we're getting there early enough today so I can get a feel for the place.

"Of course I have time. Nate and Stu should be able to handle their side of the project without me babysitting them every second."

I hear what she's saying, but I also know she *does* want to babysit. When the professor announced the groups that are working on this semester's project, Evie came home huffing and puffing about being stuck with two of the class's laziest students. She still thinks it's a conspiracy because she's one of the top students and these two bring down the class average.

"Anytime you need to go, just say the word."

Not that I have anyone else to ask for help. The only other friends I have made here have been from the program, which makes them competition. I don't believe any of them would sabotage me, but I do believe it would be very awkward to help me win.

"Kenna, darling, I cannot pass up an opportunity to boss around a bunch of hot hockey players, and you know it. You're doing me a favor."

I chuckle, because if anything, Evie loves to boss around anyone and everyone.

"That's my girl," I say, and she grins. I grab my camera bag and laptop bag, while Evie carries the external light and my tripod. After one quick look around the room, we leave.

The arena is on the other side of campus, at the edge of the school, for convenience of parking and the fact that it's used for other events in the community throughout the year. But it does make it difficult to get to when you're lugging a bunch of stuff.

"I should've ordered a car before we left the room," I say as we step out of the dorm. "Let me do it now."

We move to the side so we don't block the sidewalk just as I hear my name being called. Glancing up, I find Reese's car parked at the end of the walkway and a pretty girl coming around the front, waving in my direction.

"Who's that?" Evie asks.

"No idea," I reply. The girl has light brown hair, longer than mine, and it falls around her shoulders in very stylish waves. She's wearing a sweater, an overalls dress, and sneakers. She looks about our age. She also looks a little familiar, but I can't place her. She rushes up to us, a bright smile on her face.

"By that expression, I'm guessing you didn't get Reese's text," she says by the way of greeting.

"Umm no?" I may have been too busy to check my phone. It's inside my laptop bag somewhere, I'm sure of it. But my mind is more focused on the fact that this girl is driving Reese's car. I try to ignore the uncomfortable feeling in my chest and focus on the girl instead.

"I'm Morgan. Don's sister. The guys have practice before the shoot, so Reese asked if I could come pick you up. He assumed you had equipment to carry." She looks at my bags, then at Evie, and reaches for the light. Evie hands it over immediately with a grin.

"How considerate of Reese," Evie says, sending a look my way. Morgan laughs.

"He takes care of his own, that's for sure. Let's go." Morgan turns back to the car, carrying the light, and I see no reason not to follow.

"He sent a car to pick you up," Evie whispers.

"I can see that."

"That's very boyfriend of him."

It is. And it's messing with my mind. Did we agree to do these things for each other? I already feel indebted to him because he's helping out with my application. I nearly cried in the café because he offered without being asked. I've spent so much of my life believing I had to earn affection. But he's just there, supporting me. It means more to me than I'd like to admit. After spending so long having to defend my career choice to my dad, it's such a contrast to have someone just accept it. And encourage it.

Now this. I definitely should've made the contract more inclusive. I have no idea where this is fitting in.

"He's very nice." My friend is unyielding.

"Evelyn."

"Okay, okay."

I know she's teasing to keep me from freaking out, but it's making me freak out more.

"So Morgan, how long have you known Reese?" Evie asks once we're inside the car.

"Just since he started playing with Don three years ago. I've known most of the guys that long. Except for Tyler. He's been friends with Don since middle school."

I don't miss the way she says Tyler's name, and I wonder if there's more to it than meets the eye, but I don't get a chance to ask because Evie is on a mission. Not that I would pry. But it does make me curious.

"Does Reese typically send you to pick up… people for him?" Evie continues, leaning her face between the front seats.

"Are you kidding? I nearly had a heart attack when he asked me. He doesn't even let the guys drive his car. I said yes immediately because I simply had to meet you." She glances over at me, a huge grin on her face. "You guys made all the headlines on WentworthWhispers. But more so, I never thought Reese would find someone who makes him smile like you do, but he's such a sap when it comes to you. I immediately decided we had to be friends."

"A sap?" I ask, my voice slightly wavering. Even though I'm not looking at Evie, I can feel her staring straight into my skull with that knowing look. She's become Team Reese after the party, while still being super protective of me at the same time. I have no idea how she's managing to balance that. It's a talent, for sure.

"Oh yeah. He's super protective too, because one of the rookies could've come to get you since they finished their scrimmage game earlier, but nope. Had to be me." I open my mouth to reply but she's not done. "Sorry, I'm babbling on like a dork, but I'm just so happy to have another girl at the games. Two girls! I could've sworn those dummies would never give me any friends, but I suppose Reese was just waiting for the right one."

She's so cute, I can't help but be drawn into her energy. Even though I still don't really believe a word she's saying. He's clearly just really good at playing his role. And he's nice. I've already established that.

"Are you a sophomore like us?" I ask, and she shakes her head.

"Second semester freshman. I couldn't start until the beginning of this calendar year, so while I'm the same age, I'm a little behind."

I've heard of people coming in at different times during the year based on their circumstances. I even considered doing it myself to stay home and help Dad, but Evie and my high school counselor talked me out of it. I'm glad they did.

"What's your major?" I ask.

"Bachelor of Fine Arts. I paint. Eventually, I'd love to have a gallery of my own, maybe a small one with a shop. But I would also like to learn and utilize art therapy."

"Oh I've heard of that." I perk up immediately, because she's speaking my language now. "There are classes designed around the healing attributes of art and how it can be used for restoring physical and mental health."

"Exactly. I know how much art has helped shape me into who I am, I'd love to give people a chance to experience that as well."

"Wow, kindred spirits," Evie comments, and I agree. I love meeting other people who share the same passion. I think Morgan is right. We are going to be friends.

thirty

. . .

REESE

"Will you stop pacing? She'll be here," Don says as I skate past him for the fifth time. We've supposed to start our scrimmage game already, but Coach got pulled away on a call, so we've been running drills instead. I'm tired and anxious about seeing Kenna. Besides the small amount of time we spent together at the café, I haven't spent any time with her since the party.

I miss her.

This has become a never-ending theme in my days. I'm still trying to figure out what to do with it.

"Our boy is smitten, give him a break," Tyler says, skating by me. He, Austin, and Micah have been playing pass the puck. We could've technically started the game already, but Coach wants to be here to evaluate the rookies. I glance over to the other side of the rink and the top contenders who will take over from us when we graduate.

"Can you believe that used to be us?" Leo asks, coming out of the crease to stand beside me.

"It's actually crazy to think about. Have you talked to Weston or Noah lately? I know Wes applied to a school near the resort so he and Lily could give it a solid go." The guys graduated last May, and their absence has been felt. Leo has always been much better at keeping in touch with people. It's part of his personality that will help him as a counselor one day.

"Yeah, he got in. He should be finishing up training within the next month. He'll be teaching middle school. I think he might get to coach too."

"That's great. It's what he wanted."

"He misses the Colorado weather, but says the heat is worth it for Lily," Leo continues. "Noah and Nat will come down for Clark's first game with the Knights, so you'll see them then."

Clark is the only one who wanted to play hockey professionally, which worked out perfectly when he got drafted by the Las Vegas Golden Knights straight out of college. Noah is in med school now and only plays on the weekends.

When I was first preparing for college, I thought hockey would be my only option. Uncle Dan sure thought going pro would be my only dream. But junior year of high school, I got really interested in physical therapy and decided that's what I wanted to study. Uncle Dan was not happy. But my parents encouraged me, albeit from afar, so I stood my ground.

Meeting Weston and Noah was like a breath of fresh air. They love hockey the same way I do, but they didn't see it as their all in. They both encouraged me to pursue what I wanted. So did Leo. If I got drafted, I would one hundred percent give it my all. But if I didn't, my second option would be to play for the minor leagues for a few years and then retire to work with them as a physical therapist. If neither works out, I would go into work immediately. The frustrating part of it all is that I can't really control the outcome, just what I put into it.

I watch the rookies skating around on the other side of the rink and think of the possibilities. It's not often I dwell so much on the future, but since meeting Kenna, I'm thinking about it more and more. After our talk in the café, I haven't stopped thinking about the future.

"Alright, boys. Let's get started," Coach Warren calls out, coming back into the rink. Everyone snaps into action immediately, taking their positions.

"Your girl is here," Don says as he skates past me to take his place at center ice for the face-off. I turn my head to the side immediately, and there she is. She's wearing one of her jeans and blazer combos, her hair pulled back in a high ponytail. Morgan leans over and says something to Kenna, and then her eyes are on me.

I've had plenty of girls come to open practices and games with my name on their jerseys or painted on their cheek. But I've never wanted anything more in my life than to see my name on Kenna. The image is so vivid in my mind, I'm almost blinded by it.

The whistle blows, the puck is dropped, and we're off. The nervous energy I've been carrying around inside of me dissipates. And I can't tell if it's just the usual feeling of peace from being on the ice, or it's the fact that Kenna is here watching me.

thirty-one

. . .

KENNA

When I told Reese that I gave a hockey game a shot before, I wasn't really truthful. I stayed for maybe half a quarter and then had to leave. I saw no point, not when my feelings were hurt and the pain was raw.

But now as I watch them skate from one side of the rink to the other, I'm really paying attention. And I'm mesmerized. Granted, that might have more to do with Reese than the actual game.

Watching him is like watching a dance. His moves are fluid, precise. There's no hesitation. On the ice, he's the same way he is in real life. He's hypnotic.

It's probably a good thing I didn't watch him back then. I think it would've made the disappointment that much stronger. But now, somehow, I have arrived at the place when all of that seems unimportant. I think I've resigned myself to the fact that I can like him, even if he only likes me because I'm helping him out. In the last month, we've become something akin to friends, and I think that's enough for me. After all, beyond our contract, he wouldn't like me anyway, I'm not his type. But we can at least be friends.

I'm never going to put myself in a situation where I set unrealistic expectations.

The only response I can control is my own, so I will own up to my feelings, and that's all.

"What are you thinking so hard about?" Evie asks, leaning in to whisper into my ear. I glance over, meeting her eye, and I have no idea what she sees there, but she leans back to study me further.

"I think I'm okay now," I say, "with… everything."

Evie doesn't seem to need me to elaborate. She snakes a hand through my elbow and gives me a squeeze. I'm sure we'll talk about it later, but for now, this is where we are.

The whistle blows, and Morgan turns to me with a brilliant smile.

"Let's go down and talk to the coach. The guys will want to shower and change into game day jerseys."

She heads down the stairs, and Evie and I trail behind her. The guys wave as they skate off the ice on the opposite end of the rink, but number thirteen skates over to us. Even before he takes his helmet off, I would know it's Reese. Not just by the number Morgan told me to watch out for, but by the way he moves. I'm not sure when I've become so acquainted with his body's movement, but here we are.

"Hello, Frowny Face. Evie, Morgan," Reese says with a huge grin on his face as he greets us, but his eyes are only on me. I bite the inside of my cheek to prevent myself from smiling, because somehow, I now enjoy his playful nicknames for me. But I'm not telling him that. Instead, I narrow my eyes.

"How sturdy are you on those skates?" I ask, raising an eyebrow, and he laughs.

"Why don't you do whatever that evil head of yours is thinking of doing, and we'll find out?" Reese replies, ducking down enough to meet me on eye level. "You think you can take me?"

"Absolutely," I reply, lifting my chin. That's when I hear Evie and Morgan chuckling beside us, and I realize that I've instantly forgotten that Reese and I are not alone. I look away, really wishing I had my hair down so I could hide behind it. Evie meets my eye with an amused expression, and I round my eyes at her to warn her to stay quiet.

"While I would love to see Reese get his comeuppance, go shower. You stink," a man next to Morgan says and motions Reese away. Reese grins once more, salutes the man, and then meets my eye.

"Don't miss me too much," Reese says, then pivots and skates away.

I'm sure my cheeks are on fire when I turn to face the three people next to me. Reese sure was laying it on thick, and there aren't even any cameras around. Unless he knows something I don't about the way WentworthWhispers operates. Even though it's just an act, the teasing is pretty normal to us at this point, and I can't argue that I don't enjoy it. This isn't going to end well for me; I can feel it.

"Hello, Kenna. I'm Coach Warren," the man says, and I offer him a smile.

"It's nice to meet you. Thank you so much for letting me use the rink and your players. I mean, your players' time." The earth needs to open up right now and swallow me whole. How many times can I embarrass myself in the span of ten minutes? Apparently, the limit does not exist.

"I should be thanking you," Coach Warren says. "We haven't really cared to take any official pictures besides the headshots lately, and I think this is perfect timing for the start of the season. The PR department has mentioned it to me a time or two."

"Then I'll make sure to do my best," I say, and he nods.

"I believe you will." He turns and motions two guys over. They're wearing regular street clothes, but they skate over from the other side of the rink. "This is Charlie and Asher. They're two of my rookies. They'll help you get on the ice and set everything up."

"Great, thank you."

Charlie is blond and looks more lean than buff, while Asher is dark-haired, with the widest shoulders I've ever seen. They don't seem like freshmen to me, but maybe that's just the hockey in them. They have that hockey player vibe I'm becoming acquainted with. They also appear much taller, since they're both wearing their skates.

"Give me a second to roll the carpet out," Charlie says and glides off.

"Carpet?" I ask.

"It'll be easier than walking on the ice. They usually have it out for games, when there's a presentation or something," Morgan announces, motioning to where Charlie is rolling the red material out near the entrance to the rink.

"Is there anything else you need?" Asher asks, as Evie hands over my portable light and tripod.

"Let's go set this up and see where we're at. I need to take some practice shots to figure out my settings."

He nods and moves off, taking my equipment with him. A part of me is a bit nervous handing it off to someone not on solid ground, but he delivers the items to the edge of the carpet and then sets them down gently.

"Okay, let's get this show on the road," I say, using my high school photography teacher's favorite phrase.

thirty-two

· · ·

REESE

$\mathcal{I}$ shower at the speed of light, slamming my elbow into the side of the locker as I pull on my jersey, and nearly miss the bench when I sit down to tug on my skates like the completely unhinged man that I am.

"I'm pretty sure she can't leave until she's finished with all of us, so maybe don't injure yourself?" Don comments, putting on his own uniform much more slowly.

"I just don't want to hold anyone up," I say.

"Mm-hmm," Tyler makes a noise, exchanging a look with Don at my expense, but I don't even care. I just need to be out there already.

Our little conversation before I had to hit the showers encouraged me. She seems more at ease with me, which has to be a good sign, right? We need to have a conversation soon because I don't want her to have any doubts when it comes to how I'm feeling. But I also don't want to pressure her. From the glimpses of her past she's allowed me to see, there is baggage that she's still carrying around. I'm waiting for the day she finally shares, but until she's ready to let me in, I cannot force myself into her heart. Patience has never been the strongest on my part, but I'm willing to learn. For her.

When I step out on the ice, my gaze is immediately drawn to where she's directing Leo. They moved the carpet farther than usual, near the goal on the opposite side of the rink. The light setup is behind Kenna, and I watch as she kneels, brings the camera to her face, and tells Leo to move. The goalie skates forward almost in slow motion, as Kenna's camera makes a bunch of clicks.

Morgan is telling Austin something as they watch Kenna position Leo differently. She motions with her arms, then explains positioning, and demonstrates how to stand and shift the way she needs him to.

I'm completely entranced by the way Kenna works. She's totally in her element. She explains everything with clarity, pivots when needs to, and looks so sure of herself I can't stop grinning. Then she's on her knees once more, this time leaning back so much I'm worried she'll pull something in her back.

Asher skates over, carrying two handheld flashlights, and stops beside her, just as she rights herself. He leans down offering his arm, and she places hers on top of his forearm so she can stand.

A cold sweat washes over me at the sight of her hand on his arm, and I have to keep myself rooted in place, because I don't like that. Oh, I don't like that at all. It should be me and me only who—

"Don't cause a scene," Coach Warren says, as he comes to stand behind me. I clench my jaw, keeping my impulse in check, but this feeling is so new, I don't really know what to do with it. I've never been… territorial. But now? If Asher touches her next, I think all bets are off.

"I'm fine," I tell Coach, but even without looking at him, I know he's not buying it. He stands right behind me, while I grip the edge of the rink to keep myself in place.

"It's okay to feel protective of her."

"Is that what I'm feeling?" I turn to face him fully, because it feels like I need to talk to someone, and my teammates aren't exactly geniuses when it comes to this. Coach Warren studies me for a long moment before he finally speaks.

"It's about time you brought her around," Coach Warren says. We stand in silence for a moment while Coach gives me a chance to process my emotions. He's probably the first one, besides my therapist, who's ever encouraged me in this way.

"She's incredible," I finally manage, and Coach chuckles.

"When the mighty fall, they fall hard," he says. I can't even lie to him and say it's all fake or that we're only doing a favor for each other. He sees through it.

"You're scared," he continues, and I nod, because there's no reason for me to try and deny it. "You've talked about your uncle before, do you think he's right? About the way love and relationships work?"

My brain snags on the word love, my eyes shifting over to Kenna as I think honestly about Coach Warren's question. As I watch her, something becomes very clear.

"I don't. At least, not anymore. But I don't know what to do with that."

Coach is silent for a moment, as if he's choosing his words carefully.

"I believe our brains hold immense power. But the greatest aspect of our minds is that they never actually stop developing. Sure, by a certain age, parts of you will have reached maturity, but when it comes to this, you're not stuck in what you knew as a fifteen-year-old boy. You can learn, you can adapt, you can develop."

"Uncle Dan always said relationships were a prison. You don't believe that?" I glance down at the wedding band on his finger. I've never seen him without it. He follows my gaze, a soft smile blossoming on his face.

"I never told you this, but Rose and I met in college." That surprises me. I don't hear many successful college sweethearts love stories. "She was working at the admissions office. They handled dorm assignments and my buddy and I had issues, so we went in person to try to get them fixed. One look at her, and I knew I had to get to know her."

"Just like that?" I ask, and he chuckles.

"I didn't need more information. She, of course, wanted nothing to do with me, mostly because she didn't date jocks. But it didn't matter, because I knew we were meant to be. Even before I got to know her. I gave her space, but we kept getting thrown together. I called it fate, and still do. She's the best teammate I've ever had."

"And you think that's not a one in a million occurrence?" Because that's always been my fear. Every time I think of my parents, I believe they got the love story I won't have, and I used to live by that idea. It's why I never even bothered to try. But ever since meeting Kenna, that hasn't held true for me.

"I think every love story is a miracle, Reese. But people can miss it if they're not looking hard enough."

"So how can I stop being scared?" I ask, glancing at Kenna over my shoulder before turning back to Coach. The expression on his face can only be identified as pride, so I guess I asked the right question.

"You have to decide if staying safe is more important than taking a leap. You have to decide if she's worth it."

"She is," I say immediately, almost as if the words were waiting to come out. Coach Warren smiles.

"Then you have your answer."

Before I can process that truth bomb or say anything else, Austin shouts my name. I turn, my eyes zeroing in on Kenna, where she stands at the edge of the carpet, her eyes on me. Without hesitation, I grab my stick and my helmet and glide toward her, stopping just a foot away.

"It's my turn?" I ask, and she bites her lip, giving me a quick once-over.

"I thought you were going to take a shower and get ready," she says, cocking her head to the side.

"Are you implying I don't look ready?" I ask, and she shrugs.

"I guess I'll work with what I've got." The teasing in her eyes shines brighter somehow, and I wonder what she would do if I broke all our rules right here and right now.

"If you're done pretending like I'm not the best looking model out of this bunch," I say, folding at the waist so I bring my face as close to hers as possible, "how about you direct me to where I need to go."

She shakes her head, surprising me by holding her snarky remark back, because I can see it written all over her face. Instead, she turns to Asher and Charlie, motioning him forward.

"Okay, we'll go in this direction. Reese, you will start out over here." She points to the middle of the rink. "Charlie and Evie, I need you beside me with the flashlights. And Asher, you know what to do, right?"

"Yes." The kid nods then takes off skating to the opposite

side of the rink. I must look confused, because Kenna turns her attention back to me.

"You'll need to look tough and intimidating, can you do that?" she asks, pressing her lips together, and I swear, if she doesn't knock it off with the shining eyes and the subtle teasing, I'm going to carry her out of here. This time, probably heading for the chapel.

"So just my usual, got it," I reply, sending her a wide grin. She rolls her eyes and then moves toward Evie, who's standing beside her.

"We're going to train the light on you. If it's too much, just let me know. You can close your eyes and open them when I tell you, if that's easier."

I nod, but I don't close my eyes. Instead, I watch as she rearranges Evie to point the flashlight. The big light behind Kenna is already a bit blinding, but I don't want to complain while she brings her vision to life. She moves to Charlie next, having him kneel so the light is in a direct line in front of him, before she rearranges him too. Once she's done, I'm being spotlighted from three different directions.

"Asher will skate toward you. When he reaches the mark, he'll turn, spraying you with ice. Is that okay?"

I turn to glance over my shoulder at Asher. A bunch of other guys are in the stands, and the rest of the starting lineup are here too.

"Whatever you need," I say, turning back to Kenna. She grins at me, making my heart do that loud thudding thing again, and then she signals for me to go. I pose exactly how she wants me to and then a few seconds later, I hear Asher's "now!" from behind me. Kenna's camera begins to click, and then suddenly I'm showered in ice. Kenna pulls the camera away, looking at the screen, then she jumps a little on the balls of her feet.

"Let's go again," she calls out to Asher and then glances at me. Her face is absolutely shining, and I can read that expression all too well. It's kind of like when I score a goal. Whatever she envisioned has clearly worked out.

We go a few more times until she's satisfied, then she moves on to the rest of the team. She does a few action shots between Tyler and Donovan and then has the starting lineup come back for a group photo. We even manage to get Coach to pose with us.

"I'm assuming you're taking her home," I hear from beside me once everyone starts dissipating, and I glance down to find Evie next to me. She's watching me with an intensity that makes me feel self-conscious.

"I am."

"Hmm." She seems like she wants to say something, and at first, I think she won't, but then she moves just a fraction closer and lowers her voice. "I'm not going to be cliché and tell you if you hurt her, I'll kill you," she begins, more serious than I've ever heard her. "I mean I can. I am in plenty of science classes that will help with that. They also have taught me how to properly dispose of a body."

I pull back to look at her to see if she's serious and she is. Noted.

"But what I will say is that if you're serious—" I open my mouth to say I am, but she holds up her hand. "If you're serious, then you need to have a talk. And you need to make it very clear as to where you stand. Like talking to an elderly person while trying to explain how a cell phone works kind of clear. Patience and lots of repetition. She's not going to believe you and—well, that's a conversation you need to have with her."

There are so many questions I want to ask, but it does verify my suspicions. Something has happened in Kenna's life that has made her closed off to this possibility. Or maybe not closed off, but extra careful. Evie is warning me, but also giving me the hope I need that this isn't one-sided on my part. She wouldn't be encouraging this if she didn't at least suspect that Kenna might like me.

"Understood," I reply. She watches me for a moment longer, before she walks off to help with the clean up.

The guys have taken her equipment back, except for the camera still around her neck, and I skate back over.

"All done?" I ask, and she nods.

"Just need to make it to the side of the rink without breaking my neck. Or my camera," she says, cradling it in her arms. "The guys took my bag."

"Do you want me to call them over?" I ask, already getting ready to do so, but she shakes her head.

"No, it's okay. The girls walked on the ice. I should be fine."

But the moment she takes a step off the carpet, her foot slides a little. She's not wearing shoes equipped for this. I reach for her arm automatically, holding her steady.

"Should we figure out a better way?" I ask, and she grunts.

"I'm too tired to think," she replies with the most adorable pout. "Do I have to do everything around here?"

"Oh, so you want me to come up with a plan?"

"Well, you're the boyfriend, isn't it your job to take care of me?" As soon as the words are out of her mouth, her head jerks in my direction, sending her sliding once more. My hand grips her arm automatically as I steady her. I freeze in place, keeping her beside me, as I try to process.

She said boyfriend. BOYFRIEND! I know I've used the term loosely, but she's never said it. And I already want to hear it again. I've never been anyone's boyfriend before. Does it always feel like winning gold at the Olympics? Is it acceptable to start jumping around like an idiot?

"I—"

"You said boyfriend. No take backs," I interrupt, and she goes from shocked to annoyed real fast.

"What are you, a kindergartener?" she asks, and I nod vigorously.

"Whatever you say, *girlfriend*. Now, hold tight?"

"What?"

Without hesitation, I sweep her right off her feet and into my arms. She wraps her arms around my neck, pulling herself tightly against me.

"Are you nuts? You're on skates!"

"So?"

"So! What if you fall and hurt yourself? Put me down."

"Awe, you're worried about me?"

"I'm worried I'll end up breaking my camera."

"Kenna," I say, and just as usual the use of her name makes her freeze. I love that I have that effect on her. "I would never let anything happen to you or your camera. I've been skating practically since I started walking. This is nothing."

"But I'm heav—" She presses her lips together, cutting off the word. I can't help it, I lean forward and place the tiniest kiss against her forehead. I can feel her body shudder, and the memory of her skin under my lips is forever imprinted in my brain. I don't linger, hoping I'm not scaring her in anyway. I glance down and find her gaze on me, her eyes soft. Something shatters inside my chest, my heart cracking open and ready to pour out all of my feelings right here and now. So I readjust my grip, just to have something to do instead.

We need to have that conversation because I'm done denying my feelings. Coach Warren's words ring out loud and clear in my head. I have to be brave about this. So I give her a tiny smile.

"That's to remind you."

"Remind me of what?" She whispers, her eyes frozen big. I smile.

"Just the truth. That you're perfect in every way."

And then I skate.

thirty-three

. . .

KENNA

It's been three days since Reese kissed me on the forehead. It's been three days since he skated off the ice with me in his arms like it was the most natural thing. The moment we were off the ice, however, he got called away to see his adviser, and I had to get this project finished up. Basically, we have not seen each other since.

It's driving me a little nuts.

"Kenna, darling, what do you have against your computer?"

"What?"

Evie's voice pulls me out of my thoughts. She's on the floor in front of our coffee table, a bunch of textbooks spread out in front of her, while I'm on the couch with my laptop. We're supposed to be having uninterrupted co-studying time. Well, she studies while I work on the pictures and type out the briefs. We go for forty-five minutes and then take a fifteen-minute break, then go again.

"Has it been forty-five minutes?" I ask, and she shakes her head.

"No, it's been twenty. But you're jamming down so hard on your laptop keys, I'm just wondering if everything is okay." She's leaning forward, looking up at me, her glasses perched on the tip of her nose. She only wears them when she's really stressed studying. Her eyes tend to get tired quicker.

"I'm okay," I reply, looking away and hoping she doesn't push. No luck today though.

"Can you say that again, but more believable?"

I sigh, transferring my gaze back to her. She gives me a tiny smile, as if trying to coax me into spilling my thoughts and feelings. When I don't say anything, staring at her stubbornly, she rolls her eyes.

"Come on, baby girl, just talk to me. You like him. You don't know how he feels. You guys are still in your weird fake-but-not-fake relationship. When are you going to talk to him?"

"Well, wow, when you summarize it like that, I don't know why I haven't fixed it already." I drop my head to the right, leaning against the couch, all thoughts of my project forgotten. Not that I was making much progress when my mind just keeps going back to his lips on my skin, his arms around my body, as we glided across the ice. It felt different from when he carried me out of the party, more… influential somehow. Like an announcement, like staking his claim. But that's crazy, right? I'm definitely not his type and we've only now reached this strange friendship stage of ours.

"Kenna, I can see the steam coming out the top of your head."

"I don't know, Evie. I'm just terrified, okay? Terrified of letting myself believe that this could be real. I feel—" I stop, trying to find the words to express the mess of emotions inside of me. "I feel safe with him. Like I've never felt with anyone else. And that scares me."

Evie moves to the side of the table, reaching out and placing a hand on my arm, giving it a tiny squeeze.

"Have you noticed that I've been pushing you toward him a little more lately?" she asks.

"Yes, actually. What happened to being on my side?" I say.

"That *is* me being on your side. I can see things a little differently now. An outsider's perspective, if you like. And he's been good for you. Not only because he keeps standing up against the notions you have in your head, but because you shine brighter around him."

"I don't know what you mean."

"When we were at the party," Evie says, not a trace of humor in her voice, "I watched you walk in there with your head held high, holding his hand. And then when that PR girl was trying to make a move, you didn't allow it. For someone who doesn't know you, those things might not mean a lot. But after what happened with Rob, you started to minimize yourself. Hide yourself away. You don't do that as much anymore."

Her words pierce me right at the center, everything that I've been thinking and feeling, laid out in front of me. My eyes fill with tears, because I can't help but feel blessed that I have a friend like her. She always calls it like she sees it.

"You think it'll be okay?" I ask, reaching over and giving her hand on my arm a squeeze.

"I think you won't know until you talk to him."

She's right, of course, but that requires me being brave. And no matter how many times she says I've gotten some of my spark back, I'm still missing some fire.

My phone dings just then, and I reach between the cush-ions to pull it out. When I see the text, I drop my head back against the couch.

"What?"

"It's Alan. He said that I'm scheduled to do inventory tonight."

"On such a short notice?"

I shrug. "Honestly, he gave me four hours' notice. I should be grateful." Mrs. Lowery came to the café last week for the first time and she mentioned monthly inventory. I didn't expect it to be the job of a newbie like me, but at the same time, it is probably given to newer employees. I actually don't mind inventory that much. It's one of those repetitive tasks that's probably going to be good for me at the moment.

"Let's see how much I can get done before I need to leave. I should at least finish this brief," I say. Evie nods, accepting this for what it is, and I'm grateful. I have a lot to think about as it is.

When I step inside Coffee & Books three and half hours later, it's right before closing time. The last of the customers leave and then it's just Alan and me. He barely even glances my way as he hands me the clipboard.

"You need to…" he trails off, just as a noise comes from the back, and then Reese steps into view. "Oh good, you're here. I'll leave you two to it."

Before I can even form a coherent thought, Alan steps around the counter and heads to the back.

"Good evening, Sunshine," Reese says. I bite the inside of my lip to keep myself from melting at his soft smile. My mind takes a mental snapshot, in case this is all I ever get because he looks like a dream. His hair is perfectly messy, his lips curled up in a tiny smile as he gazed down at me with gentleness that makes me want to cry. Or maybe jump into his arms and let him hold me for an hour or ten. My emotional state is not strong enough to handle alone time with him right now. The way he watches me makes me feel like he sees through every part of me. It's becoming pointless to hide anything.

I turn away, clearing my throat before I reply.

"I didn't know you were working too," I say, grateful my voice comes out even.

"Well, unlike Alan, I'm not one to throw you in the deep end without a life vest."

"Oh, you're the life vest in this situation?" I seem to have gained some control of my emotions, so I turn back to face him. He hasn't moved, his eyes still trained on me, as if he's memorizing every inch.

"Absolutely. Frozen water, regular water, steam." He shrugs, "I can handle all forms."

"A man of many talents."

"You have no idea."

Even though there's a whole counter between us, the distance seems too close and too far at the same time. Something has definitely shifted between us, and I have no idea how to navigate it.

"Shall we get started?" Reese finally says, just when I start to think we'll be standing there, staring at each other for hours.

"Yes," I reply immediately. But before I can move, my phone vibrates. I pull it out to see my father's name on the screen, and my heart drops. We've already spoken this month, so this call can't be good news.

"Is it okay if I take this? It's my dad." I show Reese the screen but he's already nodding.

"Of course."

"Thanks."

I walk over to the corner of the café, the farthest I can get from the counter, before I take a deep breath and push the button.

"Hi, Dad," I say.

"McKenna, how are you?" It's the standard question, but there's something in his voice that makes me stand up straighter.

"I'm okay, I'm at work. Is everything okay?"

He doesn't answer immediately, and the silence on the other end of the line raises my alert level.

"I thought you were sending money," he finally says. I press my lips together to keep my immediate response at bay.

"I will. I had to pay the electricity bill first. You missed a payment, Dad."

"I have it under control."

"No, you don't," I reply, losing some of the control I usually exhibit around him. He's always like this, always says that he can handle it. But he never does. Not until it lands on my shoulders, and I handle it for him. There's never a thank you, just a way to make me feel worse about the whole thing. "They charge interest, Dad. This bill was an extra one hundred and fifty dollars. You can't keep doing that."

"I didn't ask you to take care of it."

"No, you didn't. You simply expected me to do it."

I think back to what Evie said about how some of my spark has been returning, and I try to remember the last time I stood up to my father like this. It was before Rob. I look over my shoulder to find Reese at the counter. Almost like he feels my gaze, he glances up and mouths, *are you okay?* I nod once, and then turn back to the phone, just as my dad speaks again.

"What I expect is for you to do your part as my daughter. Not run around the whole campus with some hotshot boyfriend, instead of unfulfilling your duties."

Whatever I thought he'd say, it was not this.

"What are you talking about?"

"One of the new guys at work mentioned a social account at his school, so I looked up your college and found your school's gossip page. There are pictures of you on there being carried around by some guy. Who is he?" There's so much bitterness in his voice, I'm surprised he doesn't choke on it. After mom, he started hating love. But more so, he started to hate any association with it. When he found out about Rob, he nearly lost his mind. Not that it mattered. By that time, Rob was done with me anyway.

"I thought I told you that I would allow you to go away to college if you behaved," he continues when I don't respond. "If you're going to study your pointless photography, you can at least be useful."

The pain in my chest would probably hurt less if I was stabbed with an actual knife. A useful daughter. That's my only role in this family, apparently. If I can even call it that.

The relationship I have with my dad has always been conditional. It has never been enough for him that I am his daughter, I must perform my duties and be useful. He pretends like he's in control, yet still expects me to actually take care of things. It used to drive me mad, the contradiction, but I've become used to it. Which is a sad statement in itself. But it's probably why it was so easy for Rob to get to me. He needed help with his test, I though helping him would show my affection. In the end, my acts of service were used and abused and then he found someone better.

I've dealt with a lot of this in therapy, but even so, lately I've been thinking about the kind of a person I actually want to be. Probably because I am finally surrounded by people who don't really want anything from me.

I steal a tiny glance at Reese and find that he's already watching me. He's leaning on the counter, his arms flexing as if he's holding the edge with his hands. His gaze is fiercely protective, and it fills a spot inside of my chest that was bleeding before.

"Dad, I don't have time for this right now. I'm at work. But if you must know, Reese is my boyfriend and he supports my career choices just fine. I'll talk to you next month." And then, without waiting for a response, I hang up. I put the phone on silent just in case, and take a deep breath to calm my nerves.

"Sorry about that. Where were we?" I ask, walking back over to Reese.

thirty-four

. . .

She's sad. I can see it in her eyes. She's trying to hide it, but I've learned to read her moods. Her phone call with her dad definitely didn't go well. At least when I talk to my dad, it's like talking to a pleasant acquaintance. There isn't this much hurt between us and we're working through what's there. But Kenna? She seems to be folding in on herself.

We're in the back pantry now. It's not really big enough for two people, but we're working in tandem. Just like with her photography, she's focused and efficient with this. I'm not surprised. I wish she would talk to me, but I don't want to overstep, so I compromise.

"Do you want to know how I actually got the nickname Ice Man?" My question seems to do the trick, and she refocuses on the here and now, instead of whatever is going on in her head.

"I thought it's because you're levelheaded on ice?" It kind of makes me warm and fuzzy that she's thought of me.

"Actually, no. When I was six, I was completely obsessed with ice. No matter how cold it got, rain or shine, I'd be eating ice cubes."

"Wait." She turns to face me fully for the first time, and I feel like I've won a prize. "You mean you just ate ice cubes?"

"Yep, like people eat candy."

"I've never heard of anyone doing that."

"There are actually cases where it's part of physical or mental illness, but for me it was a nervous habit."

Kenna holds my gaze for a moment and then says, "Would it be okay to ask why?"

I smile.

"I just moved in with my uncle full-time, and he didn't have an ice dispenser, just trays. I thought they looked like candy, so I tried them. But then, it became a nervous habit. And I'm glad you're asking."

"Really? Why?"

"Because it means you're curious," I reply honestly. She holds my gaze for a moment before she turns back to the box in front of her. The shelves here are metal, and floor to ceiling, so I probably need to go find the step stool, but I'm not ready to leave just yet.

"Ouch!"

Kenna's cry of pain jerks me into action. I rush to her immediately and find her pressed against one of the metal shelves.

"What is it?" I ask as I look her over. She doesn't appear to be injured.

"Reese, I'm okay." She places a hand on my chest, stopping my panicked perusal of her. I freeze immediately, and I know she can feel how wildly my heart is beating under her touch.

"I'm just a little stuck," she says and raises her hand to point behind her.

"May I?" I ask, and she nods.

I step right into her personal space, leaning over her right shoulder. She still carries that fresh bouquet smell, mixed with something akin to vanilla and strawberries. I inhale discreetly before I locate the issue. A strand of her hair caught on the metal hook that protruded from the side of the shelf. If she moves at all, it'll tear at her hair.

"Give me a minute, okay?" I pull back enough to see her face, and her eyes meet mine.

"Okay."

I reach over her shoulder using my left hand and start to pull the hair apart. She must've twisted around after it was caught, because it's pretty tangled.

"I need my other hand," I say, and I feel Kenna shudder as my breath rushes over her ear.

"Okay," she says again, this time her voice breathless.

I move in front of her, and then reach with my right hand, caging her between my arms as I lean forward. I try to keep a sliver of separation between us, but I don't want her to hurt herself. So, while every part of me is freaking out about the proximity—somehow this seems much more intimate than me carrying her in my arms—I concentrate on working quickly. It takes another minute, in which I think both of us have stopped breathing, before I'm done and step away.

"Thank you," she says, raising her hand to push at her hair. My eyes snag on her wrist, and I put out my hand instantly.

"May I?"

She looks at me in confusion but holds out her wrist to me, and I pull off the hair tie she's wearing as a bracelet.

"I can do it," she says, looking up at me.

"I know, but would you let me?"

She can say no, and I wouldn't blame her. It's a weird request, maybe. But she always seems to carry so much on her shoulders, I have the urge to take on some of that burden. This is a small thing and maybe I'm overthinking it already. But then she nods once and turns around, giving me access to her hair, and I feel like I won something precious.

A part of me is glad her back is to me because when I reach for her hair, my hand trembles. Slowly, so I don't pull on it unnecessarily, I run my hand over her hair, gathering it in one hand. It's the softest hair I've ever touched, and I wish I could just keep playing with it. Instead of giving into that impulse, I speak up.

"You know, all the guys were gushing about the pictures you took. They've been asking when they can see the final versions."

"Oh really? They said that?"

"Why do you sound so surprised?" I've noticed this before, her downplaying her photography talent. Which I don't understand. Her pictures are good.

"I just didn't expect it, that's all."

"Why wouldn't you? You're talented and precise. You have a vision, and you execute it. It's impressive." I thread the hair through the hair tie twice, pulling it a little tighter. My fingers brush her skin, ever so lightly, but I feel her tiny shiver. She's just as affected as I am. "All done," I say before I force myself to step away.

Kenna's hand runs over her low ponytail, and she throws a smile over her shoulder. "Thank you."

She steps past me and out the door, but I'm almost one

hundred percent sure there was a glimmer in her eyes. Almost like she was trying to hold back tears. I stand in place, wondering if I should go after her. We're in such a strange place in our relationship, I have no idea what I can and cannot do.

But after another minute of trying to talk myself out of it, I can't stand it. If I can help in any way, I will try. If she tells me to leave her alone, then I will. But I can't just do nothing, not when she seems to be hurting.

When I step out of the back room, I find her at one of the tables. She has the work laptop in front of her and one of the inventory sheets we filled out earlier beside her. The lights in the room are dimmed, only the twinkle lights are on. Sitting there, bathed in the cozy light, she looks soft and fragile, and my chest fills with the need to protect her from everything.

"Hey, do you want to talk about it?" I ask, taking the seat opposite of her. She doesn't look up, but her fingers freeze on the keyboard.

"Kenna."

She shakes her head but doesn't look up and something breaks inside of me. I'm on my feet immediately, kneeling beside her as I turn her toward me. She lets me take her hands in mine. As I hold them on her lap, it's her grip that tightens first.

"Sunshine, what is it?"

"I'm sorry, I'm just really tired. Give me a second, and I'll pull myself together."

Her words are barely a whisper, and I'm once again in that confusing state of wanting to protect her and wanting to go out and fight whoever hurt her. I know from personal experience, that kind of language isn't accidental.

"Kenna, you don't owe me an explanation, but if you need to take an hour and cry, we can do that. I can take you somewhere, anywhere you want to go, or you can sit here with your feelings for as long as you need to."

Maybe I'm laying it on too thick, but after going to therapy, I have learned that acknowledging feelings and actually feeling them is an important part of staying healthy. This is something I was never allowed to do when I was around Uncle Dan, and I still struggle with that aspect. But if I can encourage Kenna in this way, then it's worth it. I want to understand her, if she'll let me.

She raises her head just a little, so she can meet my eyes. Her eyes pool with unshed tears, and I feel her holding herself together as if she's doing it physically.

"You don't think crying is a sign of weakness?" she whispers, breaking my heart as her voice catches.

"No, Sunshine. Crying is a sign of being alive."

She stares at me as if I've spoken a foreign language, and I fight the urge to just simply pull her into my arms.

"But what if it's for a stupid reason?" she asks, and I'm immediately shaking my head.

"How about you tell me the reason, and we can decide together if it's stupid or not?"

She nods a little and then takes a deep breath, as if she's preparing herself for whatever comes next. I'm not sure why, but it seems like she's preparing herself for me calling her out on it being a stupid reason. Like a preconceived idea. One, I'm sure she's received from someone else.

Instead of saying anything though, I just wait. She flexes her fingers under mine, pulling so my hands move fully around hers. I give her an encouraging squeeze, and she takes another deep breath.

"My dad… he hasn't really been supportive about my career choices," she begins, her voice barely a whisper, and my heart thuds, making sure I pay attention. "When he called today, he asked about you. Apparently, someone at work showed them the school's Instagram page."

She stops, but it doesn't seem like that's the end of it. I hate that I'm right.

"When he gets mad at me, he always makes sure to tell me how stupid and useless my career choice is. He knows it's a sore spot for me, and he makes sure to push on it when it's convenient for him. When you said my pictures..." she inhales again, as if it's helping her stay in control. "When you said my pictures were good, and that others were excited, it just hit that much harder after hearing him degrade me."

She stops then and a tear slips down her cheek. I catch it with my thumb, cupping her face gently, so I can lift it. She meets my gaze, as another tear slips out.

"I knew it," I say, my voice barely a whisper, "not a stupid reason at all."

She nods, not saying anything else, and right now, words aren't needed. I just kneel beside her, staying with her for as long as she needs me to.

thirty-five

. . .

KENNA

*A*fter the inventory shift, something changed between us. There have been ripples throughout, every time I see him, every time we talk. But the way he stayed and let me process my feelings—I don't think I'm ever getting over that.

MORGAN:

I'll be there in 5

I glance at my phone at the incoming message and turn to look at myself in the mirror. It's a week later, and it's Reese's first preseason game. Or I guess it's called an exhibition game, according to Morgan. She's become a fast friend to Evie and me, and we both enjoy the chaotic artist energy she brings. She's been teaching me a bit about hockey, and tonight she's picking us up for the game. It's only about a forty-minute drive over to Hunter's College, where the game is being played, and she offered to drive us there.

Reese showed up at the café during my shift three days

ago and asked me if I would come. It resulted in another very cute picture for WentworthWhispers of him leaning over the counter, both of us smiling at each other. It was the picture that put me over ten thousand followers.

I won't admit it to anyone, but I've been saving these in my folder, along with the selfie Reese and I took together at the party, and revisiting them late at night when I'm trying to figure out what I'm feeling.

"Evie, time!" I call out, as I step into the living room out of my room. My friend skips out of her own room, a bright smile on her face. She's wearing jeans with tall boots and a hoodie with the school's name printed on the front. A big forest green bow holds her hair halfway up. I went for a more subtle jeans, combat boots, and a dark green pullover, since I don't own any school memorabilia, except for a class T-shirt. Maybe I should invest. I actually like the fact that our school colors are dark green and silver. I've never really seen the need for school spirit. But now, I'm rethinking my stance on that.

"What do you think?" Evie asks, doing a little twirl.

"It's perfect." I reach for my camera automatically but then decide against it. Tonight, I just want to enjoy what's happening on the ice with my own eyes. But after shooting the players for my project, I will admit, I kind of want to see if I can take some action shots at the game. I've never been much for sports photography, but that might be changing. I suppose I'll see at the game.

"You look amazing, as always," Evie says, heading over to the door. "Maybe even glowing."

"Evelyn." I roll my eyes, but I'm not all that mad at her teasing. At first, I wasn't going to tell her about what happened at the café, but she noticed a change in me, so I couldn't keep it to myself. Though I didn't tell her everything, just the highlights. That sent her on the 'I told you so' path, but in the most loving way possible.

"Yes, McKenna?" She smiles at me sweetly, and I wave her off. After checking to make sure I have my ID and phone, I nearly push her out the door.

We make it downstairs just in time to see Reese's car pull up. Morgan honks the horn once, leaning down to call to us through the open window.

"Your chariot, ladies!"

"He is an *excellent* boyfriend." Evie hooks her arms through mine, pulling me along. I can't even argue with that. I don't want to hope against hope, but none of this feels like a fake relationship anymore.

Evie gets in the back as I take the front. I've come to think of this as my spot, and that's dangerous.

"Wow, Morgan. You look great! Do people dress up for exhibition games too?" I say, and she gives me a bright smile at the proper term. Her hair is curled, separated into two half-up pigtails with one green and one silver bow. She's also wearing a Wentworth Ravens jersey. It has Wentworth Ravens written on the front in big green letters, with a raven in the middle.

"Absolutely. Especially at an away game, we have to fill the stands with green and silver."

"Who's your player?" Evie asks, and Morgan laughs.

"As if it can be anyone but Donovan," she replies, pulling out on the road and toward the exit off campus. "If I show up wearing a jersey with another name on it, that person might not survive the night."

"Ah, protective. I like that," Evie comments, and Morgan and I chuckle. Evie has been saying that about basically any athlete she's met recently.

"Oh, speaking of," Morgan says, "Evie, can you grab that bag from the floor and hand it to Kenna please."

Evie does so, and now I'm staring at a plastic bag on my lap.

"What is it?"

"Why don't you open and find out?"

When I pull the top open, my heart leaps in my chest. It's a jersey. I pull it out slowly, while Evie claps her hands behind me. "Wentworth Ravens" is written on the front of the jersey. I turn it around, staring at the large number thirteen on the back with the name Dawson written over the top of it.

"He wants me to wear this?" I ask.

"I'm pretty sure he wants you to live in it," Morgan replies.

The girls laugh, but I'm too distracted. Rubbing the fabric between my fingertips, I have the sudden urge to cry. Everything Reese has done since becoming my fake boyfriend has been him taking care of me. For someone who hasn't had that kind of care for a long time, these gestures get me right in the heart. The longing for all of this to be real has become a constant buzz at the back of my head, but I'm pushing through it. I have to. There is no other choice for me.

We stop for coffee and arrive at the arena about thirty minutes before puck drop. The parking lot is packed. For some reason, I didn't really expect that. It's not an actual game, but apparently the school spirit runs deep.

"We'll be in the lower bowl, about halfway up from the team," Morgan says as we get out of the car. "Since it's your first game, this will give you a good view of the whole rink."

"Is that where you usually sit?"

"I like to move around," she shrugs. "You'll find a place where you like best. We can test a few."

She speaks as if this is going to be a regular occurrence.

The game hasn't even started yet, but I also would like it to be a regular occurrence. Once again, I have to pull myself back before I start making up scenarios in my mind. Reese and I haven't had our talk yet.

I pull my sweater over my head, grateful I decided on a tank underneath. My tolerance for the cold is pretty high overall, so I almost didn't. When I pull the jersey on, it falls down my thighs, swallowing me whole. Yet, somehow it feels as comforting as a sweater. I run my hand over the front of it with a little smile.

"Look at her, all grown up," Evie comments, and I glance up to find her and Morgan watching me with matching smiles. I throw my sweater back in the car and shut the door.

"I'm not sure if I appreciate you two ganging up on me," I say as we start to make our way inside.

"We're not ganging up, we're supporting you as a united front," Evie replies, and I simply shake my head. As we walk inside, I see that I'm not the only one with Reese's name on my back. I have no idea how to feel about that, so I ignore it.

The moment we're inside the arena, I feel the excitement. We take our seats, with the girls putting me in the middle.

"So Reese has really never dated?" Evie asks, leaning forward. I glance at her, rounding my eyes in warning, but she ignores me.

"Nope. I think there's been a few girls who have tried to catch him, but he was pretty against it all. Well, there was that girl last year." Morgan glances at me, and now I'm fully locked in.

"What girl?" I ask. Morgan glances back at the rink, before she looks at me and leans forward.

"Okay, I'm not really supposed to know about this. I overheard him and Leo talking about it. But apparently, Leo dragged him to some blind date experiment and he met someone there. I use the word "met" loosely, because he never saw the girl, just talked to her through a screen."

I'm pretty sure my heart is beating so loudly, everyone in the arena can hear it. Evie reaches over and places a hand over my own, giving me a tiny squeeze, but I can't look away from Morgan.

"He talked to a bunch of girl, but only one stood out to him. He really thought they connected, and he left his information for the date, but then he heard nothing else. Apparently, the girl didn't feel the same. He was pretty bummed about it for a while, but that's it. That's the closest he's ever come. But girl, the moment he met you, he hasn't stopped talking about you. I probably shouldn't even have said anything. Should I have said something?"

She looks so worried that I force my brain to work again as I shake my head.

"No, thank you for telling me. It… umm… brings more light to his personality."

"Right?" She sits up straight, smiling. "Honestly, that's what I thought. But sometimes, when I'm comfortable with people, I kind of word vomit information."

"You didn't," I smile, hoping it doesn't looks as crazy as I'm feeling.

Morgan turns to the rink, just as the guys come out. "Here they are!" she says, joining the other people in cheering.

I don't move immediately, trying to process the information I've been given. It feels like my whole body is on fire.

"Kenna, are you okay?" Evie leans over, concern in her eyes.

"I am," I reply, and realize that I mean it. I've already decided to let the past go, but now knowing it wasn't his fault, that somehow he never got my information, makes everything I know about him that much bigger somehow. The only girl he connected with while in college is me. Then and now. There's no way everything I feel for him is one-sided.

Morgan reaches down and pulls me beside her.

"Look, there's Reese," she says just as number thirteen makes a round on the ice, bringing him back to the player's bench. He looks up into the stands and his eyes snag on mine. Everyone else disappears as we watch each other, my heart filling to the brim. Maybe I'm wrong about him once again. Maybe there's something real here after all.

thirty-six

. . .

REESE

"Y ou're antsy," Don comments, and I shrug.

"Pregame jitters!" Micah calls out, but Don shakes his head.

"Nah, it's girl jitters."

"That... sounds awful. Please don't say that again." I stand just as we're called onto the ice. Leo falls in step beside me as we head down the tunnel.

"You good?" he asks.

"Yes." Because I am. Kenna will be here. She'll be wearing my jersey. I couldn't sleep last night, thinking of what she'll look like with my name written on her back. When I did sleep, I had my family dream again, except this time, Kenna was beside me, wearing my jersey.

Whatever happens, I can't wait any longer. Tonight, I have to tell her how I feel.

The moment we step out on the ice, my body feels calmer. Being in the rink has that effect on me. But then my heart thuds loudly in my ears as I start looking for her. Morgan never answered to tell me where they're sitting, and I know Don's sister likes to move around. I don't see them immediately. Maybe they're not here yet.

But then, there she is.

They're in the lower bowl, a few rows above the players' bench, and I can see Morgan grinning in satisfaction. I should've expected her to sit here. It's the best view for Kenna, and it's the best view for me.

I see Morgan pull Kenna up beside her, and our eyes meet. Kenna is wearing the jersey.

I take off my glove and point at her, before I make a twirl motion with my finger. There's a moment of hesitation, and I see the second she realizes what I want. She turns around slowly, gathering her hair to the side, and there it is.

My name. She's wearing my name.

Mine. Mine. Mine.

Every part of me screams to simply jump over the barrier and go claim what's mine.

Kenna turns back around, sending me a brilliant smile. I actually don't think my heart is in my chest anymore. She's holding it hostage.

"Reese, you're good to go?" Coach Warren's voice penetrates my epiphany, and I glance over at him to find him and my teammates all grinning at me. I pull my glove back on and take a hold of my stick, turning to my team.

"Let's do this."

I need to go get to my girl.

But first, I need to crush the Sparrows. We go through the opening ceremony; I'm itching for the game to start. Leo and I exchange a look as he takes off toward the goal. None of the guys on the team are big fans of the Sparrows. Mostly because we hate their captain.

Kyle is an aggressive player and he's not afraid of penalties. He does his best to skirt around them, just close enough to not get ejected. Even in an exhibition game, he's drawn blood more than once from other teams, even though we're not allowed to fight. Somehow he knows exactly what to do to get around the rules and he thrives on that. He's one of the few players that might actually get through my ice man exterior one of these days.

"There he is," Kyle calls out as we take our positions. It's just my luck that he's the right defenseman for the Sparrows. It's almost like he did it on purpose. I don't engage, instead focusing my attention on the referee.

"Heard you got yourself a girlfriend. She must have a heart for ugly strays," Kyle continues. Thankfully, the whistle blows and we're off, shutting him up.

This is the part I like. When my brain shuts off and my body takes over. Maybe it sounds stupid to outsiders, but it's almost like I become one with the game. There's nothing like the high I experience gliding across the ice, knowing my teammates and I are working in tandem.

We're the first to score, which, as usual, means that the Sparrows get more aggressive. Not in the fun, hockey way. In the mean, angry way. When Austin gets checked against the wall, my annoyance goes up three notches.

"I'm looking for a day when I no longer have to play against the Sparrows," Micah says when we come together at the edge of the ice as the first period finishes up. I glance over my shoulder long enough to make sure Kenna is still there before I go down the tunnel. For the first time in my life, I kind of wish we weren't playing a full game.

Thankfully, the second period goes off without a hitch, but it's in the third when the Sparrows step up their aggression.

It's 4-1 to us. Our newbie goalie let one sneak by. But I'm not even upset about that. He needs the practice.

When Kyle comes after me, I'm ready for him. He's been egging me on all night. It takes half a period before he finally gets what he wants.

We're about second from scoring, Don on the go, when Kyle slams into me, driving me against the wall. The whistle blows immediately, and I hear the penalty being called out, but Kyle isn't letting me go. I push him away, but he drops his gloves and comes at me, grabbing me by the collar and reaching for my helmet. I let him take it off, unbothered, which makes him even more mad. I manage to shake him off, but I won't raise my hands. I need him to be the only one breaking the rules here.

"Come on, man. This is the year. Or are you too pansy to fight in front of your girl? You think she'd like a manly man instead? I should find her later." He moves forward, but Tyler and Austin catch him, pushing him back. They hold his arms as the rest of the team and the referee skates over.

"He really has it out for you," Micah comments, and I shrug.

"It seems that anger is the only thing he has going for him."

We beat them 6-1. The high score makes it that much sweeter. The PR department decided that tonight's game is a good opportunity to get some pictures for their promotional materials, so instead of skating off the ice, the fans are let on.

All I want is to be done with this day and be with Kenna. I search for her through the arena, trying to make sure I smile and pause as people take pictures. When I finally spot her, my heart settles immediately.

She rushes over to me, pushing through the crowd. We

stop, facing each other. She does a quick once-over, as if making sure I'm intact.

"Kenna—"

"I'm about to break a rule," she says, just before she launches herself into my arms. I catch her easily as she wraps her arms around my neck, and I lift her right off the ice. Even through all the gear, I can feel her pressed against me, and it feels like the most perfect feeling in the world.

"Don't tell me you were worried about me, Sunshine?" I ask in her ear and then place her back on the ice as she pulls back to look at me.

"Of course not. Why would I worry about you?" she replies, cocking her head to the side. I wonder what she'll do if I break all the rules and kiss her right here, in front of everyone.

I can't even believe it myself. I'm falling in love with this girl.

thirty-seven

. . .

KENNA

 e end up at Reese's house for the afterparty. Apparently, beating the Sparrows is a celebration-worthy event, even in preseason. After watching that guy come after the Ravens, and hearing Morgan talk about it, I'm not surprised. When he grabbed Reese, I thought my heart was going to jump out of my chest.

Now I'm sitting in the living room at the guys' house with Morgan beside me, while she discusses plays with Don. By the looks of it, the two of them are really close, and I find that heartwarming. I don't even have any cousins I can be close with.

"Hey," Evie comes back, kneeling beside. "I need to head back to the dorm. No surprise to anyone, but Nate is incapable of doing one thing right, and I need to go check the graph we were supposed to submit by midnight tonight. I'll need to meet them early tomorrow at the lab."

"Okay," I stand immediately, "we can call a car."

"No, no," she pushes me back down. "I didn't mean you too. Just me. You stay and enjoy."

"But—"

"No, buts. There's absolutely no reason for you to head back now." She leans over, whispering directly into my ear. "And you no longer seem to fear parties, or am I wrong?"

She's not. When we came inside the house tonight I didn't even think about my past. I was only excited to see Reese. Which is actually more terrifying than any party, ever.

"Also, baby girl, you have a conversation to have, remember?" She continues.

This is what I get for telling Evie my thoughts before we went down to the ice to see the team. After hearing Morgan talk about Reese's "one that got away," Evie is even more Team Reese.

But am I ready to tell him the truth? The fear in my heart is so potent, I can almost taste it. What if my dad and my ex are right? What if I'm not enough as a person and I have to work to earn affection? It's the only response I've ever had, especially when it comes to my dad, so I'm not discarded. Yet, Reese and I have been in a mutually beneficial relationship that I *think* has turned into a friendship and he has never made me feel like I had to perform in order for him to stay. But is that enough?

"Maybe tonight isn't the right time," I say, because I can't shake off the doubts.

"I think he might have something to say about that," Evie replies.

I follow the direction of her eyes and see Reese come into the living room. He went to pick up pizza and drinks with Leo. The place they ordered from wasn't doing delivery today.

The moment he's in the room, his eyes find mine. He

moves toward me, almost automatically, when he's stopped by someone. I glance over to find that girl, Alicia, hanging onto his arm. I watch as he shakes her off, not taking his eyes off me, and steps back enough to put distance between them. She doesn't look happy, but he's already walking toward me. The movement is intentional and my stupid brain can't help but feel hopeful.

"Reese, I'm leaving Kenna in your capable hands," Evie says the moment he is within earshot. "Kenna, you behaved well today. Your curfew is lifted. Bye, Morgan!"

Morgan jumps up and follows Evie out, while Reese takes her vacated seat.

"You were a good girl today, huh?"

I like the way he says that, his breath ruffling the side of my face. I shrug, facing him, bringing our faces just a few inches apart. Just like that, he's beside me and all of my fears go quiet.

"It happens once in a while."

Reese grins, but before he can say anything in return, someone calls him from the kitchen.

"Sorry, I promised the guys I'd take care of everything for this party, so I'm on duty."

"No worries, Morgan's back," I say, just as she returns and takes Reese's empty seat.

"Oh, we're playing musical chairs?" she asks, and Reese shakes his head.

"I'll be back," he says.

"I'll be here," I reply.

He holds my gaze for a moment, as if making sure I'm serious, then finally walks away.

It's about an hour later when the noise of the people gets too much. I should probably head back to campus, but I promised Reese I wouldn't leave. He had to drive a few people back to campus. When I tell Morgan I'm not feeling well, she sneaks me upstairs, showing me to a room.

"You can rest here. No one is allowed up here, so you're good. I'll come and check on you in a bit."

"Are you sure?"

"Yes." Morgan grins and then slips out the door, shutting it behind her. I sit down on the bed, suddenly so tired I can't even keep my eyes open. All my missed sleep is catching up to me. There's only a single light on, located on the bedside table. I trust Morgan won't steer me wrong, so I slide back on the bed, take off my shoes, and curl into a small ball. I decide to lie here for a few minutes in the dark and hopefully, my headache will subside.

———

When I wake, I'm not alone. At some point during my sleep, I moved up to the pillows, and I look over my shoulder to find Morgan sleeping beside me. I pull out my phone and see that it's after one in the morning. The house seems quiet, so the party must be over. Reese mentioned he wanted everyone gone by midnight, but I didn't think it was possible. I guess people do really listen to the captain. I sit up carefully so as not to disturb Morgan, and I grab my shoes before slipping out of the door.

The upstairs is dark, but there's a light on downstairs, so I walk down the stairs. The kitchen is straight in front of me and I head there first. My throat feels dry, so maybe I can grab some water before I head out.

"What happened to being a good girl?" The voice comes from behind me, and I jump, slapping a hand over my mouth to stop myself from making a noise.

"Reese! What are you doing awake?" I whisper, before swatting at him. "You almost gave me a heart attack."

"I was finishing cleaning up. You were supposed to be asleep. Was the bed not comfortable enough?"

"No, that's not it—"

"The pillow not fluffy enough? The bedding? I guess forest green is just not your color, huh?"

I narrow my eyes, when it dawns on me. "It was your room."

"Yes." He grins, and I don't even know why I'm surprised. Morgan and Evie seemed to be on a mission.

"I'm sorry I commandeered your room."

"Well, I know it was Morgan." He doesn't seem to mind, and I realize that we're all alone for the first time since the café shift. Suddenly I feel very self-conscious.

"Would you like to see the stars with me?"

Reese's question takes me completely by surprise. He's looking a little unsure of himself, almost like he's afraid I'm going to say no, but I find myself saying yes.

"Wait right here," he says, before dashing up the stairs. For someone so big, he sure moves quietly. I put my shoes on while I wait, and he returns not a minute later with blankets.

"Come on." He motions toward the glass door to my right, and we step outside. The weather has definitely cooled down a lot in the last couple of months, the cold front coming in. I shudder a little bit but then feel the blanket placed over my shoulders. I meet Reese's eyes, and he motions me forward.

I didn't make it to their backyard during the party and I'm curious to see it. It's not big, but it seems well maintained. At the corner opposite the house is a wooden platform. Reese steps up on it, spreading out one of the blankets he brought out here. He sits on the blanket, then motions for me to join him, and I do. Once I'm seated, he takes the last blanket and places it over our lap.

"Lie back," he says, before he does so himself. I follow. When I do, my eyes lift up to the sky, and I gasp. Somehow, this spot in the backyard perfectly blocks off any light. Since the house is also dark, the stars seem close enough to reach. I've found that to be one beauty of Colorado. The stars are always reaching down to us.

"This is perfect. But why do you have a wooden platform in your backyard?"

"For a jacuzzi," Reese replies. "The guys were determined to get one over the summer, so we did, and it broke. Almost immediately. They were outraged, it was a whole thing. So, for now, we just have a wooden platform."

I chuckle, because I can somehow imagine it. Reese sighs in contentment, and I can feel my own body relaxing as well. Somewhere in the last few weeks, he started to have that effect on me.

We lie in silence for a few minutes, but then I can't seem to take it anymore. I told Evie I was going to talk to Reese, so I need to talk to Reese. But being brave enough to start the conversation—that's scary.

"Reese."

"Kenna."

We start speaking at the same time, and I turn to find him watching at me.

"You go first," he says, and I actually do think that's for the best. But I can't do it lying down, so I push myself up and stand. I feel Reese moving behind me. It's his quiet, encouraging presence that finally makes me say the words.

"I have to tell you something. I'm not sure how you'll react. You might not want anything to do with me afterward or—"

"That will never happen."

"Please, just let me get this out." I still haven't turned around but I can feel he's moved closer.

"Last year, you took part in a blind date event," I begin. I hear his sharp intake of breath. Deciding to face it head-on, I turn and find him watching me in shock.

"How—?"

"I know because I was there. Number two seven three."

"You were her?" His brow furrows as he tries to process.

"I was. And you were number one two nine." He jerks again, and I really can't read him in this near darkness. So I push on. "I want you to know that the conversation, the connection you felt, it was real. I felt it too. And I was so curious about you, I cheated. I saw you leave the booth, and I heard you talk about your ideal type."

Realization washes over him. He opens his mouth again, but I hurry on.

"I gave them my information, told them I still wanted to meet you, and then I got the message two days later. I went to the café and waited for you for two hours. You never showed up."

"Kenna."

"I just found out it's because you didn't know. Something must've happened, I don't know what, but I was going through a rough patch. My ex," I pause taking another calming breath. "My ex used me for his own benefit. It started with him needing to pass midterms and I thought I was doing him a favor anytime I went out of my way to help. Anyway, then at a party, I found out he was cheating on me the whole time. This girl was everything I'm not. You know, tall, blonde, athletic—kind of like your type so you get it." I chuckle, because that's better than crying. "When I called him out on it, he humiliated me in front of the entire group of people, making sure to shout my insecurities at me."

"Kenna, I—"

"I know it wasn't fair to put you in the same category, but when you were talking to your friends about your ideal type, it brought all of that to light again and then your rejection felt like the end of the world. It crushed me, and I carried that with me this whole time."

"That's why you didn't like me?" His voice is barely a whisper as he processes all this new information.

"I'm sorry for misjudging you, and I'm sorry for putting my own insecurities on you, when you didn't know who I was. It was unfair and childish of me."

He doesn't say anything at first, just watches me in that steady way of his. I don't look away either, because I owe him at least this.

"And now?" he asks.

"Now, I don't feel that way anymore."

"How do you feel?"

He's going to make me say it first. I can't blame him. I hurt him by misjudging him and I don't ever want to do that again.

"Now, I think that whatever I felt back then doesn't begin to compare to how much I feel now. You've become important to me in a way that makes me terrified of losing you. And if that's not the way you feel, I totally understand, but at least now you know the truth. About all of it."

His gaze seems to study every inch of my face, as if he can't believe I'm saying this. There's so much softness there. He looks at me like his eyes are dripping with honey. I want to capture that look on film, so that I have it with me always.

"I need to start out by saying that you're wrong," he says.

"What?" I definitely wasn't expecting that.

"What you overheard, the whole 'my type' comment, I can't even remember it because I know for a fact I was just placating the guys without thinking it through. I was too wrapped up in thinking about you. If I was ever to describe my type to anyone it would be you. The moment I met you, I thought you were the most gorgeous girl I've ever seen. And you've only become more beautiful."

I'm pretty sure I have lost all senses and am now just a blob of emotion floating through the air because Reese has just told me I'm beautiful. That I'm his type. I need about three to five months to process that. But he's not done.

"Also, I need you to know that it's different for me."

"What is?" I seem to have regained some senses. I'm afraid to ask, but I need to know everything he's thinking.

"My biggest fear isn't losing you."

"I—?" I lose all words, not knowing how to respond. I knew it was too good to be true. But then he places his hands on the side of my cheeks, keeping my face turned toward him.

"Kenna, my biggest fear isn't losing you. My biggest fear is hurting you." He takes a deep breath, his body shuddering. "Because it's not about me, your happiness and well-being are more important than my broken heart. Losing you would kill me, but I'd die happy knowing you're okay."

There's a moment of stillness around us, as if the whole world is holding its breath while I let that sink in. His expression is so open and earnest it makes me want to cry.

"But—"

"You have no idea how much it drove me crazy last year that I couldn't find you. But all of this, the pull I felt toward you the moment I met you, it makes sense now. It was fate, it was destiny, it was all those things people write about. I just didn't know it. Not in my head, only in my heart."

It's his turn to take a deep breath, and I can't really come up with any coherent responses as he continues.

"I know we signed a contract, I know this was supposed to be fake, but it wasn't for me. It hasn't been for a long time. Maybe since the beginning. But I didn't want to push, I didn't want to make you uncomfortable.

And honestly, I didn't know where you stood and I was prepared to walk away if that's what you needed. I obviously didn't know about your ex, but I can never imagine treating you like anything but like a princess. If you didn't feel the same, if you needed space, I'm ready to do whatever it takes to make sure you're happy."

I blink up at him, memorizing every word he just said. I place my hands over his on my cheeks and pull them down. Then, before he knows what I'm doing I smack him on the shoulder with all the power I have in me.

"Hey! What was that for?" Reese looks at me in complete shock.

"That's for thinking any of this would be okay if you're not. What kind of stupid sacrificial mumbo jumbo is this?" I snap, my eyes flashing as I try to blink away the tears that have pooled there. "I could never be happy without you." I continue. "This is your big confession? That you were ready to walk away? Is that what you want?"

"Never."

"Then why even suggest it, why even think about it?"

"Because you're my number one concern. Even more so now, that I understand what you've been through, I won't ever push you into something you don't want."

That spark that Evie was talking about is back and it's a roaring fire and I feel it burning through every part of me.

"Then how about instead of assuming things, we both decide to talk about them? I don't need you to sacrifice your happiness for mine. I need you to hold my hand through it all as we figure it out together. That right there, that's the sacrifice I want, that's the sacrifice I'm willing to make. To be an equal partner in all of it. Life, love—"

"Kenna?"

"What?"

"It's my turn to break a rule," he says right before his lips crash over mine, stealing the breath from my lungs. His arms wrap around my waist, lifting me into him and I reach up to run my hands up his shoulders, plunging them into his hair.

He kisses me with ferocity that matches my own. It's like we've both been deprived of this one precious thing our whole lives and now we finally have it. His lips are gentle, yet firm. As if he's making sure I know he's serious. This isn't a passing thought, this kiss is a commitment. It fills up every part of me that ever felt unwanted or unloved. Reese worships me with this one kiss, solidifying every word he has said. I make sure that I give him just as much in return. Not because I have to in order to earn his love, but because I want to.

My hands tug him closer and he lifts me straight off the platform, holding me suspended against his chest, as he places his arm behind my thighs. I pull back, completely breathless, before I'm the one leaning forward again. I place a kiss to one corner of his mouth and then move on to the other, before he captures my lips once more. I can feel his smile blossoming and it matches my own.

"I think I'm officially addicted to kissing you," Reese whispers against my lips.

"Oh yeah?"

"Mhhm. What are we going to do about that?"

I pull back just slightly, so I can look straight into his eyes. Somehow, he's still holding me suspended, his arm pressed firmly against my thighs, so I can place my arms around his neck, our eyes on the same level.

"Are you sure?" I ask and Reese nods.

"Absolutely."

"Hmm, I think we need to assess the situation a little better," I say, leaning closer once more, so that our noses touch for a moment. "Maybe another million kisses can give us more in-depth information on how you're actually feeling about this. You know they say, collecting data—"

Reese's lips meet mine once more, shutting off my ramble. This time, the kiss is more gentle, more like a promise.

"You seem pleased with that idea," I say, coming up for air once more.

"I might need to renegotiate the 'million kisses' clause," Reese replies, and I chuckle.

"It's a good thing we're good at contracts."

Reese chuckles once more, shaking his head a little, before he lowers his head and kisses me like I'm the most precious person on the planet, while I answer in kind.

thirty-eight

. . .

REESE

er kisses are all I need to stay alive. I decided that last night and now, it's the decree I want to live by. We stayed up and talked for hours before I sent her back to my room, and I went and crashed on the couch. Today is Saturday, and neither one of us has to work, so I'm determined to make today a new beginning for us.

I can't believe I was so foolish not to see what's been in front of my face this whole time. No wonder she felt familiar, no wonder I gravitated toward her like a magnet. Everything makes sense now.

"Are you just going to keep sitting there and staring off into space with a goofy grin?" Tyler asks, coming into the kitchen. I'm at the table by the doors, a cup of water in front of me. I haven't even made breakfast yet.

"He's been like that since I came down," Don says as he takes another spoonful of cereal.

"Did Morgan stay?" Tyler asks, pointing to the jacket hanging over one of the chairs.

"Her and Kenna crashed in Reese's room," Don replies.

"Ah, that explains all this," Tyler waves a hand in front of my face in a circular motion and continues into the kitchen. I obviously can hear them talk, I just don't care. But then I hear Morgan's voice, followed by Kenna's, and I'm on my feet instantly.

"Wow, he's completely gone," Tyler comments, just as the girls step through the doorway. Kenna's eyes find mine immediately, and I have to restrain myself from rushing over to her.

"Good morning, all," Morgan says, looking first at me and then at Don, completely ignoring Tyler. She tends to do that. They've had some wild rivalry since they were kids. We're all just used to it by now.

"Good morning!" Micah and Austin bound down the stairs, stopping short at the sight of the two girls. "Well, I can get used to this view every morning," Micah comments, and I can't stop the growl that escapes. Every single person in the room turns and looks at me.

"We're leaving," I say before I walk over to Kenna and take her hand in mine.

"Oh no, do you think he's going to make me do extra drills?" Micah asks the room.

"I will!" I call back.

"He won't!" Kenna yells to them. The sound of laughter follows us out of the house.

"You can't keep taking Micah's side on things. I'm going to get jealous."

"You're already jealous," she replies, shrugging. I've thought this before, but I love the way her hand fits in mine. It feels even more fitting somehow, now that there are no secrets between us. No wondering about the other's feelings, either.

"Where are you dragging me off to so early?" she asks as we reach my car. I open the passenger door for her. I've noticed how much this means to her, and I intend to never stop doing it.

"Well, I was thinking coffee and then your dorm."

"My dorm?"

"I assume you'd like to take a shower and change." I glance over at her as she nods. "And then, if you're up for it, I was thinking Northanger Park? They're having a farmers' market there that should be fun to check out. And the small lake is really pretty, if you wanted to take pictures."

She doesn't respond. After I pull out into traffic, I spare her a glance. She's staring out the windshield, slightly frozen.

"Kenna?"

"Yes," she turns to me quickly. "One hundred percent yes to all of that. Well, actually, instead of coffee could I shower first and we can get coffee at the farmers' market?"

"That sounds better." I reply, reaching over and offering her my hand. She looks at it for a moment before threading her fingers through mine.

This, this is exactly how I want to drive everywhere now. When we reach her dorm, I drop her off, but instead of going far, I park my car and then get out to walk. Usually, I do a run on Saturday morning, but today I was much too riled up to leave the house.

I'm so lost in my own thoughts that when my phone rings, I don't even look at the caller ID.

"Reese."

The voice on the other side of the line is one I don't really want to hear right now.

"Hi, Uncle Dan. How's it going?"

"I saw the game. You need to work on your crossovers, some of them looked sloppy. If you were paying more attention, that kid wouldn't have gotten a drop on you."

"You know he would've," I reply. "You know how Kyle is, and you know he doesn't play clean."

My uncle grunts, a noise I'm very acquainted with, because he tends to do it anytime he thinks I've said something stupid.

"Regardless of that fact, you need to be quicker. This season is make or break. If you want to join the big leagues—"

"Do we have to do this early on a Saturday?" I interrupt, because I swear I've heard this all before. He's never satisfied when I'm on ice. No matter what I say, I have never been able to get through to him, and it's getting more evident every time we talk.

"Why? You have a hot date with the photographer?" That stops me cold, but I don't know why I'm surprised. He watched a live stream of an exhibition game. He definitely checks the gossip account. I should actually be more surprised that he hasn't driven to campus to read me the riot act.

"I do, in fact, have a date, Uncle Dan. She's great." I lean against my car, as I run a hand over my face.

"She's a distraction. Break up with her now, and get your head on straight."

I swear, he really does have just the one tune.

"No, I will not be breaking up with her. What I will do is take her on an amazing date, so if you excuse me—"

"You're really throwing it all away? I told you, romantic relationships are a crutch. She'll ruin it all for you. You have to get rid of her."

I've heard him talk like this my whole life, but it's never

made me as sad as it's making me now. He really lives his life thinking that. I feel sorry for him. I wonder if this is who I would've become if Kenna didn't come into my life. Would I have believed the same lies Uncle Dan lives by? It's possible, but now, I'm grateful I will never have to find out. I will also never walk away from Kenna, no matter how much my uncle would demand it. I'm not afraid to tell him as much.

"Uncle Dan, I love you, but I need you to know that she's not going anywhere. I intend to do my best to keep her. You won't be able to stop me. I'll talk to you later."

With that, I hang up. I turn back to the door only to find Kenna standing there. She must've heard what I said, but she doesn't comment. She gives me a brilliant smile, and I walk around the hood of the car to open the door for her.

"That was fast," I say as she gets in.

"I'm magic," she replies and the way she's looking at me, I'm helpless to do anything but follow my immediate impulse. As she settles in her seat, I bend down and place a quick kiss to her lips. She looks at me in shock as I shut her door and jog around to my side.

"What was that?" she asks the moment I'm inside the car.

"Magic."

thirty-nine

. . .

KENNA

$\mathcal{H}$olding Reese's hand with admitted feelings between us as we walk around the stalls at the farmers' market feels incredible. It seems silly to me that I feared letting him know how I feel. It's so easy to get stuck in my head and focus on past experiences, when all I should've done was talk to him.

Maybe things would be better with my father if we'd ever learned to talk through things, instead of letting them pile up. I'm not sure, but I know that after overhearing a part of Reese's conversation, he has carried a lot on his plate as well.

"Do you want to talk about it?" I ask as we wait to pick up our coffees. As I assumed, there's a coffee cart here, and from the looks of it, it's a popular one. Maybe it's because it's so early, and everyone still needs their caffeine.

"How much did you overhear?" Reese asks.

"Not much. But from what you told me, you and your uncle have a pretty strained relationship."

"We do," he sighs.

I wish I could just reach over and smooth out all the worry lines. The guys were making fun of him this morning for being smitten, but I'm just as guilty of that. He drops my hand just long enough to let me take some pictures, but the moment I'm done, he reaches for it again. Which brings me immense happiness. Such small actions, but they make me feel desired in a way I never allowed myself to dream.

"When I was little, maybe five or six, it was the first time I remember my uncle ranting about romantic relationships being a wasted time," he begins, and my heart immediately goes out to him.

"He called them toxic and unnecessary, his two favorite words. Back then, my parents traveled for work a lot, and since I was in training, I stayed with Uncle Dan. By age six, I moved in full-time so we could train. Even though my parents love each other, I've never been around them long enough to see it for myself, you know? That kind of upbringing rewires the brain. It leaves a mark."

I don't comment, simply giving his hand a squeeze, encouraging him to keep going. All of this sounds so familiar that my heart hurts because he too had to experience it.

"For the longest time, I thought that falling in love was a curse. So many people I know don't seem happy after a while. So, it was pointless for me to even try. But then Leo dragged me to that blind date experiment."

"And you—"

"I met someone I simply clicked with. I don't know, there was something about you that drew me in instantly. I wasn't afraid to try with you. I wanted to try."

"But then we never met."

"I think I know what happened," he says. "One of the girls on the committee, she's an avid hockey fan and has tried to get with me or the guys on the team more than once. I can't prove it, of course, but I think she might have had something to do with it. I suppose she could've just not text you with a location, but it probably felt better to her knowing that you were waiting for me and I would never show up."

I nod. I had a similar thought after I went to bed last night. It was beyond our control then, but it's in our control now, and that's what I'm determined to concentrate on. I know I need to ask about the other part that's been bugging me and even though I just resolved myself to have conversations with Reese instead of making up the scenarios in my mind, I'm still hesitant.

"What is it?" But of course he reads me like a book. I give him a soft smile and a little shrug.

"I saw you that night, the night of the date," I say and Reese jerks in surprise.

"Where?"

"Coming out of Coffee & Books. You were with a girl," I hesitate for a second before I push on, "Tall, blonde, athletics—your type. Well, you know, the type you said at the event."

I'm feeling shy as I say the words, even thought I believe Reese's words last night. His declaration has silenced much of the annoying self-deprecation voice. Reese just stares at me in shock and then his expression changes. Understanding turns to adoring in a blink, and I don't know if I can even keep standing under that intensity.

"I'm so sorry, Sunshine. What bad luck that was. That was my cousin. Pamela. She's about seven years older than me and was in town for a work thing. We haven't seen each other in years, so we grabbed a coffee while she was coming through."

Now it's my turn to stare at him in shock.

"I'm so dumb," I say, dropping my face into my free hand,

letting my hair fall to the front. I hear Reese's laughter and I want the earth to open up and swallow me whole.

"Not dumb," Reese says, as he pulls me into his embrace. My forehead rests on his chest, as I snuggle against him. "I would've jumped into the same conclusion if I were you."

"So we're both dumb then?" I ask into his chest and he shakes with laughter. He pulls me away, placing his hands back on my cheeks and raising my face so he can look me straight into the eyes.

"Not dumb. A little jaded, but we're working through it." He drops a quick kiss to my forehead and I'm back to grinning like a fool.

"It doesn't matter, because we still found each other despite all that," I say, looking up at him to make sure he knows I mean every word.

"It was meant to be," he says. "And, just in case I wasn't clear last night, don't you ever forget that you, McKenna St. James are my type. More perfect than I could've imagined. I'll keep telling you that every day, multiple times a day, so you know I mean it."

"You're kind of sappy, huh?" I tease, but I'm warm all over. He went straight to the heart of the problem, somehow understanding exactly what I need without me having to spell it out. He's making me feel a hundred things at once. My face is probably beet red by now.

"You know it, I hope you're ready for more of the same," he declares with a big grin.

Just then our coffee order is called out, and we walk over to pick it up before we continue our walk through the stalls.

The air is crisp, and it feels like a new beginning. One where I'm not afraid to follow my heart. I never want to end up in the same loop of self-doubt ever again.

"We did find each other," Reese says, almost like he had to

voice it all of a sudden. "And I hope you're ready to be stuck with me forever." He steps in front of me and starts walking backwards, so he can see my face. "I'm going to be very much the opposite of nonchalant about any of this. Find me a stage, and I will scream it at the top of my lungs: *McKenna St. James is my girlfriend*! I'll even use your government given name, so people know I'm extra serious. Oh, I should also make, like, fifteen hundred Instagram posts. Just so everyone is aware I'm taken and I intend to stay that way. How's that?"

I grin, reaching out a hand to him, and he threads his fingers through it immediately. He pulls me beside him as he turns to face forward again and we stop to look at the carts in front of us. But my attention is still mostly on him.

"That's perfect. I wasn't built for a nonchalant man," I say.

"Good." He wraps me in a side hug, drawing me into his body and places a lingering kiss on my forehead and honestly, I now know what it means to melt. I'm a complete puddle of emotions, and I didn't think that was ever going to be possible.

"What is it?" he asks immediately, almost like he can read me. But then, I think he can. Looking back at our interactions, even when I tried to hide away, he always seems to call me out. And just like that, there are tears in my eyes. "Kenna."

"I'm okay. I don't know when I turned into such a cry baby…" I realize it happened the moment I decided to be honest about my feelings for him. He became my safe place, before I even knew it happened.

Reese tugs me by the hand and leads me away from the stalls and toward a bench. When we sit down, I duck my head, trying to get control of my emotions. He reaches out and places one finger under my chin, raising it so I can look at him.

"You never have to hide from me. Tell me what's on your mind."

I want to tell him so many things. I never wanted to share this much with anyone. But it doesn't seem fair, to just over share like that. Evie is used to that from me, but this thing between Reese and me is new.

"This is supposed to be a light, fun date. Not trauma dumping," I say.

"I dumped my trauma, you can dump yours." He smiles.

"Do you think we're moving too fast? Sharing our deepest and darkest secrets?"

He's shaking his head before I even finish speaking. "No. Coach Warren once told me that he knew he'd found his person the instant he met his wife. They've been together for thirty years. I'm not a pro at this by any means, but I'm learning that it seems foolish to hold things back just because of timing or fear. If you want to say something, say it. Can we make that a rule for our relationship?"

"Should we draw up another contract?" I tease. "Make a *to-do* list this time?"

"There will only be one other contract between us, but I think that conversation can wait, for now."

I stare at him with my mouth open, because he's thinking a million steps ahead. As he places a quick kiss on my nose and then tucks a hair behind my ear I realize that the whole time I thought I was the only one falling, he was falling right along with me.

Without a second of hesitation, I reach for him, catching his lips with mine. Now that I've had a taste, I don't think I will ever get tired of kissing him. I hope he's ready for me to be just as non-nonchalant about the whole thing as he said he'll be. I need a stage to shout from as well.

forty

. . .

A month later

REESE

It's been a little over five weeks since Kenna and I decided to make things official and I don't think I have ever been happier. The more time I've spent with her, the more I realized that I didn't know anything about relationships. The only thing I was ever taught were the ravings of a bitter man. Being with someone, finding a person that's yours and yours alone, is magic. The guys have been teasing me nonstop, but none of it fazes me. They're just jealous, and I remind them of that on the daily.

When my sports psychology class finally ends, I nearly jog out of the room. I'm supposed to be meeting Kenna for some study time at Coffee & Books, but we both know she's just nervous because she's supposed hear back regarding her contest results today. My phone buzzes and I pull it out as I step outside the building.

DON:

which one of you losers finished off the
orange juice and didn't replace it?

MICAH:

pretty sure it was your sister

DON:

you can't keep blaming everything on her

MICAH:

it could also be Kenna

REESE:

leave my girlfriend out of this

TYLER:

notice how quick he is to throw the title
around

MICAH:

well, he is smitten beyond repair

REESE:

and proud of it

MICAH:

is proud what you really should be?

REESE:

you'll learn one day

MICAH:

no way, I'm never settling down

TYLER:

you say that now and then boom, you're
Reese

DON:

hello, orange juice?

LEO:

I'll bring some home after I'm done at the
library

DON:

thank you

MICAH:

yes, thank you. You are the best husband
ever

REESE:

I give you permission to assign whatever
punishment you deem enough for Micah

LEO:

perfect

MICAH:

hey!

I'm chuckling to myself when I glance up and freeze. Uncle Dan is leaning against his car, parked in front of the building. I've been ignoring the majority of his calls for the last month. Last time I picked up, I got an earful about how I need to break up with Kenna or I'm doomed for a life of despair.

"Reese, we need to talk about that girl," Uncle Dan says, pushing away from the car and walking toward me.

"We really don't," I reply, "I'm not trying to be disrespectful here, but this is one thing that I will not listen to."

"So you're ready to throw everything we worked toward away?"

I sigh, because he's a broken record at this point. I can't even find it in myself to fight him on this. He's never going to listen to me. It's like talking to a wall.

"I'm not throwing anything away," I say, because this much I will always repeat, just in case it gets through to him.

"I'm gaining something. You can't understand that, but I ask you to respect it."

He doesn't say anything at first, his eyes hard on me.

"You're really choosing her over me? Over hockey?"

"If that's the way you want to look at it, then yes. If you're making me choose, I choose her every time."

I'm tired of living as some second chance for Uncle Dan. He's put everything on me without asking my opinion. Kenna and I have that in common—father and father figure being selfish jerks. But she's shown me that love isn't about keeping score or being useful. We're learning that part together.

"I can't believe..." Uncle Dan trails off, looking at something over my shoulder, and I turn to find Kenna walking toward us.

She smiles and all the clouds roll away. My sunshine.

Kenna steps up beside me, threading her fingers through mine.

"Hi, Handsome."

"Hi, Sunshine," I reply. She smiles and then turns to my uncle.

"You must be Reese's uncle. It's lovely to meet you." She puts out her free hand and at first, I think he won't take it. But then he does. He shakes her hand, looking between us with an unreadable gaze.

"You've raised a great man," Kenna continues, tucking herself back against my side. "If you come to his next game, we should sit together."

There's a moment of silence and then Uncle Dan grunts and turns toward his car. Without a word, he gets in and drives off. As we watch the car disappear, I exhale fully, releasing some of the tension I was holding inside.

"Are you okay?" Kenna asks.

I bend down to place a quick kiss to her lips.

"I am now."

We start walking toward the café slowly, savoring every second of being together. Uncle Dan could never understand, but I don't need him to. Even though that would be the desired outcome, I have resigned myself to the fact that we will never see eye to eye when it comes to relationships.

"I thought we were meeting at the café?" I ask.

"I decided to surprise you, since I got out earlier."

"I'm glad you did."

Her presence is exactly what I need. We seem to have that healing balm response to each other. She's been dealing with her own family issues, and I've been there for her. I can't imagine dealing with things on my own. I know how that makes me sound, but I don't care. I love our partnership. I understand Coach Warren's stance now—Kenna is my perfect teammate.

"Are you sure you're okay?" Kenna asks as we reach the front of the café. She steps in front of me, so she can look at my face, and I nod.

"I am. I think I've come to terms with the fact that I'll never have a good relationship with him, that he's no longer my home. But, that's okay, because I've got a new home. I have you."

She takes my face into her hands, bringing us just a breath away.

"Everyone deserves a love that feels like home," she whispers, healing all the pieces that were hurting.

"Thank you for being mine," I say and then I kiss her. She melts right into me, and I don't care if WentworthWhispers takes a million pictures. I will kiss my girlfriend every chance I get.

"Come on, let's go see if you won that competition, shall we?" I say, then follow her into the café.

forty-one

. . .

KENNA

The noise of the music reaches us while we're still on the other side of the parking lot. The Autumn Festival is in full swing, with a live DJ and a large variety of booths for food and activities. It's like a full-blown carnival.

Evie and I are walking through the area set up for pumpkin bowling and apple bobbing. I'm not sure how many people are going to be dunking their faces into cold water in this weather, but to each their own I suppose. We stop every now and then so I can take some pictures with my new camera.

I didn't win the contest, but I did tie for third. The cash prize and my savings were enough for me to buy a new camera without breaking the bank. I haven't told my dad he'll need to take care of groceries on his own this month, but I'm working up the courage. Reese has been encouraging me to stand up for myself, whenever I'm ready. Which is not tonight. Tonight is the Autumn Festival and time with my boyfriend and my friends.

"You keep cradling that thing like it's your baby," Evie comments, chuckling.

"I love her. She's my one true love."

"Don't let Reese hear you say that, he'll cry himself to sleep every night," Micah says, coming up beside us.

"If you tell him, I'll make sure he makes you do a hundred of those bag skates." I point a finger at him. I still don't really know what bag skating is but I remember Micah being scared of it the first time we met and it seems to work. He raises his hands up in the air.

"I'm only here to lead you to the theater, please don't hurt me."

Evie shakes her head at him, but we turn to follow. One of the booths set up an outside theater, away from the loud DJ, and they're showing *Practical Magic*. I don't particularly care about the movie, but I'm excited to see Reese. He's been busy with his clinical shadowing lately. We haven't had as much time together.

But even busy, Reese is the most considerate man I've ever met. He's teaching me every day how uncomplicated and lovely love can be, if two people are determined to communicate and put each other first. We made that decision, and we're both all in.

I told him everyone deserves a love that feels like home, because I found my home in him.

My dad still hasn't really come around to the idea of Reese and I, or my photography, but I no longer seek his approval to my own detriment. I know he loves me in his own way, but we have a lot that needs to be worked through first.

Evie, Micah, and I reach the makeshift theater, and I spot the hockey players immediately. They've found themselves a place on the right of the screen, with blankets and chairs set up. When we get closer, I see that there's also a lot of food.

"Kenna and Evie have arrived," Micah announces dramatically, presenting us to the guys as if he's presenting us in court. Reese is already on his feet, reaching for me, and I go to him automatically. He holds me close, placing a tiny kiss to the top of my head, before pulling back to look at my face.

"Hi, Sunshine."

"Hi, Handsome."

After all the nicknames, he stuck to the most surprising one. Evie told me once that I shine brighter around him and he saw that in me, before I realized it myself. But truth be told, I should call him sunshine instead. He makes everything in my life so much brighter and more beautiful. He kisses me then, and the jeers start immediately.

"Down in front!" Tyler shouts.

"My eyes!" Micah echoes. Reese smiles against my lips, but he pulls back. We take a seat on the blanket, and I glance around to find Evie roll her eyes as she moves past Leo. He watches her go but doesn't say anything, and my curiosity rises.

"What's the deal with you and Leo?" I ask when Evie takes her seat on the other side of Reese. I lean right over him, and she follows suit. She sends one very lethal glare toward the goalie, then looks me dead in the eye.

"I don't know what you're talking about."

"Sure, Evelyn."

"Just pay attention to your boyfriend, McKenna."

"Do you want to switch seats?" Reese asks, looking between the two of us. We glance at him and then we glance at each other, and shake our heads in unison.

"No, I kind of like you being part of our gossiping sessions," I say, and Reese grins.

"Come on, Reese, we all know you're one of the girls now anyway," Evie says and Reese isn't even fazed.

"Then, by all means, continue," he says, all serious-like.

I press my lips together to keep from laughing and turn back to my friend. "Seriously, Evie. Spill the tea."

"He's annoying, that's all. The communication seminar combines our classes, and he seems to think that he deserves preferential treatment because he's in school to be 'a real doctor' or whatever, simply because I'll 'only be a veterinarian'."

"Did he actually say that?"

"He might as well have. He told the teacher that my participating in the final presentation was unnecessary. As if! I get better grades than he does, and he thinks I can't speak in front of a room full of people? Where did he get that idea from?" Evie rolls her eyes. "He's currently blacklisted. I don't want to talk about it. I'm going to go get apple cider."

"Do you want me to come with you?" I ask immediately, and she waves me away.

"No, stay and snuggle with your boyfriend. I'm a big girl." She stands and heads for the cart. I turn just slightly to find Leo watching her.

"Should we do something about that?" I ask Reese, snuggling into his side. He wraps his arm around me, bringing me close and places another kiss to the top of my head.

"I think we should let that develop naturally."

"But what if they kill each other?" I'm slightly concerned. "Evie does know how to dispose of a body."

"Ah yes, I remember her telling me that."

"She didn't," I gasp.

"She did. But don't worry, we'll step in if there's a threat on life," Reese says, and I can tell he's trying to hold back his laughter.

"This isn't funny."

"No, it's very funny. But also, very serious. Both things can be true, you know."

I lean my head back, looking up into Reese's face and purse my lips a few times, making sure he sees me doing it. He chuckles and leans down to oblige.

We've talked a lot about the future. We're determined to make this work. He'll be graduating first and if everything works out, he'll be drafted by the NHL. There have been a few offers since he did the photoshoot for GoGoSports. The guys have been heckling him about that one, but I know they're proud of him.

As I watch him lean back to say something to the guys, I can't help but smile. They're a family and by extension, they've become mine. No matter what happens with my dad, I have that now.

And when it comes to Reese, I'm determined to make it work. There's no going back. I'm going to prove his uncle wrong in every way possible.

Reese turns back to me and catches me watching him. We haven't said the words outright yet, but they've been on the tip of my tongue for weeks. As Reese continues to watch me, the lights around us dim and the first sounds of the movie start up, but I can't look away. There are twinkling lights in the tree behind him and he looks so handsome, his face earnest and caring as he gazes at me and it nearly brings tears to my eyes. Maybe now is the moment, maybe now I—

"I love you," Reese says, his words soft, but sure. His eyes soften even more, sparkling with love that's mine and mine alone. My body feels alive, as if the words ignited all the dormant parts of me.

"Are you reading my mind again?" I whisper, unable to break my gaze, even if I wanted to try. Reese's hands flex around me, as if I surprised him. "What? Cat got your tongue?"

"Do you mean—" he doesn't seem to be able to finish and I can't even bring myself to torture him any longer. I kiss him gently on the lips, my hand coming up to cradle his cheek, before I lean over and speak directly into his ear.

"I love you, Reese Dawson," I say. When I start to pull away, I don't go far before his lips capture mine in a soul-branding kiss. He pulls me even closer somehow, lifting me slightly off the ground, and I give him my whole heart in this one kiss. With every part of me, I want him to know that I mean the words and I'm determined to mean them for the rest of our lives.

When Reese finally pulls away, I'm grateful for the shadowed surroundings, because I completely forgot we're not alone. There's a wicked grin on Reese's face and then he leans down and whispers into my ear.

"So how about we work on a new contract to sign?"

forty-two

. . .

It's been a long day, and it's still not over. Technically, I could put everything away and go watch a movie with Evie, but I can never resist looking through the pictures after a photoshoot. No matter how tired I am, there's something necessary about me sitting down and seeing the fruits of my labor. One of the cafe regulars gave my information to her parents and they in turn passed it on to a couple with a three-year-old. The family pictures turned out so cute. The kid was so adorable—and easy to work with—which is something I don't say very often. Even though it was fun, I'm always exhausted after a shoot.

I'm deep in the perusal cave when my phone vibrates with a message. My heart leaps in my chest at the possibility of who it is and when I pick up my phone, I'm not disappointed.

REESE:

you haven't seen my face all day, are you
surviving okay?

KENNA:

oh just fine

REESE:

then it must be me, I'm the one struggling

KENNA:

that sounds about right

I can't help but grin at my phone. Reese has kept up with his daily check-ins, even when we're both busy. He's very diligent about making sure I know he's thinking about me. I'm never going to get over being so thought about.

REESE:

okay, meanie, can you put me out of my
misery and come downstairs?

I bolt upright, staring at my phone. Reese was supposed to be at clinical shadowing all evening. Jumping from my bed, I grab a hoodie and dash for the door.

"Are you off to see your Prince Charming?" Evie asks without looking up from her computer as I race past her in the living room.

"Wait, how do you know?" I ask, eyes narrowing.

"Just a lucky guess," Evie shrugs with a little furrow between her brows. I pause to give her a quick once over.

"Are you okay?" I ask. I know she's been working hard on her project lately, but maybe there's something else going on? "I can stay if you need to talk."

She waves me off, "Go see Reese. He needs a daily dose of Kenna to survive."

"That's a very Reese phrase," I comment.

"That's because I've heard him say it at least three times this week alone."

Evie grins at me and I wave in her general direction, shaking my head.

I zip up my combat boots before I'm out the door. When I reach downstairs, I can see Reese through the glass doors. He's standing right in the middle of the sidewalk, grinning at the building.

"You look like a lunatic," I say as I step outside.

"Well, I'm *your* lunatic, so…" he shrugs.

"Don't you ever forget it," I point at him just as I reach him. He grabs my extended hand and tugs me toward him, and I step into his arms automatically.

His arms pull me tight against his chest, his hands tugging me upward as his face drops into the space between my shoulder and neck. There's a moment of stillness and then he exhales, his whole body relaxing, as if he's been holding onto tension all day and he's finally letting it go.

I love the way he wraps himself completely around me, shrinking down to my height to keep me comfortable. I hug him back just as tightly, breathing him in. He's freshly showered, carrying that signature Reese scent with him and I feel better than I felt all day.

Sometimes in the last few months I've stopped caring about WentworthWhispers taking secret pictures of us—which they still do regularly, except now they just put us in the weekly updates carousel—or what my dad thinks about this relationship. Actually, that last one, I haven't cared about since the beginning. Maybe that's harsh, but I can't live in the same fear my dad can't seem to get out of. Reese has become my family, the kind of family that loves and cherishes each other, and I intend to hold on to it.

"Feel better?" I ask when Reese finally pulls back. He doesn't go far, keeping me in the circle of his arms, as he gazes down at me. His gaze is soft and full of love and I run my hand up into his hair at the back of his neck, giving him a gentle squeeze. His lips curl up, before he drops a quick kiss to my forehead.

"Always," he replies. Then, he steps away, reaching for my hand and pulls me after him. "Now, let's get going."

"Going? Where are we going?" I ask, falling into step beside him. He glances over long enough to give me a blinding grin, before we reach his car and he's opening the door for me. After shutting the door, he jogs around and climbs into the driver's seat. I turn to look at him, leaning over the middle console, placing my chin in my hand.

"You're acting mighty suspicious. Is this another attempt to try to get me to ice skate?" We tried it once and let's just say, when I do try it again, it definitely will not be with his teammates watching me crash and burn.

"No, but that's a great idea for a different date."

"Oh, so does that mean tonight we're going on a date?" I sit up immediately, clapping my hands together. It's funny how embarrassed I used to be about these types of emotions, but now, I want to be giddy around Reese. Whatever walls I had around my heart, he tore them down and cleared away the rubble.

"We are going on a date," he says, before pulling off campus onto the main road. I sit back in my seat, presenting my hand to him and he threads our fingers together almost automatically.

There are definitely certain things that we have started to do instinctually and while I'm experiencing them, I still can't believe it. Reese's gentle, comforting love has healed so many parts of me. Even now, thinking about it, I have to keep myself from crying. Reese squeezes my hand as if he knows what I'm thinking and I turn to give him a quick smile.

Whatever I thought we'd do for a date, I did not guess we'd be taking the interstate.

"How far are we going?" I ask, reaching over to place Reese's hand on the steering wheel and extracting my hand to my lap. He looks at his hand and then at mine, staring at me like I've offended him.

"Eyes on the road, Dawson. You're in the fast lane," I say. He's already watching the road, but he makes sure to shake his head at me.

"We're not going far, Sunshine. There's something I want to show you. Trust me."

I do. I lean back in my seat, watching the cars pass us by. Colorado is a beautiful state, full of mountains and trees and winding roads. But even more amazing to me is the man beside me. So I turn my head just slightly so I can watch his profile, once again itching for my camera so I can take a snapshot. Every time I look at him, a light hits him a certain way or he moves his head to the side, and suddenly, I'm desperate to photograph him. I love that he's game for it every time. The sun is almost finished setting, bathing him in the perfect golden light. It would've been nice if I brought my camera, but for now, I guess I'll just enjoy the moment.

When we pull off the Interstate I realize we're in a more remote area. Reese takes us off the main road and into a forest, driving slowly up the mountain. It takes us about ten minutes to reach a small clearing and then he parks. I glance around, but can't see much past the trees.

"Come on, it's just a little walk."

Reese gets out of the car and walks over to the trunk. He's pulling things out before I'm even out of the car, but then my phone rings. I glance down at the number, my mood instantly souring. I really don't want to talk to my dad right now.

"Kenna?" Reese is in front of me, peeking down at my face, as if he can feel the emotions surging through me.

"It's my dad," I say, looking up at Reese. We've talked about our families a lot and Reese has been very patient as I try and figure out how to deal with all of my unresolved issues with my dad. In the past, I would've walked away and taken the call, but as Reese continues to watch me, his steady presence gives me comfort.

And a bout of bravery.

"Hi, Dad," I say, as I reach a hand out to Reese. He takes it instantly, threading our fingers together, moving to stand right in front of me.

"McKenna, how are you?" It's been a month since I've talked to him, even though he called last week. But he sounds exactly the same.

"I'm good, Dad. How are you?"

"I'm fine. Work is the same. I saw you won the competition." Ah, of course. He's started following WentworthWhispers and by extension, he's started paying more attention to the news coming from campus.

"I didn't win. I tied for third," I say. Reese squeezes my hand in encouragement and I glance up to find him smiling softly at me. I square my shoulders almost automatically, standing up straighter, instead of folding in on myself like I usually do.

"There was a prize, right?" Dad asks and here we are again. He's fishing. It's that push and pull again, when he's too proud to ask for help, but does it anyway, and then somehow turns it around on me like I'm the bad guy. Is it any wonder that I've always thought I had to work for love?

Reese gives my hand another tiny squeeze and I meet his

tender gaze, so full of encouragement and understanding that all I want to do is hang up this call and jump into my boyfriend's arms. He would protect me from it all, if I just said the word.

"Do you want me to talk to him?" Reese whispers, proving my point almost like he can read my mind. I smile and shake my head.

"You standing beside me and holding my hand is exactly what I need," I whisper back.

"Kenna, are you there?" My dad asks and I take a deep breath.

"Yes, Dad, I'm here. I actually need to go. But yes, there was a prize. I was able to buy a new camera, which is something I needed for a while. I won't be sending any money home this month. I think it would be good for you to sit down and figure out your budget. You can talk to the finance department at your job or go to a bank. They have staff there who can help."

My words are met with silence and I've shocked even myself. But I can't keep tiptoeing around his issues because I want him to care about me.

"That's very disrespectful, McKenna," my dad finally says and I'm not sure why I was expecting anything else. "Is that your boyfriend's influence?"

Reese must've heard him, because he takes a step forward, his expression fierce, but I squeeze his hand. He looks at me, trusting me and supporting me, as I handle this.

"No, Dad. This has nothing to do with him and everything to do with me. You are my father, it should've been you taking care of me, not the other way around. I can't keep bailing you out, I have to live my own life. Which means I need to focus on graduating college and building my portfolio. And yes," I meet Reese's gaze once more, "creating a life for myself with someone I love. I love *you*, Dad, but I need you to look after yourself. I can't keep putting my life on hold for you."

I almost say "I'm sorry", but then I stop myself. I have apologized for things that I had no business apologizing for my whole life. It's time for him to be the one who realizes he's in the wrong.

But he doesn't.

"I see. I'll talk to you later," is all he says before he hangs up the phone. I stare at the screen until it goes dark, not sure what I expected out of that. But I said my piece and now, I'll have to stand my ground. I don't believe all is lost. I think that if Dad and I keep communicating, maybe he'll seek out professional help eventually and then we can both heal from our past.

"Sunshine, are you okay?" Reese's soft question pulls me back to the present. I look up, as my lips curl into a smile.

"I am very okay," I say, and it's true. Having Reese here, having him in my corner, is exactly what I needed. Because I have to handle this myself, but I don't have to go through it alone.

I feel tension in my hand and I glance down to find that I'm still holding onto Reese.

"Oh my gosh, is your hand okay?" I exclaim, as I realize I've been squeezing his for all I'm worth.

"Of course, Sunshine. I'm a big, tough hockey player, after all." He raises our clasped hands to his lips, placing a soft kiss against my knuckles. A simple gesture that hits me straight in the heart.

"Well, now that I've gone through quite an ordeal—" I begin.

"And I'm very proud of you," Reese interjects.

"Thank you. But can you tell me why you drove us to the middle of nowhere?"

"Ah, yes." He leads me around the back of the car and my eyes zero in on the last item.

"Wait, is that my camera?" I ask, pointing at the bag still inside the trunk.

"It is."

"But how—I left it charging on the table after the photoshoot."

"I asked Evie to bring it down before I texted you."

So that's how Evie knew where I was going.

I take the bag before Reese can reach for it.

"I'll carry this. You seem to have your hands full."

I can tell he wants to argue but there's a backpack and a large tote bag at his feet, so he lets me grab it. He closes the trunk before reaching for my hand with his free one. I take it immediately and then he leads me around the car to a small path I didn't see before.

After a few minutes of walking through the peaceful night forest, the trees in front of us thin out. When we step out into another clearing, my breath catches in my throat. The view in front of me is breathtaking.

We're about halfway up the mountain, with a sea of trees below and a sky full of stars as far as I can see. I've never experienced anything like it.

"Reese—"

"I told you I wanted to take you to a proper stargazing spot."

He did. A few days after we had our conversation under the stars that changed everything for us. But I haven't thought of it lately, since we've been so busy.

I rise to my tiptoes and place a quick kiss on his cheek.

"It's beautiful," I say and am rewarded by a kiss on the

mouth. Reese steps forward, shedding the backpack and the tote bag. He pulls out a blanket and spreads it on the ground, before he pulls out another one and motions me forward. I take a seat on the blanket and he wraps the other one around my shoulders, before he proceeds to pull things out of the backpack.

"Are these strawberries?" I exclaim. "I haven't been able to find any at the store."

"I looked around for a pick farm and found one that still has them."

I stare at the box of strawberries in my hands, my eyes stinging from unshed tears.

"Hey, what is it?" He ducks his head, so he can peer into my face, but I can't look at him. Not when I'm so overcome by his kindness.

"Sunshine…" I shake my head as he cups my face in his hands, raising it gently, giving me all the space to move away if that's what I need. But I don't. I meet his gaze, struck all over again to find concern and love in his eyes.

"I just…I can't get used to it. To the daily check in texts, the way you open my car door. To you, remembering my favorite berry and going out of your way to find it. These all seem so small, but to me, they're surprises every time."

I really don't have to spell it out, he knows just how neglected my father has made me feel for years. It's almost like Reese is determined to make up for every time I was overlooked. His thumb swipes gently across my cheek as he leans down to place a soft kiss to my forehead. He's very fond of it and so am I when it comes to his kisses.

"If you can't get used to it, then don't. You can be surprised and emotional and whatever else you need every time. Because I'm going to treat you like you're precious every single day of my life."

The tear sneaks past my defenses and then I'm the one who reaches up to catch his lips with my own. I pour all of my love into this one kiss, making sure he knows just how important he is to me, sealing his promise—and the one I make—with the kiss. Because I'm just as determined to treat him like he's precious. I'm going to love him with every part of me.

forty-three

· · ·

REESE

$\mathcal{I}$ watch Kenna set up her miniature tripod with the camera attached, pointing directly upward. She's at the edge of the blanket, sitting on her heels, hair pulled back with a hair tie so it doesn't mess with her concentration. We ate the strawberries and drank some hot cocoa, before Kenna announced she needed to set up her camera. Watching her work is one of my favorite pastimes. I've been to a few photoshoots with her, besides the hockey one, and she has surprised me every time. There's something about the way she handles the people and the pictures that is fascinating. Her artistic eye never fails to amaze me.

"How exactly are you taking pictures of the stars?" I ask, when she glances over her shoulder to throw a quick smile my way. I've noticed she does this a lot when she works, almost like she's making sure I know she's not ignoring me. It's adorable.

"I'm setting the shutter to stay open for a longer amount

of time. I can use a timer but I like using what is called B-setting. It allows me to keep the shutter open manually. I'll set the f-stop to the lowest of this wide angle lens and then keep it open for about 20-30 seconds. I'll need to play around with it to see what looks best. I'll take some—sorry, I'm rambling."

"Please never stop. Well, I would like you to stop apologizing. But I want you to never stop telling me everything that's on your mind," I say and she sends another smile my way.

"Well, when you put it that way," she says, before she continues. "Basically, if I want to capture the stars without any trails, I need to test to see how long to keep the aperture open. I'll take a few shots and see which one looks the best."

"What would you like me to do?" I ask.

"Hmm," she turns, tapping her chin with one finger. "Sit there and look pretty?"

"Done."

She blows a kiss my way, before she turns back to the camera. If it wasn't so dark, I'd take out my phone and snap a picture of her. She once told me that she likes taking pictures every day, because it reminds her to stop and appreciate the life around her. For me, she's the center of what I appreciate about life.

The guys tease me about this daily, but I can't help feeling all the sappy emotions when it comes to this girl. She saved me, even if she doesn't know it. I didn't realize how much effort I was spending trying to take care of everyone else and cater to what they wanted, until she showed me what it feels like to have someone take care of me. What it feels like to go after what I want. Coach said even my game is more focused, which I'm not sure how that could be possible when I'm constantly thinking about Kenna and our future together. Maybe that's the point.

I came to the conclusion that I want to give hockey more time, not for my uncle or my parents, but for me. I love working with patients, but my first love is still there on the ice. The more time I spend around Kenna, the more I learn about what kind of a man I want to be.

"What are you thinking about? You have that little crease between your brows." Kenna returns to my side, pushing at the place between my eyebrows gently. I wrap an arm around her shoulders pulling her to me.

"You."

"Sappy."

"And you know it."

I drop a quick kiss to the top of her head, before I lay down, taking her with me. The stars seem to be within reach, the lights from the small towns too far away to disturb the darkness.

"Thank you for bringing me here," Kenna says, snuggling into my side. Her body is pressed tightly against mine and somehow, I want her even closer.

"Anytime."

"Is it because you're obsessed with stars?" She asks, lifting her head just a tad to look at me.

I shake my head.

"It's because I'm obsessed with you." I laugh as she rolls her eyes, poking me in the side. "And stars, I'm obsessed with stars."

"I knew it," Kenna says, laying back down.

I could keep things to myself here, but I don't want to. I want to tell her everything.

"I've always associated stars with good memories," I say and I feel Kenna's body tense a little, as if she's making sure to listen to every word. "My happiest memories of my child-hood revolved around stars. The last time my uncle was happy with my aunt, the one time my parents took me to a planetarium. Small memories, but very vivid."

Kenna squeezes me around the middle, before she sits up a little, to look down at my face.

"Then we'll keep up with the tradition. Stars are officially our thing, I'm claiming it."

"Just like that, you claim the whole sky?"

She shrugs. "Sounds reasonable to me."

I grin at her enthusiasm, before I tuck a strand of hair behind her ear and pull her to me. Our lips meet with the same intensity as if it's our first time. I will never get tired of kissing her. My arms pull her closer still and she wraps around my body, putting her whole heart in our kiss. I answer in kind. I can't wait to spend the rest of my life with her.

"I'm also very proud of you," I say against her lips. Her body relaxes against mine, as if that's exactly what she needs to hear.

"Couldn't have done it without you," she whispers, but I shake my head.

"You could. You can do anything. But now, you don't have to, because I will always be by your side, supporting you."

Her arms squeeze me tighter and I capture her lips with another kiss, sealing my words as a promise.

Two hours later, when I finally pull in front of her dorm, I wonder if she'll think I'm insane if I propose right here and now. Maybe lying under the stars, talking about nothing and everything, has made me a little unhinged, but it seems I'm ready for the one thing I never really wanted.

"Reese, what is it?" Kenna asks, when I don't immediately let go of her hand.

I shake my head, because I don't think I can keep the impulse inside if I speak now. Instead, I lean over and give her a soft kiss, before I get out of the car and open her door.

"I'll see you tomorrow," I say, wrapping her in my arms, before I step back and pull out the camera bag. She takes it from me and then rises to her tiptoes to place a quick kiss to my cheek.

"Get going."

"I'll wait until you're inside," I say.

"No, I want to watch you leave." She gives me a little pout and I'm helpless against it. After another quick kiss, I walk over and get into the car. She waves as I pull away, staying at the edge of the sidewalk so she can watch me. I drive about ten feet, when I can't control myself.

I reverse, stopping right next to Kenna. She rushes over, just as I roll down the window, leaning down so she can see me.

"Did you forget something?"

"Yes."

And then I kiss her. I pour all of my promises into this one kiss and the words it's not time to say yet. There will be a time when we're both ready, I truly believe that. But for now, I'm just going to love her passionately and without bounds.

"I love you," I say against her lips and I can feel her grin.

"I love you," she replies, before she pulls herself farther inside the car through the window, kissing me once more.

When I finally do drive away, I'm thankful no one can read my mind, because if my teammates were calling me smitten before, it doesn't compare to how captivated I am now. Although, I'm not sure I care, because Kenna and I are it. We can handle their teasing along with whatever else the world throws at us. As long as we're together.

272

epilogue

. . .

We're in Las Vegas for a Friday game, and while I'm excited to play and then go to the Knights' game to watch Clark, I miss Kenna. We've been spending nearly every weekend together for the last three months and it feels weird that she couldn't be here. She has a family photoshoot this weekend and she can't miss it, or I would've begged Coach to let her come with us. Most of the away games are close enough that even when she can't come, I can be home within a day. This time, we'll be apart for four days. It might not seem like much, but I'm dreading it.

I reach for my phone, seeing that I have a text from her, almost like she knows I'm thinking about her.

KENNA:

make sure you keep safe, Mr. Ice Man

REESE:

I'll do my best

REESE:

I wish you were here

KENNA:

I'm sorry I have plans

REESE:

you don't need to apologize. I'm just whining.

KENNA:

okay, your secret is safe with me.

REESE:

all of my secrets are with you

Ever since we said I love you I have to stop myself from typing it every single time we text. It's almost like I've been carrying those words inside of me my whole life and now they're bursting to come out at every opportunity. When it comes to Kenna, I might've been carrying them inside of me since the birthday party at Coffee & Books all those weeks ago. With those three little words, Kenna has chased away all of my doubts about the future. It's a precious gift, just like she is.

KENNA:

I'll keep them tucked away in my heart

REESE:

you're the best

KENNA:

I know

"Stop grinning at your phone and gear up," Leo says, and I send Kenna one more emoji, then dim the phone.

"Stop being jealous and do something about it," I reply,

raising my eyebrows at him. But he's unfazed. He waves me off and finishes getting ready.

When it's time to get on the ice, we walk out for warm-ups, and I realize I really can't stop grinning. My face muscles are sore. Never thought I'd see the day.

I begin the warm-up, starting with stretches on ice, before I stand to skate. All of us have our own routine and this part, just like the game, makes me feel alive. It feels strange to know that I might not be doing this next season.

"Reese, eyes up," Don says, swinging by. I look over at him, confused. But then I see her.

Kenna. My sunshine.

She's at the edge of the rink, leaning forward just a little, and it takes me a moment to realize I'm not hallucinating. I skate over to her, stopping just a breath away.

"You weren't supposed to be here," I stare at her in wonder. No matter how much time we spend together, she keeps surprising me.

"Oh well, I told Micah I'll come see him play." She shrugs, and I throw my hands down to get rid of the gloves so I can take her face in my hands, squishing her cheeks.

"Don't you dare."

"Or what? You'll fight me?" I grin at her trying to be intimidating while I hold her cheeks captive. I lean down and steal a kiss, making her eyes grow big.

"Reese."

"That's my name," I say, then steal another kiss. "You came to my game. My away game. My far away game."

"Okay, okay, don't make it a thing."

"Oh, it's a thing." I cup her face more gently, tugging her toward me, and she comes willingly. This time when I capture her lips with mine, I linger. She tastes like coffee and white chocolate, and she kisses me back with just as much fervor as I kiss her.

"Wait for me after the game?" I whisper over her lips.

"Always," she replies. I hear my name called, and I reluctantly let her go. I pick up my gloves before I move away. She gives me the softest smile and blows a kiss my way as I skate away backward. I don't even care that I look like the biggest sap in the world. She's worth it all.

"I love you," I call across the space between us, and I watch her whole face light up.

"I love you back," she says and my whole body feels energized. I skate over to her immediately, capturing her lips with my own. The kiss is passionate and hungry, and I pour every bit of my love into it. When I come up for air, it's too soon. But I have a game to win.

"That was some display," Leo says when I'm next to him.

"I hope you're powered up to win, because I am," I reply, making the guys chuckle. They can't even make fun of me for this, not when I'm going to make sure we crush the other team.

Because I have a girlfriend waiting for me. A smart, talented, and beautiful girl who loves me. My own sunshine.

I can't wait to build a future with her. Whatever comes, we're in it together. My forever teammate.

———

THANK YOU FOR READING KENNA AND REESE'S STORY! STAY tuned for book 2 in the Wentworth Ravens Hockey series, coming soon!

note from the author

Thank you for reading my book! If you have enjoyed it, please consider leaving a review. Reviews are such a big help to authors!

They help books get more visibility, and help readers make a decision!

And, if you'd like to stay up to date with all of my shenanigans, sign up for my newsletter today and receive a free prequel novella!

Go here to sign up: https://dl.bookfunnel.com/63dsekx62f

Thank you!

about the author

Viera Hope is addicted to HEAs, K-dramas, Hallmark movies, hockey and coffee. She writes sweet, clean romantic comedies, with lots of angst and banter! Her aim is to make her readers laugh and swoon!

You can find her on Instagram @vierahopeauthor, where she shares her love for romance in pictures and quotes. You can download a free copy of her sweet romantic comedy novella by signing up for her newsletter!